A Stitch in Crime

Justin Robinson

Candlemark & Gleam

For information, address
Candlemark & Gleam LLC
38 Rice St. #2, Cambridge, MA 02140
eloi@candlemarkandgleam.com

Library of Congress Cataloging-in-Publication Data
In Progress

ISBN: 978-1-936460-93-9
eISBN: 978-1-936460-92-2

Cover art and design by Kate Sullivan

Illustrations by Fernando Caire
www.artstation.com/artofern

Editor: Athena Andreadis

www.candlemarkandgleam.com

For the Owl and the Turtle

ONE

The hole was the size of my fist. Big enough to fit my whole life inside. It poked through the plaster, fractured the wooden bones of the living room wall. Fault lines of cracked paint haloed it. The hole was the first thing I saw when I opened my front door, and the last thing I thought of before my two hours of sleep at night. Two hours, not enough even for a meat golem like me. I tried to look away, ignore it, pretend it wasn't there. I couldn't. It was a gouged-out eye staring at me. Daring me to face it.

It had been there for a week. No—it was there before I punched it in. Waiting for the rage that would reveal it. I'd been pretending it was a clean, unbroken wall. That there was no hole for me to fall into. That the life I wanted, that I thought I was living, wasn't balanced on a precipice.

In the split second it took to put that hole there, everything went into it. Lost forever. The rest of my days to think about it, to hate myself, to wallow in regret.

The worst part was, I didn't even remember doing it. In my mind, I existed perched on a rock surrounded by a roiling green sea. The waves never stopped crashing in, and sometimes I went under, the green closing in over my head. While my mind drowned, I was the oldest story in a young book. Another dizzy skin-dolly about to put someone in the hospital. It happened from time to time no matter how much I wanted to keep it at bay. Someone getting a little too fresh, the sound of that slur "skin-dolly," or even just a misplaced comment. The waves thundered higher and higher until I couldn't keep my head above water. Then I was gone.

There were a couple things that could lower the water, at least. Ella Fitzgerald songs. Wind blowing through the leaves of trees. Old paperbacks. And one person in particular.

The worst part of the hole was that it wasn't there because some phantom decided I was his true love and he was going to put his hands on me. No, it came in a razor-blade instant when I nearly killed the one person who could normally make that water fall faster than the mercury in an icebox. The only safe person in all the world.

Nick.

That's Nick Moss, the only human private eye in town. My boyfriend. Or he had been my boyfriend until it all went away in a crash of green. He'd said something about my birthday. I don't even remember what. Didn't matter. Those waves had been getting higher and higher all week, and I was going to break the next person who said "fire."

I pushed my head above the green, gasping for air, and there Nick was, cowering under the hole, plaster dust drifting over him like the snow Los Angeles would never see. He clutched his lighter in his hand, the tiny flame like a blade spearing my borrowed heart. I found myself hissing like a whole alley full of cats as I scrambled backward. Then I put the pieces of the last few seconds together.

The hole. The fear in Nick's eyes. The fire he'd never, ever pull on me.

I had almost hit Nick. Had I connected, he'd be dead. My Nick, and I'd almost killed him. In an instant when the piece of me that truly deserved the name "monster" was in charge. I wanted to explain, to apologize, but I had no voice. My slate was out of reach. So I could only stare at Nick, more frightened than he was. And then he was gone.

I stared at the hole as though I could make him reappear beneath it and we could pretend it never happened. We could go back to what we were, finding love that no one wanted to be real. Between a living man and a woman made from the dead. Make believe we could be together. That we were normal. That there was nothing wrong with me. And know it was that pretending that put the hole there in the first place.

I picked at the stitches between the middle and ring fingers of my right hand. They had been loose for years, and that punch had jarred them something fierce. The two patches of skin they bridged were different colors, one sort of greenish, the other kind of gray, and they were coming undone, like a zipper. The flesh underneath was frayed and bloodless, like a bolt of cloth ripped in two. I knew I should try to restitch them, but every time I sat down to do it, I found myself staring at the hole, desperately trying not to see the space beneath it, where Nick wasn't and would never be again.

Hell of a birthday present, too. Nearly kill the only man who didn't treat me like a joy girl or a stitched-up pile of corpses. Happy fifth birthday, Jane Stitch.

Yes, I was five years old. Kind of. Not really. It's hard to explain. See, meat golems get made, the same as other monsters, out of people. But with every other monster, it's a one-for-one ratio. With us, it's six corpses: five for the body and one for the brain. We're a new person, but we still have a few things left over from the old. Like old voices on a tape recording. I didn't have to be taught to read, or to eat, or even to drive. I just knew all of those things. I even knew who the president was, that the handsome fella in *Notorious* was Cary Grant, and that I shouldn't buy the Brooklyn Bridge, no matter how good a deal the nice man was offering. I also knew a creep when I saw one, which might have saved me in the first moment I opened my eyes.

So I was five, but it was a hard five. A worn-out five. A five that didn't want to deal with the memories bounding around her noggin, and who wanted to pretend that she could have a life with a strange little man who loved her.

What a joke, right?

That touch of verdigris in my complexion said it all. I was a monster, and monsters don't get happy endings. Nothing Nick would have said could have justified me hitting him and he certainly never did anything to send me under. I'd lost time before, more often than I cared to admit, but when it happened, there was usually a spark. Like I said, the green waves would close up over me and I'd wake up mashing some phantom's head into the pavement.

But no. This time, my Nick had simply opened his mouth about my birthday and I'd nearly killed him for it.

My birthday. September 15, 1951. Five years since the night a sizzling bolt of lightning shot white-hot life into me. Since my eyes opened and I was a new kind of person. Five years since I started running from that life and only stopped when I'd run out of land. Five years since I'd left sand for tinsel.

The hole, yawning across the living room, got bigger and bigger as I watched it. The edges crumbled away, the hole devouring everything around it. Then, in the middle, where the wood in the walls broke like ribs, a spot opened so black no light would ever get out. Not even the black of the night. No, this was a black that didn't exist in the deepest parts of the war, when monsters chittered in the dark. This was the black of anti-light, of anti-life. I'd punched my way to it, and now it wanted to swallow me, frayed stitches first.

Even as the chemicals running through my veins turned cold, I realized what I had to do. There was nothing for me until I did it, and I'd been avoiding it for five years. Five years too long.

I had to stop running.

Two

No one would have said Nick was much of a looker. Truth is, he looked a bit like a weasel. Short, shifty, and a little furry. But, as the saying almost went, he was my weasel. Only he wasn't, not anymore.

I had one picture of him, creased from its home in my wallet. He hated pictures of himself; he said he didn't like what he saw. I thought at first it was vanity, but it wasn't. Once, when he'd had a little too much to drink, he told me everything. Told me the things he saw in the Day War, the things he'd done in the Night. Listed all the lives between D-Day and this one, and he remembered each and every face. Told me about all the people he'd let down, too, those he couldn't find or the ones he'd found too late. They still whispered to him when he closed his eyes. Nick had a ledger in his mind, and he was always in the red.

"I don't like what I see here," he'd said, pointing to his eyes with wavering fingers.

I held him until he was counting sheep. Then I held him for longer because I had to. When I looked into his eyes, I didn't see failure. I saw the man who stopped me from burning. I saw the man who wouldn't leave justice to someone else if he could find it. And I saw the man who would never see that in the mirror.

In the picture, he was asleep on my couch. Funny, because that was how we'd met. Well, we'd actually met a couple times before that, but that was the first time we'd really talked. I'd pulled him out of a beating at the hands of three gangsters and brought him to my place as a thank you for saving me from a fire. That old story. When he woke up, he thought I was going to turn him. He didn't know then that I'd never turn anybody. That I was nearly as scared as he was. For all I knew, he was a gangster too, one of Mickey Cohen's boys. And unlike every other mug in the City of Angels, he didn't have a fear or a weakness to prey on. I'd taken off his jacket, heavy with wards, herbs, and weapons, and hung it on a hook like a leopard I wasn't sure was dead or not. These were the weapons of a killer.

But he had stopped me from burning.

The picture had been taken on a Sunday in May. He was in his shirtsleeves, arms crossed over his chest, mouth slack, eyes closed. Peaceful. That had taken him a month or two. Even with me, he often shuddered in his sleep, or woke up in a flash, ready to fight. Like most meat golems, I don't sleep much, so I was awake for all of it. Then, slowly, he started getting more and more comfortable with me. It got harder for him in his neighborhood. The other humans called him a real Christine Daaé—you know, the dame from *Phantom of the Opera*—for taking up with a monster, and he preferred to stay at my place. I did too. The other monsters looked at us funny, sure, but they all assumed I was playing some kind of long game. I wasn't. I had the Nick I wanted, and he had the Jane he wanted.

My finger traced a greenish path over Nick's face as the red car rattled into Hollywood. I wondered where he was. Probably at his tiny office on Flower Street. Nick was more like the private eyes in the books than he wanted to admit. His secretary, a siren by the name of Serendipity Sargasso, was so nice that I thought she was putting me on at first. Nope, it turned out she was just happy that Nick was happy. That made me like her. And now she probably hated me. With good reason.

I wanted to go see him, but I couldn't. I was the same person who'd thrown the punch. I couldn't see him until that danger was past. Until I'd never raise a hand to Nick or anyone else who didn't deserve it. Until I was me.

Whoever that was.

The red car dropped me off in Hollywood, on Sunset. Daytime had stripped the glamor away, and it left a street looking like a party after everyone had gone home. Two vampires walked by, shielded by their parasols, eyes hidden behind chunky dark glasses.

My destination was the art deco façade a block away, the one marked THE NOCTURNIST. Even the defining nightspot of the Sunset Strip looked sad in the light of day, a thin layer of smog hovering over it in a haze. I went through the front. Unlocked as always. Anyone who came into the Nocturnist looking to cause trouble was going to get far more than they could ever dish out.

The antechamber was empty; Hargoth wouldn't get in until an hour before sundown. Just as well—he tended to think the waitresses here might like to make some time with an ogre. Some of the girls did, and the rest of us just had to put up with what an ogre thought were clever come-ons. I opened up the inner door, and the sounds of the Salem Sisters fluttered out.

My heart flopped over. They'd been Nick's find. Three gorgeous witches in perfect close harmony. I might have been a little jealous of them at first, but I wasn't going to admit it, and Nick never let on they were anything but friends. They were rehearsing, the club's nearly all-phantom orchestra behind them. It was a hell of a sound, and one I'd never gotten over. A side benefit to working here.

I passed them by, going up the stairs by the back of the stage. A few more twists and turns led me to a staircase heading down into the basement suite of rooms Nyx Nocturne used as an office. The staircase was narrow, and I clomped my way down to the bottom and knocked on her door.

The slide over the peephole hissed open and a jaundiced eye crawled over me. Then the door opened, revealing a slender ghoul, baring snaggleteeth. She wore a suit top with a flared skirt and boots that looked like she should be tromping around the Night War. She carried a gun, but she wasn't pointing it anywhere. This was Holly Thorne, Miss Nocturne's majordomo.

"Jane. What do you want?" Holly asked. "Not dressed for work."

I wasn't. Shorts, a checked t-shirt tied at my waist, and a scarf corralling my hair weren't exactly Nocturnist wear. My shoes were flats, too. Plus, I was wearing my slate like the world's least fashionable necklace. Made me look like a schoolkid from thirty years ago, but it was the most effective way I knew to talk to anyone who wasn't also a lady meat golem. It was just a framed bit of blackboard hung around my neck with a piece of twine, a stick of chalk hanging from a second piece. It was also verboten at the Nocturnist. Destroyed the glamorous image here, of whistlebait who couldn't talk back.

I wrote on the slate, *Need to speak to Miss Nocturne.*

"Miss Nocturne's sleeping. You know that," Holly said.

I resisted the urge to make only real sound I could: an angry hiss. Holly was lying through her broken teeth. Miss Nocturne wasn't sleeping because it was still early enough she'd be totaling the receipts from last night. She wasn't going to catch a wink before she was damn sure nobody's finger was in the till.

Please, Miss Thorne. I showed her, then wiped it away with the heel of my hand and wrote, *It's business.*

The ghoul sighed, then stepped aside, gesturing to the room. "I'll get her, but don't expect her to be in the friendliest of moods."

Nyx Nocturne being friendly to an employee would have been a first. I walked in, but couldn't sit. My limbs always felt too long to me, like they belonged to someone else. They did, I suppose, but they'd been mine long enough you'd think I'd be used to them by now. So I stood in the middle of the room, shifting coltishly on stolen legs while I waited for Miss Nocturne.

I had to give it to her; the room was lovely. She'd kept with the decor of the rest of the place, trying to pretend this was some old-world castle in the haunted woods of Transylvania. The furniture was all heavy stained wood; the walls looked like stone, hung with woven tapestries. Of course, instead of the Battle of Hastings, the tapestries showed the Night War, except how it might look to some medieval artist.

Nyx Nocturne herself swept into the room, keeping me waiting only long enough that it wasn't a question about who was in charge. In a nod to what she was supposed to be doing, she was wearing an elegant dressing gown, but her coal-black hair was still it its lacquered side part from the evening, and her gold eyes were as bright as a newly polished British sovereign.

"Jane, yes. What can I do for you?"

I wrote on the slate with a jittery hand, wishing I'd done it while she was out of the room. I felt the vampire's attention on me, heavier than a lead weight. *I need time off.*

"Time off? I didn't know meat golems got sick."

Not sick. Personal difficulties.

Nyx Nocturne raised a perfectly sculpted eyebrow. "Perfectly sculpted" described the whole package. She really did look like an ivory statue someone had painted only sparingly, black over her hair, gold over her eyes, crimson on her lips, and nothing anywhere else. "Personal?"

I nodded, wondering if she was going to pry any further. I couldn't cough up the truth to anybody but a good friend. But lying to a vampire was tough under the best circumstances. It's why they made such great lawyers.

"How much time?"

I shrugged, giving her my best "I'm not sure" face.

"I see," she said, considering. "Take what you need, but your job isn't going to be waiting for you forever. There are a lot of girls with stitches in this town who need jobs, and this is a good one. If you're back in a couple days, maybe a week, you'll have it. Longer? No promises."

I understand. Thank you, Miss Nocturne.

"Use the time well."

I left her office behind, but I wasn't going to leave the club quite yet. There was one person I needed to talk to. Needed to talk to her more than I did with Nyx Nocturne, in fact. I passed through the club, where the Salem Sisters were taking five. Two, the maiden and mother, sat at the edge of the stage, while the platinum blonde crone was having a low conversation with the cornet player. "Crone" was a bit of a misnomer; Hyacinth Salem couldn't have been older than her mid-twenties. Their familiars, a robin, a blue jay, and a sparrow, perched on the microphone stand singing their own little ditty.

None of the other girls were in yet. That made it easier. We were friends, united by our shared experiences. We talked in a sign language only meat golem women knew. We'd teach it to the new ones in a sacred trust. No one else spoke it; I don't think most monsters even knew we had our own way of communicating. They might have understood what I had to do...or they might not, and I'd feel even more alone than I already did.

I opened up the door to the kitchen, where the ovens were just starting to be heated up. The head chef, Wyeth Wyrd, issued orders to her staff of zombies, calling them "dear" and "honey." Next to her, a raccoon stood on its hind legs, its gestures mimicking those of its master.

A confused frown rippled over Wyeth's features as she saw me. "Jane? What are you doing here so early? You're not dressed for work."

Taking some time off.

"Miss Nocturne let you?" I wobbled my hand at her in a more or less gesture. "What's going on, dear? You look perturbed."

I glanced around. More than one of the zombies was surreptitiously watching us. While I didn't mind Wyeth knowing, I didn't really want an entire kitchen staff gossiping about me, even if all they could say was "Brains."

Wyeth read me perfectly, like she always did, and ushered me to the little alcove by the back door. The raccoon clambered onto the counter and watched the zombies, his furry paws on his Rubenesque hips.

"Now, what is it, dear?" Wyeth murmured.

Going back, I wrote. Then, hesitating, I wrote another word. *Home.*

"Where is home?"

Arizona. I didn't get any more specific than that. Most people hadn't heard of the place I'd been sewn together. They were better for it, as far as I was concerned.

"Why? Did something happen?"

My stomach flopped over. Wyeth knew Nick, but she didn't know why I was so hung up on him. As far as she was concerned, he was the crazy human who came into the Nocturnist, practically daring any of the monsters present to turn him. Still, I didn't want to say, because I didn't want her to diminish what I'd done. I didn't want her to try to comfort me.

I need to talk to my creator.

"You've never spoken about...him?" I nodded. "What do you want to ask him?"

Everything. I need to know who

I stopped writing. It was nearly impossible to get out. I forced myself; not answering was the same as running and I was done running.

I need to know who I was.

Wyeth's gaze fell to the train tracks of stitches that ran over my body. "I see," she said. "You know, if the memories are troubling you, I have hexes that can make you forget."

I shook my head and tapped the need on my slate. She thought it over. "Be careful, Jane. Who you were and who you are are different people."

I erased everything except *I know.*

"I can tell there's nothing I can say that'll talk you out of this, so instead, I'll just tell you good luck. Now come here." Wyeth wrapped me up in a hug. It would have been so easy to quit right there. To surrender to it and let her comfort me, let her be the mother I'd never had. Let her take the pain away. But I deserved that pain. Needed it, even.

I parted from her and nodded. It was all I could say.

THREE

My train left Union Station around noon like a slouching caterpillar. I packed a single bag, just a rucksack cobbled together from half a dozen different bags, stuffed with a few changes of clothes, my toothbrush, and a detective paperback nearly thumbed to pieces. I liked the bag; it was well-made, even if a stitched-together woman holding a stitched-together bag invited unfunny jokes. At least it never put a hole in my drywall.

I didn't know how many changes of clothes I was going to need. Not too many, hopefully. I only had to ask one question, but the thought of doing it made my stomach twist into burning knots and threatened to pull the green waves up over my head. One question. One answer.

He'd cough it up. He had to. Although my desperation to convince myself told me he wouldn't. I knew a creep when I'd seen one, some memory lurking in the depths of my borrowed brain. It whispered not to trust him and I'd listened. And stormed out on the knowledge I needed to mend my life.

The ghost conductor checked my ticket as I boarded the noon train to Phoenix. Wouldn't be going the whole way, but it wasn't like anyone sold a ticket to my hometown. It was barely a point on the map. It would have been forgotten if anyone knew about it in the first place.

I rested my head on the cool window and watched the city give way to the desert as we chugged into the east. The train jostled and rattled. The civilization of Los Angeles dwindled to the endless dun of the Mojave. I wasn't just going home; I was going into the past. I only wanted five years, but it looked more like twenty, thirty, fifty.

When Los Angeles was nothing but a glittering memory, the giant anthills became a regular sight stretching into the horizon. Occasionally, an ant the size of a Studebaker would poke its head out, or scuttle down the surface to forage through the landscape. Some mad scientist deep in the Arizona desert had made those things at the tail end of the Night War. Now they were used like cattle, raised on the rantches that dotted the Southwest. Eating giant ant was an adjustment the world had made quickly; the Nocturnist was famous for its ant bisque, and Musso & Frankenstein served an incredible ant steak. Tasted a little like lobster, only meatier. We passed a few of those rantches, marked by cement anthills and wide-open fields where swarms of giant ants scuttled to and fro, watched over by a new breed of cowboy.

The sight of the Springfield Shape announced that we were almost there. The last time I saw it, I was going in the other direction, maybe even on the same train. The Shape crowned the Dome Rock Mountains, its formerly gelatinous form flash-frozen in the particularly cruel winter of 1950. I couldn't imagine what kind of damage that monster would have done if it had made it to the coast. Blobs were never the most reasonable of creatures, and once they got that big, they tended to see Armageddon as a finish line rather than a cautionary tale. The Shape was dead, but there was far too much of it to move. Parts of it were dusted with dirt, and I could have sworn I saw the beginnings of bushes sprouting on its surface. In another ten years, it would just be part of the mountain that killed it.

Then, as we passed both mountains and Shape, I caught the first glimpse of my hometown, the place I saw for one night and one morning five years ago. Quartzsite, Arizona was little more than a scattering of low buildings in a baking wash between two different stubby mountain ranges. The structures had been thrown up haphazardly since whites settled the area, using whatever materials were cheapest at the time. Some of them had a distinctly Old West look about them, with chipped paint and rotten beams. Others were whitewashed, but like everything else in the desert, the whitewash had been yellowed like an old tooth. The town wasn't much to look at, but at least it was honest.

The train stopped with a squeal of brakes. Halfway between Phoenix and Los Angeles, as far as possible from anywhere on either side, stuck in the middle of a desert that didn't care one way or the other. I picked up my bag and stepped from the train to the platform. The sun was close, the air dry enough to catch fire. I didn't sweat anymore—didn't do a lot of things, really—so the heat just stuck to me. It took a truly perverse meat golem to settle in the desert, so at least that part added up.

It was mid-afternoon by the time the train got in. I squinted into the blinding sun. My left eye guzzled in the light; I always had to squint that one, giving me a cockeyed look whenever it was bright out. I put on a pair of sunglasses. I'd just have to put up with the fact that my right eye would have to work a little harder to see through the darkened lens. It would have been too much effort for him to get me a matching pair of eyes, I supposed. Some of the girls had death's own cataract on one of their peepers, so I shouldn't complain.

Quartzsite was baking. It was difficult to say if this was the place I remembered. I had barely been here. My hometown that I had lived in for maybe twelve hours. Something looked wrong about it. Something that kept wriggling away when I tried to put a finger on it. The few monsters on the street, mostly ghouls with a smattering of zombies, walked with their heads down, their steps quick and furtive. I ambled north past Main Street, passing three spectral chargers tied to a hitching post. The beasts pawed the ground, smoke and an occasional blast of fire coming from their nostrils. Whenever they did that, I nearly bolted like a spooked mare.

I couldn't go right to his office, even though it was the one place in this town I could have found blindfolded. There might as well have been an invisible wall all around it, pushing me away. He would be there, going about whatever business he had. As far as he knew, there was nothing drawing me back to the place of my birth.

So I ignored the whole point of my train ride, of possibly losing my job. I turned my attention away, facing the sun sinking into the Dome Rock Mountains, glittering off the pink crystal that was the Springfield Shape. Instead of going to his office, I wandered the streets. About half of them were paved; the rest were packed dirt, sometimes little more than tracks worked into the desert soil. Tumbleweeds somersaulted between the cactus. Lizards sunned themselves, diving under rocks as I approached.

I passed an old church that looked like it had originally ministered to this place when it was Mexico. It looked as hungrily empty as the hole in my wall. I never felt right around churches. Every part of me had been taken from a dead woman, presumably gone on to her eternal reward. What was left didn't have any of that stuff anymore. Nothing in a church for any part of me.

I passed by the grave of Hi Jolly, the copper camel at the top turning crimson in the dying sun. Once upon a time, a man from Syria was the most exotic thing Quartzsite had ever seen, and all he'd done here was die.

I kept walking until I ran out of town. It was hard to see where Quartzsite really ended. The structures just sort of petered out, finally surrendering to the indifference of the desert. On the horizon, at the distant edge of the wash, a sheet of dust rose into the sky like a storm that would never get any closer.

This piece of town where I found myself was different. Other than the clustered buildings of Main Street, most of Quartzsite was scattered buildings in ones and twos, built wherever someone had been inspired to do so. This, though, was a cluster of shanties, cheaply constructed even by local standards, slapped together out of clapboard and battered sheets of aluminum, all simmering in the sun. An artificial moat surrounded the whole thing, filthy water running briskly in an endless circle, powered by a clever aqueduct built from trash. Just inside the border was a fence made of exposed wires connected to an aging generator. Evil eye wards hung from eaves and dried roses were suspended in glass bottles, sitting on every windowsill. Gold coins were shockingly common, glittering in the late afternoon sun. The whole thing reeked of vinegar and I couldn't figure why.

The people inside gazed sullenly back at me. There wasn't even defiance in their stares; they had been beaten. Before Nick, a person staring was a threat. A person with their head down was nothing at all. Now, though, I saw them, and saw the truth of what had happened to them. They were locked up in their own homes. Safety was a few square feet of garbage.

"Well aren't you a morsel." The voice was juicier than a fresh-cut cactus.

The speaker was a spidery ghoul reclining in an old rocking chair he must have dragged out into the desert sands. He wore a Hawaiian shirt caked yellow with desert dust, and a pair of shorts that showed off knobby knees. His wide-brimmed hat, the front brim pinned to the crown, looked like something a prospector would wear in a campy movie. His shoes were old wingtips he'd cut the toes out of. A pair of wire-framed glasses balanced on a snub nose, and it took me a glance or two to see that yes, they were just frames. He clutched a cigarette in a holder between his teeth.

And his teeth were impressive, even for a ghoul. These weren't sharp, but they were big and blunt, and he was missing a few. Mold grew around the gumline, but that didn't stop him from showing off his chompers. Once I'd talked to him for a bit, I realized this was because he didn't have enough in the lip department to close his mouth. He was already staring at me, blinking out the sun. His big, watery eyes were the color of mold on old steak.

"We don't get many meat golems around these parts. Are you perchance acquainted with our local doctor?" I shook my head. He didn't need to know my business. "Shame. You certainly found Fort Meatstick with admirable alacrity." I frowned. I'd heard the slur often—who hadn't?—but even before Nick, I'd never used it. Now it washed a wave of green up over my feet. The ghoul took my frown to mean something else. "If you like the looks of one of them, they're free for the taking. Although you'd need five, I suppose."

I resisted the urge to let the green deal with him. I wasn't looking for conversation, but it often found me anyway. Something about a woman who couldn't talk always brought out the raconteur in men.

6

"Wrote that quickly." Now the green was touching my ankles. "Now where are my manners? I'm Barrow White. Yes, *those* Whites." He leaned over and offered a gray hand to shake. His nails were filthy and chipped.

I didn't know who "those Whites" were, and I wasn't about to ask. I took the hand anyway. It felt like paper, and I knew I could crush every bone in it if I wanted to. He leaned over and brushed his lips over the back of my hand. I mostly felt his teeth.

"And your name, my dear?"

Jane. Not dear.

"I meant no offense, Jane. I'm pleased to make your acquaintance and even more pleased that you will be adding some lovely scenery to our community. Like I said, if you like the looks of a meatstick, there's no line. I have my eye on that one there." He pointed his crooked finger at a woman who was pulling filthy rags off a clothesline. She scurried back inside as soon as she noticed Barrow's attention. "Then again, if you harvested those stems for a daughter, I wouldn't be displeased." His grin was an icy finger on my spine.

I turned away so Barrow wouldn't see just how much he was turning my stomach. My eyes met those of a kid on the other side of the fence. A tiny girl with filthy feet and tired eyes. And then I wasn't there anymore, I was walking down Not My Memory Lane, a gift from the woman who'd given her brain up to me. I was holding a little girl who couldn't have been more than two, with hair like sunlight. I was lifting her up, to the too-green leaves of an orange tree. One of her chubby hands reached for a fat orange and...

"Jane? Is something troubling you?"

Barrow was a few steps closer, his expression at the edge of worry. He knew the stories. They all did. The way we skin-dollies could turn violent at a moment's notice. Might be thinking I had just about lost the reins on the beast in my mind, and he was right. I blinked and shook my head.

I walked away. I couldn't stay at Fort Meatstick. I couldn't do much of anything.

FOUR

ometimes the only option is buried under a fifth of whiskey. I can
drink a gorilla under the table, so long as he isn't fifty feet tall.
Benefits of a dead girl's liver, I guess. Not that I thought I was
working up the courage to see him that night. No, this was more about
drinking away cowardice than throwing gasoline on any moxie.

I found the Sugar Shack on Quail Trail Street. Looked to be the place
in this town. The walls were a coat of dented plaster over weatherbeaten
wood, and the sign, buzzing with neon, was a lot newer than the building
itself. The bouncer was a beefy zombie who told me "Brains" when I
walked in. He was a lot more right than he knew.

The place stank of anything you can spill in a bar, and that stench
had sunk into the floorboards. Fighting, drinking, passing out—all of
it haunted the place like the ghost of an Irish prizefighter. The people
drinking were mostly ghouls, with a couple zombies, gremlins, and what
I was fairly certain was a witch. The place didn't have a stage. Instead, a
phantom had taken over a corner, warbling some ballad about how his wife
had left him and he'd enacted an elaborate revenge on both her and the
man she'd run off with. He strummed an acoustic guitar, his cowboy outfit

somehow looking both lived in and bunk at the same time.

The bartender was a human fly, her insect head poking out over a western-style shirt unbuttoned far enough to show off generous cleavage. She wiped down the bar with a rag attached to her insect arm, lazily taking the orders of the slumping regulars. Whenever she mixed a drink, the tip of her fly arm lingered in the glass. Before long, she came out from behind the bar, a lanyard tipped with a collection of cards hooked to a metal ring bouncing against her chest.

"Bzzzz," she said, but at the same time, she selected a card without looking and held it up with her human hand, the right one. The cardstock had probably been white at one time, but time had yellowed it like everything else in town, and a dark water stain crept in from the bottom. She tapped a nail with cherry red polish against it. Her head was mostly green, her huge compound eyes taking up the bulk of the available real estate. Her insect mouthparts quivered unnervingly as she buzzed. I forced my gaze south to really look at the card in the dim light of the Sugar Shack.

{*What will you have?*} The writing was bold and black, not especially tidy.

I responded on my slate. *Whiskey neat.*

The human fly made a different kind of buzz, this one stuttering. She flipped the top sheet of her order pad over, moistened her pen in her mouthparts, and wrote, then flipped it over to show me. {*Ain't we a pair.*}

I had to smile. First time since coming here. I wondered if human flies had a way to talk to each other the way we meat golem ladies did. They were so new it was unlikely, but stranger things had happened. Were happening all the time.

The human fly put her pad away and got me my whiskey. There wasn't anyone else working in this place, other than the phantom crooner. She could probably have used an experienced waitress, but I was allegedly on vacation. She returned, set a double in front of me, and flashed a card. {*Name's Sugar Kane. This is my joint.*}

Jane Stitch. Nice to meet you.

Sugar tapped the table with her chitinous claw. I took that as a "same to you." She went back to what she was doing, and I started drinking. And drinking. And drinking. Problem was, it didn't drown anything. It just made me dwell on what had sent me into this spiral in the first place. The phantom's maudlin country dirges didn't help either, pulling my thoughts again and again to that hole in my wall and the poor, sad, wonderful man beneath it. I stared at the far wall, wet with shadow, as though it, too, had a hole I'd punched into it. I stared into that hole, out into the town and my eventual destination. If I could work up the brass to do what I came to.

Sugar kept bringing me drinks. Sometimes she'd stop for a word or two. Not often the canned phrases on her cards, unless she was flashing the one that said {Another round?} Usually ones she had to write out. {Doing OK?} or {New in town?}

I didn't know how to answer either one of those, and offered the same halfhearted shrug to each. Sugar seemed like an okay sort, but her questions only led to stories I wasn't sure I could tell. Especially to a stranger, no matter how nice she seemed. It all came back to that picture in my wallet.

The mood in this place was the same as everywhere else in Quartzsite: beaten down. The ghouls and zombies slumped on their stools and chairs, listlessly nursing the booze-flavored water Sugar set in front of them. I don't even think they were listening to the phantom. They were lost in the exhaustion of being.

Until the door boomed open. This was maybe a couple hours after I'd parked my keister at a high table in the corner. I'd seen everything there was to see in this place, and heard every variation of the phantom's tales of abandonment and revenge. The more they wheedled into me, the more they'd made me think of my own lost love, the more like a sap I was feeling. Just when I was beginning to think I should find a place to shut my eyes for an hour or two before dawn, the door opened. The bouncer flinched; never a good sign. Four people moseyed in.

Headless horsemen, all of them. Hard to mistake those, even when their demonic steeds weren't around. Where there should be a head, there was just a ragged stump of desiccated tissue. The muscle had gone gray, a bit of white bone poking from the middle like a cut of meat. Other than that, human. The one in the lead was the shortest of them, and more than a head shorter than me, no pun intended. His western-style shirt was tucked into a tight pair of blue jeans crowned with a thick belt buckle that glittered silver. His cowboy boots were scuffed with use and tipped in more silver. A bowie knife hung on his belt, the handle bone, the blade thick and heavy with promised murder. Every horseman had a weapon they brought back from the change and, for some reason, that this one had a knife made my nerves jangle more than a sword would have. A knife was something I understood; a knife was something you used. There was no doubt in my mind that this horseman had put his knife to work.

The others were two men and a woman, each dressed like the one in the lead, though their buckles were more tarnish than silver. Their weapons were different, one man carrying a double-bladed wood axe, the other a noose, and the woman had a shotgun sheathed across her back. I didn't need to be a local to know these were trouble; the way everyone tensed like a guitar string was enough. Even the phantom's song petered out. Everyone was motionless, staring at the headless horsemen, though desperately trying not to look like they were staring.

The green moved in at the periphery of my vision, the waves beginning to crest. I felt the wind kicking up over the fields of Kansas, across a gulf of memory. If it swallowed me, I'd be tearing this place up, so instead I swallowed more whiskey, hoping to burn away the echo trying to drag me under.

"What's the matter?" asked the lead horseman to the room. Like all of them, his voice reverberated, as though he was calling from deep inside his chest. "Ain't everybody having fun? You, play another 'un." This last was to the phantom, and the musician obligingly started another song, though at considerably lower volume. "Got me about a week's worth of pay to drink off. Sugar? The usual for us."

Sugar obediently filled up four glasses. It was the same stuff I was drinking: amber liquid that was more whiskey-adjacent than whiskey, poured from a label-less bottle, and tasting like burnt cinnamon and old pond water. The pour was a lot shallower than what Sugar had given me. The horsemen brought up the glasses as though they had heads sitting on top of their wounds, tipping them back over invisible lips, and the liquid just vanished as though it was going down a human gullet.

Conversations, what few there had been, started up after that, but they were quieter now. I'd seen this kind of thing before, though not quite to this level. The Nocturnist wasn't a mob bar, but it was neutral ground. So when one of the bosses came in, whether it was Titanio Mab or Mickey Cohen, things got a little quieter as everyone watched the shark cruise by and hoped they wouldn't be mistaken for fish. These four were sharks, but there was a livewire quality to their energy, a violence that wasn't constrained even by the mob's petty notions of decorum. The mob were murderers, sure, but these were killers, and there's a difference.

"Hello there, what have we here?"

The lead horseman didn't need to have a head for me to know what he was talking about. Murphy's Law would compel him nicely, or just the simple fact that I was a new pair of legs in a dead-end town. The horseman pushed away from the bar and approached, moving with a distinctive John Wayne limp. The others stayed at the bar, maybe watching me, maybe watching everyone else. Their violence could explode anywhere, and that's what made it so gut-churning. He carried a smell around, this acrid miasma that stank like fake fruit somehow gone bad.

"You're new here, ain't ya?" he asked me, only he wasn't really asking. "Guess you don't know who I am."

"Tell her, Tod," said one of the horsemen. He pronounced the name almost like "Toad." One of the others chuckled, but judging from the sound, he'd never heard a joke in his life.

"I'm Tod Dullahan," the horseman said. "That's a name you should put right on your tongue. Or, I s'pose, that slate."

The horseman was next to my table then, and he picked the slate up between his thumb and forefinger. The slate was mine. You didn't just touch it without permission. Or at all. Wasn't hard to see what the room said, that these four would pull those weapons with no hesitation or worry about the consequences. But I couldn't quite control myself, even if the green hadn't drowned me yet. I yanked the slate back, and wondered if he knew how lucky he was that I hadn't just crushed every bone in his hand like a paper cup. His stink filled up my nose.

He didn't make another grab for the slate. Maybe he saw something in my face, or maybe he was done with that part of the conversation. "Got a name, dolly, or are you too new for that?"

I bristled at the "dolly." It was right next door to what he wanted to call me. The implicit promise was that he was going to pick one or the other, and I got to choose by whether or not I answered him. So I did, and burned with the capitulation.

Jane.

"Plain Jane, huh?" Tod said. "Well, Plain Jane, if you ever get a hankering to see what a real rantch looks like up close, you just let me know. I'll show you everything." The woman whistled, and it sounded like a boiling kettle. "Come on now, Morgan," Tod said. "I'm just bein' neighborly."

"The doc's gonna be hot, he knows you're makin' time with his new moll," Morgan said. She spoke with a faint Irish lilt.

"What's the doc gonna do, charge us double? Ain't no one else in this town needs him. Not anymore," Tod said. That last was with cruel amusement and his friends laughed appreciatively. No one else did. In fact, the room had gone silent, everyone else desperately pretending that this wasn't happening. Grateful that it wasn't them. "So whaddya say, Plain Jane?"

Not here long.

Tod guffawed. "Now if that's not the least surprising thing I've heard all week." He leaned in close, and I could smell...not his breath. No, it was whatever horsemen had instead. It came from the neckhole. The whiskey was there, an undercurrent of spoiled meat, and beneath that, the whiff of brimstone. "Dropped the doc, huh? Can't say as I blame you. More to this town than a broken-down old meat golem."

I didn't have anything to say. It reminded me, maybe too much, of being home. My real home, my new one. At the Nocturnist, our uniforms are halter tops, shorts so short they barely have legs, and fishnets. Gives some people the wrong idea, that we might like to be touched when it's really only an invitation to the peepers. Here, I was maybe dressed a bit more modestly, but the reaction was the same. Some monster thought if he got friendly enough, he was going to taste the eye candy. Though Miss Nocturne wasn't keen on us breaking anything on the customers, she was also fine with inflicting a little pain, so long as it didn't become a habit. Kept the dangerous reputation of the place intact. Miss Nocturne was far away, with a job that might or might not be mine.

"So, Plain Jane. How long you with us?" He slid one hand, rough, backed with big, ropy veins, over mine. The green was coming in now. The hand bucked slightly, all of its own accord, before I could take back control. Times like these, the body wanted to make the point that I was only renting.

"Don't have to be rude, Plain Jane," Tod said, in what he probably thought was a purr. "I could be good for you." The body wanted to put him through the wall, and the brain wasn't far behind. But my eyes kept going to the bowie knife on his belt. Wasn't the knife exactly. It was what the knife meant.

I looked at my right hand, between the middle two knuckles, right where my flesh was coming unzipped. I'd like to have blamed my creator, but those stitches had come loose so many times I'd lost count of how often I'd repaired them. Underneath, the muscle and tendons peeked out, some gray-green with decay, others dyed the unnatural colors of the industrial broth I used for blood. I focused on that torn flesh, because I knew if I looked up at the faded pearl buttons on Tod's shirt, I was going to grab him, wad up that flesh like an old newspaper, and show him precisely what Plain Jane could do.

And then have three more headless horsemen on me, each with their own weapon from the pits of hell. Meat golems are tough, and yes, only electricity can kill us in a single shot, but we can be hurt. Do enough to us, we will die. Just takes some effort. These four horsemen had the tools to do it, and the time it took could be clocked with my pain.

"Kinda quiet even for a dolly, ain't ya? I like that. You ain't lived until you seen the sun come up over the desert when the swarms come out."

The hand ran over mine again. My skin wanted to unzip itself and crawl away in sheets. He wasn't pawing, not exactly, but he was close enough that I could read the old agony in his neck. Looked like it had been flash fried when it was cut, the edges of the muscles burned black, the stuff beneath gray like a cooked steak.

"Beautiful sight," he whispered, and I caught a kiss of brimstone.

I swallowed, my throat burning from whiskey and hate. Then, salvation. An arm, covered in iridescent green chitin and brillo hairs, slapped a sheet of paper on the table in front of me. I blinked at it.

(Pay up.) said the card.

It was impossible to read emotion in the fly's head. Sugar buzzed, and I was beginning to think that was involuntary, her mouth parts restlessly working. The dim lights of the room shined off her red compound eyes. She held up the card again.

"Sugar, come on now—" Tod said.

Sugar raised the chitinous claw, beckoning to the door. The wall of zombie got off his stool and shambled over. "Brains," he told me in no uncertain terms.

Sugar held up the *(Pay up.)* card, then followed it up with *(Or you get the bum's rush.)*

That was right about when I figured out what she was playing at. I wanted to thank her, but that would have ruined the whole farce. So instead I patted my shorts where I didn't even have any pockets and made a helpless gesture. Sugar pointed to her muscle, and the zombie grabbed me by my upper arm. Reflexes, born from another life, nearly made me tear the arm out of his grasp. A zombie tried to herd me, the best thing he could look forward to was a broken arm and an earful of hissing. But this one was part of the cavalry. So I let him pull me up from my seat. I snagged my bag as I got up and played the helpless gamine as he marched me to the door.

"Sugar, don't you worry about nothing," Tod said.

Sugar flashed a card at him, and I only got a glimpse. *(Sorry.)* Then another, this one decorated with a crude drawing of a full cocktail. *(Next round is on the house.)* That got Tod to back off, leaning up against my former table, his ghostly attention on me as tangible as an unwelcome hand. So I went, as the zombie took me to the door and shoved me out of it onto the street.

"Brains!" he said, the tone implying "And stay out."

Good advice if ever I'd heard it.

Five

It took some time to find a flop. I wandered past Fort Meatstick, and I swear that wasn't my intent. It was out of my way, out of every way, but I still went. Maybe it was the monster part of me, the part that wasn't any of the dead girls. The piece that wanted to make more meat golems even if the conscious me never would. As I walked, Fort Meatstick pulled on me with its own gravity, and before I knew what I was doing, I was there.

The wards were active now, which meant the fence was buzzing and the torches were lit. I hissed and shied from both. Most humans in Los Angeles used the fears, keeping the weaknesses for emergencies. Nick's policy was that the monster decided for him which he would use. That these were openly using electricity and running water pointed to a far more deadly struggle. A lawless one.

Monsters gathered around the sad little fortress, silently staring in. The vast majority were ghouls, licking their chops whenever a human showed themselves beyond the battered walls of their hovels. But there were others: zombies, gremlins, mutants, and witches. The only thing I didn't see that surprised me were headless horsemen.

Barrow wasn't too far away, still in his rocker, peepers focused on the house of his chosen. Nick had told me all about it, the monsters surrounding his house every night, hunting for a way in, teasing him, harassing him. I wouldn't have believed it if any other human had told me that, and I never went down to the human neighborhoods. This was the first time and now I was seeing it for myself. If anything, Nick had undersold the spectacle. My skin crawled just as badly as it had under Tod's hand. Nick had always said it was so much nicer at my place. He had been right. Until I'd ruined it.

I walked away from Fort Meatstick, finding a motel near the outskirts of town, and I was pretty sure it was the only one for miles. Not exactly a booming tourist trade in Quartzsite. A series of sagging bungalows arrayed outside of a dirt parking lot, it looked just like I felt.

I went into the office and rang the bell. Wasn't too much later that a ghoul shambled from the back, licking his green teeth.

"Help you?" he asked.

A room, please.

He named a price I could live with. The bungalow was two tiny rooms: a bedroom and a bathroom. Two people couldn't have stood in that bathroom at the same time, and there was scarcely space for three in the bedroom. The bed creaked on old springs, and the wood-paneled walls looked ready to give up. It didn't matter. I threw my bag into a corner and collapsed on the bed. I was counting sheep in no time.

Six

I counted a total of three sheep before I was positive I wasn't going to sleep that night. The sun came streaming through the threadbare drapes a couple years later and the merciless day had caught me. I pulled myself out of bed and rubbed eyes that were dry even when it rained. I glanced at the bathroom and decided against it. I wanted him to see me at my worst. I didn't want him getting any ideas that I had dolled myself up in any way.

I left my stuff behind, taking only my purse—a beat-up handbag that was as much alligator as I was—and went out the door. In the early morning, when the air was still blue from the night, my hometown was almost nice. The rot I saw in the punishing light of day wasn't quite as apparent. I made my way across town, and once again, I found the invisible shield in place. It was weaker this morning, as I was at least able to look in the general direction of my eventual destination. I had a debt to pay first.

As rationalizations went, it was a good one. At least the debt was a real one, incurred so recently I felt compelled to pay it. That's how I ended up in front of the Sugar Shack. Like any bar in the regretful light of morning, there was something faintly sad about the place. The holes in the plaster, the stained walls, and the wear on the building were visible in the morning sun. The neon, once glitzy, was now dark and silent. The place looked rundown. Tired. Like everything else here.

I knocked on the front door. There was no answer, and I didn't really think there would be. No property lines demarcated any of the lots—there was just open desert until the next buildings, a small market and a shack, rose from the dirt. I went around the side of the bar. An exit toward the back was marked with cracked soil that had been wet and dried many times, but the door itself looked to come from the bar. On the back end, I found what I was looking for. An outdoor staircase, made of sun-bleached wood, led up to a door, over which hung a lightbulb partly shielded by an aluminum cap.

I took the stairs, hesitating as they creaked dangerously, but growing confident when they didn't collapse into the dust. I knocked on this door, and was almost immediately rewarded with the sound of someone moving inside. A moment later, the door opened. Sugar Kane stood in the doorway, buzzing, drawing an old flannel robe around her. She cocked her head in surprise at the sight of me and held up one finger from her human hand.

She ducked inside, emerging a moment later with a pad and pen. *{Jane. Got home okay?}*

Staying at the motor inn.

{Sorry to hear it.}

I shook the concern off. *Thank you for last night. Came to pay my tab.*

Sugar named a sum I was pretty sure was less than what I owed. I fished my wallet from my purse, peeled off a couple bills, then held up a hand to refuse any offer of change. Sugar reflexively tucked the money in her cleavage. I did that from time to time myself, though that was mostly because I didn't have much up top, and so there was plenty of room for tips. Sugar, though, looked like she could have used her chest as battleship ballast.

{Realized you didn't know who you were dealing with,} Sugar wrote.

Figured it out. At least some.

{Last night you met Tod Dullahan. Number two of Ambrose Dullahan. Owns the town.}

Everything?

{*Everything. Doesn't own my joint, but that's about it. Owns all the rantching land in the wash, buys anything in town whenever someone up and leaves. If he thinks it's valuable.*}

How many Dullahans are there?

{*Too many. Steer clear of them.*}

How do I recognize them? I asked.

{*You see a hollow around here, they're a Dullahan. All report to Ambrose. They run this place any way they like.*}

What about the cops?

Sugar buzzed and I took it to be bitter laughter. {*Ambrose Dullahan owns the law.*}

I shook my head. That was certainly nothing new. Even the cops in LA, supposedly straight as arrows, had more than their share in the pocket of a gangster. Out here, there weren't even the vague checks that the city had. Someone with enough money or force of arms could run this place like a medieval lord. Sounded like Ambrose Dullahan worked that out.

{*Don't think you're here to deal with Clan Dullahan, are you?*} Sugar wrote.

No.

{*Mind my asking, then?*}

Here to talk to my creator.

{*The doc,*} Sugar wrote.

You know him?

{*Everybody knows the doc. Only one around here, so he treats everybody who needs it. Doesn't matter if you're a hollow or a bug.*} Sugar stopped writing, then added, {*Don't know him well or anything.*} Sugar's wings, transparent as cellophane, rattled against her back.

Just need to sort a few things out. Then I'll be gone.

{*Good idea. Quartzsite ain't a safe place to be. Don't matter who you are.*}

SEVEN

owhere else to go. No way I could invent to avoid it. If I kept orbiting the place, I might as well just go home, get my job back while it was still waiting for me. Spackle over the hole in my wall and try to pretend that I couldn't see it out of the corner of my eye, yawning open like a mouth. I'd still be the same monster who had nearly taken Nick's head off. Counting the days until I inevitably tore that hole wide open again. It was time to do what I came to.

Though I tried to keep in mind what I wanted, I couldn't. The noble emotions weren't strong enough to carry me. Anger was. I could hold tight to my rage, ride it as long as I could and hope it didn't throw me off.

I walked unerringly to my destination, proving that, five years later and in the daylight instead of the dark, I could find the place unassisted. I passed the church on the way, a weary congregation heading inside for their sermon. I hoped they found whatever they were looking for, and I wished it would be that easy for me.

My destination looked like it had once been a garage or possibly a gas station before it had been repurposed to a doctor's office. A picket fence, like a sagging and weatherbeaten dotted line, partly traced the boundary between the dirt road and the property itself. Outside, a few piles of spare parts rusted gently in the sun. The only intact vehicle was an ice cream truck that was twenty years old if it was a day, battered in desert dust and fried in vicious heat. Islands of asphalt peeked up from beneath a thin coating of sand. The front of the building featured two doors, one for pedestrians and one rolling gate for vehicles, but that one was chained shut, the chain long since rusted the color of a scab.

My heart, taken from someone I didn't know, hammered in my similarly stolen ribcage. I took a deep breath of hot desert air. It would have been so easy to turn away, to go back to my motel room, grab my bag, and catch the next train home. I wouldn't have to think about him, or this place in the sun. Back to the nightlife, of making clothing with someone else's talent. Back to being too close to Nick but unable to talk to him.

That made me walk across the yellow dirt to the door. I paused there, momentarily unsure if I should knock. I opened the door, the bell jangling to announce my presence. Must not be many phantoms out here if he was using one of those. A few exhausted chairs were lined up against the wall to my right. A short wall stretched partway in front of me, then gave up. This looked like it had once been a waiting room of some kind, but had its walls knocked out to add it to the larger room beyond. What had once been a mechanic's shop was now filled with metal beds, stained curtains, and medical and scientific tools. In the back, glass jars lined up like soldiers on parade, filled with what looked like water but stank like an old cat. In the center of the room was a winch with a table that would rise up to the skylight overhead. I shuddered when I saw that; my first memories were of waking up on that very table, steel cuffs over my wrists and ankles. A mountain of machinery stood next to it, covered with dials, gauges, and radar dishes. Directly in front of me, a short staircase led up to another door, to what looked like an apartment.

A chain clanked to my left, and I whirled, ready to fight. A giant ant, though small for it, chittered as it tried to get close to me. About man-sized, it was covered in a railroad of medical staples. In LA, the must-have pet for meat golems was a wolfhound, custom-assembled by the owner; out here, it must be ants. The mandibles worked, and I couldn't tell if it was happy or angry, or if these emotions even applied to a stitched-together bug.

The door to the apartment opened and a meat golem stepped out. She was curvy and small, but her outfit wasn't doing her any favors. The short black dress was a few sizes too small, and no matter how she moved she looked like she was ready to pop out of it somewhere. Her hair was brittle, black and high, her two skunk stripes rising up like candle smoke. Lines of stitches ran over her body, but these were far angrier than mine. Maybe because they were fresh. Her complexion wasn't quite right, either; her skin was a uniform gray-pink rather than the patchy quality we meat golems tend to have.

She wobbled down the stairs and fixed me with pale brown eyes. "Can I help you?"

I started when she spoke. If there was one thing I hadn't been expecting, it was that. I signed to her in our language. *How can you talk?*

"Well?" she said, putting a hand on her ample hip.

I signed again, and she kept staring. To those who didn't know it, the way meat golem ladies talked looked like restless fidgeting, and not a single bit of understanding dawned in her eyes.

"You gonna use that slate or just stand there like a boob?"

How can you talk? I wrote.

She clomped a little closer on her chunky meat golem heels and squinted at the slate. "I ain't what I look like," she said. "Just changed a little bit. Gotta go along to get along, you know? Now whaddya want?"

My gaze swept over the lines of stitches. They weren't holding her together. They were marking her, making her present to the world as a meat golem, only she was still human. She pulled at the hem of her dress, and threatened to spill out the top, where more stitches dipped into the neckline.

"Whaddya want?" she prompted me.

Looking for Burke O'Hare.

The not-meat golem jerked a thumb over her shoulder. "He's in there."

Can you get him for me?

"Who should I say is calling?" she asked, straightening up.

Jane.

"Got a last name, Jane, or should I make something up?"

I added a *Stitch* after the *Jane.* She didn't quite give me a harrumph, but she came close, tottering back across the lab, up the stairs, and disappearing through the door. I waited, keeping an eye on the ant. Occasionally, it rattled its chain, but didn't seem to want to do much more than that.

The first thing I heard from the apartment was a bellowed, "Who Jane?"

Of course. Most important person of my life, and I don't even rate a memory. A moment later, the door burst open and I saw him. Burke O'Hare, my creator.

Whoever had made him hadn't spent much time ensuring he matched. He should have been as tall as me, but a hunchback ruined that. His right arm was longer than his left, and far more powerfully muscled. His legs were wiry and bent. His kisser was cobbled together and looked more like a flesh-and-blood collage than a real face. I don't even think his skull came from a single person. A line of stitches dipping to his lip gave him a permanent sneer, or perhaps a leer. He lurched out of the back and glared at me with jaundiced eyes. A terrycloth bathrobe flapped open over his boxer shorts and a stained undershirt. The loathing slithered through my body right on cue.

"Who you?" he demanded, holding the railing of his stairs. Behind him, still in the apartment, the woman shot me a defiant look. I held up the slate where my name was still written. Burke stumbled down the stairs, staring at the slate with a cockeyed expression. No recognition lurked in his mad stare. "Who you?" he said again.

I tapped the slate. Burke moved closer, then, frustrated, he limped off to the left side of the office, past the platform where I'd been brought to life. He wheeled out an old blackboard, the surface cloudy with the ghost of chalk. Signing would have been easier, but I was glad he didn't know how we could talk to each other. I wanted to keep that where he could never find it.

He wrote on the blackboard, «Who are you?» His writing was messy, the lines of the letters all struggling to escape.

I think he must have seen the hatred in my eyes because he flinched, just slightly. I wrote, You made me.

Burke squinted at me. Recognition glimmered in his right eye, which was a swampy green. He nodded. "Jean good," he decided.

I suppressed a shudder. Inside, I felt the hot wind coming off a burning town. I concentrated on the stifling atmosphere of the doctor's office. Jane, I wrote, and tapped it on the slate.

"Jane good. Why here?" he asked.

"You made her?" asked the woman, clomping down the stairs. She stayed in the back half of the lab, as though I had claimed the front. I wanted to tell her that none of this place was mine. Burke nodded, making a rumbling in his throat. "Couldn't find a smaller nose?"

Burke's expression grew stormy. "Jane good," he insisted. The woman quailed.

I turned to her. I'm not staying.

The woman nodded, then turned hard. "Of course not."

"Frances nice," Burke said. I took that to mean "Frances, be nice." At least I had a name for the woman now. Frances, for her part, submissively ducked her head. "Jane back," he said.

Not staying.

"Jane good," he said. "Why here?"

I have questions, I wrote.

Burke frowned, then gave me a "go on" gesture.

Who was I?

"Jane now," Burke said, and then, frustrated, returned to his blackboard and scrawled, «Doesn't matter. You're Jane now.»

It matters. Then I underlined Who was I?

Burke shook his head and looked to Frances. She was watching the both of us with interest. I still felt the haze of hostility, but now it was tinged with curiosity.

6 women. Who were they?

Burke shook his head, then swept one hand out. "Not matter!"

Matters to me.

Burke paused, then opened his mouth to speak. He shook his head and returned to the blackboard. «*You left. Now you come back? Why now?*»

Doesn't matter.

«*Matters to me,*» Burke wrote, and his ruined lip curling back to expose rotten gums.

I want to know who you made me out of. Either you tell me or I go.

"You leave?" he asked.

I turned, ready to prove my point. It was a bluff, but one I wanted to be true. If I walked out that door, I'd never see him again. I'd never come back. In all probability, I'd never know who I was. Whose memories were in my mind and whose life occasionally drove my body. I'd be back to being Jane. Batty Jane, whose last stab at happiness would be gone as soon as she saw the sunlight on the other side of that grimy door.

"Jane wait!"

Tell me, I wrote, holding up the slate with barely contained anger.

Burke shook his head, but held up a misshapen finger. He wrote on his blackboard. «*Not now, but I will tell you. I need a favor.*»

I shouldn't have been shocked at the nerve, but I was. Guess I was a sap for thinking he'd have any decency. Green waves lapped at my ankles.

He saw the look in my eye and nodded, a defiant gleam in his gaze. «*I made you,*» he wrote. «*One favor, and I will give you what you want.*»

I should have known it wouldn't be so easy. I didn't even really know Burke, but still, I should have known. The kind of person who makes a bride for himself out of corpses, then tries to insist on a short engagement when she hasn't been alive for a day was the kind of person who used anyone for anything. He wasn't going to give up something, even something worthless to him, without extracting value in return. I should have left. I knew it even when I was making the decision to stay. I should have gone through with my bluff, but I couldn't. He knew it, too. He must have smelled it on me like sweat.

What kind of favor? I wrote, the hatred I felt bleeding into my fingers.

"Easy favor," he rumbled. He waved at the apartment. "Fetch box."

This last was directed at Frances, as she wobbled back across the room to the apartment. She didn't balance well on those heels. I don't know why they were in fashion for meat golems; they took a hell of a long time to learn to walk in. Left to my own devices, like now, I wore a comfortable old pair of saddle shoes.

Frances returned with a beat-up cardboard box. She handed it over to me. To my meat golem muscles, it was light as air. When she was right next to me, the blonde roots beginning to grow out under her black and white dye job were obvious. I frowned at Burke, raising the box.

He got the hint. «*Take Sunkist Trail out of town. Make a left when you come out of the wash. Follow the trail up, turn right at the cactus that looks like a devil's fork. Deliver that box to Phobos.*»

What is it? I asked.

«*Doesn't matter. Give it to Phobos. She will give you $. Bring $ to me and I will tell you everything you want to know.*»

It wasn't too late. I could still leave. But I knew I wouldn't. This was the price of knowing, so this was the price I was going to pay. Then I could leave Burke O'Hare to the desert. Let him get swallowed up by the same dust that was eating up his home.

I'll do it.

EIGHT

The ice cream truck coughed and sputtered like a martian with hay fever, but it drove. After I convinced Burke that I didn't have a car, he agreed to loan me his, and it turned out to be the hulk outside his office. Against all appearances, he had been maintaining it fairly well, so at least it could still move without being pushed. The icebox in back appeared to be in working order, too, but I wasn't going to go digging around in there. Let the contents remain a mystery.

Just like the box sitting on the floor beside the single seat up front. It rattled a bit when I went over uneven ground, and since the whole way was uneven, there was a lot of rattling. I wasn't much of a driver, truth be told. I didn't own a car in Los Angeles—with the red car you didn't need one—and I had only gotten a little practice recently, when I drove Nick's old Ford coupe. And that was something we only did rarely, just because my mind and body weren't always my own. Driving, like so many other skills, was something I carried from the women who'd made me, hidden in my brain or body, or maybe both.

As I made my way into the desert past the northeastern corner of the town, I started to see what Tod Dullahan had meant. The wash that held

Quartzsite was crisscrossed with ant fences. Like the barbed wire of the previous generation, but this stuff was far hardier, made of one of those alloys the mad scientists are always dreaming up. Weathered wooden posts with what looked like wires strung around them enclosed vast swathes of baking land. A look at them set my nerves to jangling as I imagined the current that could end me.

Meat golems existed on that irony: a bolt of lightning brought us to life, but the next would end us permanently. Made living in an electrical world a unique danger.

From time to time, I spotted a swarm of giant ants on the horizon. As they moved, they kicked up sheets of dust dyeing half of the sky yellow. I didn't see any of the artificial anthills; this looked to be on the edge of Dullahan land, if that even meant something. The Dullahans likely laid claim to whatever they could see, and there wasn't anyone around to tell them different.

As I bounced over the uneven track out to the hills, my mind started wandering. Maybe it was looking for an excuse. Because I was looking for it, it wanted to find me. The light, blinding, through the windshield turned into the sun coming between the leaves of an orange tree, a chubby hand reaching for them. Then it became the scorching glare of martian death rays scything over a burning city. In my first couple years, I hunted for that city in magazines and almanacs. I thought if I learned the genesis of that memory, I could exorcise it. Break its power over me. I finally found the city in an old issue of *Life*, a picture of the Glassing of Wichita. It had been in June of 1951, when a trio of martians in their mighty tripods had burned Wichita to the ground. The soil itself had been turned to glass, a beautiful and awful remnant of the Night War.

I had been there. Or, more accurately, my brain had. My daughter's sweet weight bowed one arm; a weight that would be like a feather to me now, but then was as heavy as all the world. She was too big to carry, but that didn't matter to either of us as we watched the monstrous machines stalk through the smoke. Her little head was buried in my shoulder, crying the kind of sobs that said nothing would ever be okay again. Wichita wasn't our home. I felt no particular attachment to it, no sense that I was seeing my life go up in the inferno, but that was the moment the woman whose brain I had knew the Night War was lost.

Nick told me that every human had that moment, and it was uniquely awful for every one of them. For him, it had been the arrival of a fifty-foot ape in Los Angeles, throwing cars around like toys and smashing buildings into rubble. For me, it was the Glassing of Wichita, and it happened before I was even made.

The searing wind whipped through my hair, my dress fluttering around me. Like every other time, I tried to see my hair, to see if I was a blonde, a brunette, something to give me a connection, but I couldn't. The world was dark, the only light was the hellish glow of Wichita's Viking funeral.

I blinked, and I was back on the sun-drenched road. Good thing there was nothing to run into out here. The land started to rise ever so slightly. A small depression betrayed a turnoff, and I followed it. Burke's directions had been perfunctory, sounding like the kind of thing I couldn't miss, so I had to take it at least a little on faith that it would be. He didn't want me to get lost. This was his errand and he wanted it finished.

The road started to climb into foothills. The mountain range that bordered this side of Quartzsite—though after seeing the Rockies, "mountain range" seemed to be overselling it—was still in the distance. The terrain began to vary as I went up and down, dust giving way to rocks. I wondered when I was going to see this devil's fork of his. Cactus was hardly a unique sight out here, same as tumbleweeds and joshua trees. But then I saw it, and I knew it had to be the right one. A cactus, with three perfect prongs stabbing the noon sky. I made the turn there and began to snake into the foothills.

I drove, wondering what I was going to find. Ogres ruled the hills and mountains around LA, but Phobos hardly sounded like one of their handles. So I kept going, assured that eventually I would see something that had to be my destination. And I did, as the day bled into the afternoon.

I found my destination soon after, and I knew it as soon as I slapped eyes on it: an old mine dug into the side of the hill, a few weatherbeaten beams struggling like Atlas to keep it up. Arizona was honeycombed with old mines, but this one looked a mite too clean to be abandoned.

The truck stopped with a protest of its aging brakes and I turned off the engine. If I were still human, I'd have been sweating. Old sense memories trumping the new. I stepped out, stretching my legs. I reached in through the open window of the cab and honked the horn twice.

Turned out, I didn't have to. They were all around me, waiting, revealing themselves only when I was out of the truck. Mutants. They stood up from behind rocks, one emerging from the shadows of the mine, another from the lip of terrain overhead. Mutants are predominantly blue, with hard heads sculpted in the shapes of massive brains. You'd think this would make them rivals with mad scientists and brainiacs for the smartest monsters. You'd be wrong. Mutants are generally muscle for those types, and in that role they perform admirably. Their faces are alien, with wide circular eyes and a mouth that's just a wobbling sheet of pink tissue. Their bodies are covered in blue chitin trimmed with red veins, their arms ending in crude pincers. Supposedly, they have some kind of psychic connection with insects, making them ideal keepers for the giant ants. I didn't see a giant ant anywhere.

I just saw their guns, modified to fit in their two-clawed hands. One was holding a shotgun, two others a strange cannon with tubes leading to shiny metal tanks they carried on their broad backs. The last held a three-foot prod ending in two sharp metal points. Scorched ozone of an exposed wire wafted from it. I shrank from the weapon, even though it was far away.

"Stay where you are!" said the one with the shotgun.

"Before you think of anything, I got an antprod," said the one with the prod. He jabbed it into a slender cactus, and with a crack and hiss, it burned right through the trunk, knocking a good foot of the plant into the dirt.

I grimaced, momentarily picturing the green skin of the cactus as my own flesh with its touch of verdigris. Then I showed them my hands.

Nothing in them. Of course, a meat golem didn't need to be armed to do serious damage. Slowly, I reached into the truck, and brought out the box. They tensed, but no one fired.

"You from Doc O'Hare?" asked Shotgun. I nodded, held the box up again, mimed handing it over.

"Phobos gonna want to talk to her," Antprod said. "Go fetch some more antprods. Keep her nice an' gentle."

"Yeah, you comin' with us." The two cannons ran back inside, and the one with the shotgun stopped pointing it at anyone in particular. Didn't matter. My attention was on the one with the antprod, just waiting for him to decide that maybe a meat golem was much less trouble when she wasn't moving.

A second later, two mutants came out of the mine, carrying three antprods. They might have been the same ones from before. I couldn't tell. They passed an antprod to the one with the shotgun, and now all four of them were armed to kill. More than they needed. I just wanted to make Burke's handoff. I wasn't looking to make anyone bleed.

"All right, dolly, march," said one. I obeyed, approaching the mine cautiously. One came up to walk ahead of me, out of arm's reach. Not that I had a free arm to throttle anyone, what with the box in my hands. The others formed up behind me, and I could hear their distinctive shamble, each one running electricity up my spine.

Natural light was gone pretty quickly, the mutants using old oil-burning lanterns to see. The flames made me shy away, but at least they were behind glass. They weren't using torches, which would have sent me fleeing back up to the surface. Instead, I had to put up with a tighter and tighter knot in my belly, and the memory of Wichita burning ever brighter in my mind.

The central shaft was wide enough for several people to walk shoulder to shoulder, with an old rusted track for mine carts going down the center. They passed several side shafts but then one said, "Turn left." And I did. There were a few other turns after that one, and I had the impression this was just to hide the precise location from someone. I made no mistake here: these mutants were hiding in the hills around Quartzsite. There seemed to be only one person worth hiding from, too. I already knew more and less than I wanted to. I cursed Burke. I asked him one question, one he should have answered without hesitation, and instead of answering, he sent me into the earth with a bunch of mutants armed to kill.

After a few more turns, we found our destination: a hollowed-out chamber repurposed as a camp. Half of the stuff in there—the stained canvas tents, the battered cookware—looked held over from the Old West. The rest of it was modern edging into the futuristic, the kind of thing that you saw with the smarter monsters, machines whose purposes I could only guess at. I was pretty sure none of this was their handiwork: mutants were scavengers, not innovators.

"Phobos! This one here's got a package from O'Hare!"

The biggest tent in the chamber parted open, and a mutant stumbled out into the golden light of the surrounding lanterns. Phobos was craggy with age, the furrows in its skull deep and rough with a faint azure dust. The eyes, normally a metallic gold, had dulled to copper.

There were only the five of them total, the four outside and this new one. The camp was big enough for a lot more. Those numbers could have been away from there, but somehow, I didn't think so.

"O'Hare sent you?" Phobos asked. The voice was deep, but feminine and rusty. I nodded, and tried to hand the box to her. "Demos," she said, gesturing with a claw.

One of my escorts snatched the box from my arms and brought it to Phobos. The mutant took it in her claws, surprisingly agile for being nothing more than a pair of curved pincers. She held it with one, dimpling the cardboard, while the other pulled the panels of the lid open. She reached in and pulled out a skull, claws through each eye socket. The surface of the bone had been etched with designs, the curves and whorls stained with deep reds inside. Phobos dropped the box and turned the skull over, inspecting it from every angle.

"This is good work. Really, it is," she said, and then she cast it away like garbage. It made a sound like pottery breaking as it vanished in the thick shadows of the mine. "I'd almost believe this was Tod Dullahan's skull if not for that bunk you passed off as Morgan Dullahan last week!"

I held up my hands, trying to placate her, my eyes telling the story that this wasn't me, I wasn't a part of this. It didn't help.

"What are we gonna do with her?" Demos asked.

"Send her back to the doc," Phobos said. The mutants made noises of dismay. "I didn't say in one piece," Phobos went on. "Doc's gotta know what he done ain't right. Gotta know that even out here, he can't cheat us and think there's no recompense. No, we ain't down by a long sight."

The antprods hummed as they closed in. I fought to hang onto myself, to keep the green from crashing over me. I grabbed the slate and scrawled a message, showing it to them.

Not me. Him.

The hum of the antprods grew louder, and I shrank away, but there was nowhere to run. Phobos held up a claw. "You got something to say in your defense, hon? You say it now."

I wiped the message away with the heel of my hand and wrote another. *I'm not with O'Hare. Just doing a favor for him.*

"Why would you do the doc a favor?"

He has something I need.

"She's lyin'," Demos said. I shook my head as emphatically as I could manage.

"Got every motivation to lie, hon. You know what antprods can do? Why, they can go right through a carapace and encourage an ant to do what you like. Got a charge like a bolt of lightnin'. Never seen it used on a skin-dolly before, but I seen it on a ghoul. Zzzz, pop! Stops their hearts dead. A little charrin' to show you was there."

I thought of the cactus being decapitated and I shuddered. Dimly, the persistent buzz of the antprods began to sound like the death rays of martians, sweeping over a town. Green washed in from the corners of my eyes.

Not lying. I swear. I don't know what O'Hare did. I'm not a part of it.

"Don't know what he did? I'll tell you what he did, hon. Maybe you're new. Maybe you don't know that I used to own this place. The whole wash was mine. The swarms out yonder? Mine. Quartzsite? Every goddamn stick of every goddamn shack? Mine, mine, mine. I was making a good living, an' everyone was getting a share. Then Ambrose Dullahan and his hollows come out of the east, and they decide they should take instead of earning."

"The La Paz War," said Demos.

"Oh, you knock it off with that stuff," Phobos said. "Make it sound like we're hellbound for glory. We ain't. Just two different rantchers with a difference of opinion. I think he should be dead and he thinks I should be dead."

The mutants laughed appreciatively.

"We killed us a lot of them," Phobos went on, "and they killed a lot of us. Ambrose and his boys are doing a bit better than we are, because every time one dies, two more take his place."

"Like a hydra, only without the heads," said a voice, younger than all the others.

Phobos faltered, turning to the mutant who spoke. He quailed. She turned back to me and started up again, the pink tissue around her mouth shuddering. "Anyways, your friend, the doc, he makes us an offer. He tells us he can get his mitts on Morgan Dullahan's own skull. We get that and Morgan starts dancing to our tune, right before we encourage her to take a little dip in the nearest river."

She was talking about something we all knew. Supposedly, if you took a headless horseman's skull, you could control him. It was illegal, at least in California, but I didn't think these mutants cared overmuch about legality.

"That little moat out by Fort Meatstick!" said one of the mutants. They all laughed.

"Be fun for everybody to watch little Morgan come apart in that current, I think, after she kills all her friends," Phobos said. "So we have the skull, and we set us up our little ambush. Gonna catch Morgan with

Tod Dullahan and his gang, maybe make her use that scattergun on them for a change. We spring the trap, but Morgan ain't doing what we want. And she kills Thebe and Charon! Two of my own is dead, thanks to the doc! And he thinks he can snare us with the same damn con, only now it's Tod Dullahan's skull? No, I think all I can do is pay him back by returning his ladyfriend in the very same box!"

Please. Not his ladyfriend!

The antprods sparked. Green engulfed me. I was looking through a pinhole at Phobos now, and all around me, the rush of flames, the hot wind, the screams of metal and people. I held on, only barely, knowing the instant I lost control was the instant I died. I focused on Nick, the terror in his eyes after I punched that hole in the wall. Then I had been the lightning; now it crackled all around me.

"Phobos?" ventured the young voice. He sounded not quite as bruised from their existence down here, a little hope left in him still.

"What is it, boy?"

"Why ain't she attackin' us?"

"What?"

"Skin-dollies. They go bugs when you back 'em into a corner, only this one ain't fightin'."

"Could be she's yellow," Demos said.

"No, Ophelios might be right," Phobos said, peering at me. "We don't wanna do nothin' to the doc that ain't gonna hurt. So what about it, hon? What was you sayin'?"

I tapped the *Not his ladyfriend!* on my slate as I hunched up from the antprods all around.

"You really ain't with the doc?"

I shook my head, now underlining <u>*Not his ladyfriend!*</u>

"What do you think the doc's reaction would be, if we sent him you all cut up?"

I shrugged, trying not to let the casual brutality of her words sink in too deeply. *He didn't remember me.*

"You said he made you." I nodded. Phobos laughed. "Oh, hon, I am sorry. I've made me a whole brood, as you can see...used to be more, mind, but this'll give you an idea...and I remember all of them. Whenever a Dullahan cuts one of my boys down, a piece of me goes with 'em. Ain't much left, truth be told."

I tried to put a sympathetic look in my eyes. It was difficult, because mutants were alien enough to provoke an instinctive loathing, and this one had just been talking about butchering me. That outcome was still on the table if I didn't play my role to the hilt.

"Doc O'Hare conned you, too," Phobos decided. "Here's what we're gonna do. You're gonna go home. You ain't getting a dime for that fake skull you brought, neither. And you deliver a message to the doc. You tell him, the next time we see him, he's a dead man."

"Quartzsite ain't too safe for us," Ophelios said.

"Shut it, kid," Demos told him, followed by the clack of chitin on chitin.

"Quartzsite ain't gonna be Dullahan land forever," Phobos said. "O'Hare's days is numbered. He never should have tried to cheat us. Guess you can tell that to him still alive."

I exhaled, giving her a grateful nod. The antprods receded behind me.

"But know this, hon. If we find out you're more to him? That anything you said to us is a lie? Well, you're gonna get real acquainted with those antprods, and we're gonna make sure it takes a long time for you to die."

Nine

I don't remember very much about driving back. I know I had the accelerator kissing the floorboards. I know the tires shrieked and threw dust at every turn. I know the sun was giving up and the giant ants were marching back home over the horizon.

The rest was lost under the roiling green. Burke had sent me in to be killed. He knew what was coming. That's why he didn't go himself. He knew the mutants had gotten wise to his con, or he believed they might. That was enough for him to throw me to the wolves. My first conscious thought about any other individual was that Burke O'Hare was a dirty son of a bitch. Babies, real ones, get to think their parents are the greatest people in the world before disappointment. My father tried to kiss me within minutes of birthing me, and now he set me up to die.

That memory, at least, was mine. It was in the part of my secondhand brain that was specifically me, Jane Stitch. My experiences and no one else's. I'd opened my eyes in the blinding haze of the thunderbolt. I had been clamped to the table, naked, and I was up and out of the skylight. Overhead, lightning flashed in a dry sky. I found out later he had a machine to take care of that, bought from a mad scientist whose lair was deep in the southern Arizona desert. The pulleys squeaked and the chains clinked as I descended into the room. The skylight closed, two metal doors thrumming shut like a coffin lid. Then he came into view, gaze crawling all over me like hungry maggots. I suppose I should be happy he undid the clamps before he tried to get fresh.

He'd stitched me out of corpses to be his little toy. He thought I didn't have a choice in the matter. Told me as much. That's when I slugged him. That was after several hours of him trying to break me down. The funny part was, I should have crumbled, but there was one thought that never went away. The one thing I wanted to get back to. That wanted to wake me up from the nightmare I'd been born into. It was the little girl's hand, reaching for the orange.

More came back after that. Nothing useful, though. Just flashes of the little blonde girl, spurring me to lose what control I had. For years, I thought I might have two kids, but lately, I think it was just the one. I was seeing her at different phases of her life, her face reshaped first by growing up, then by the Night War. That was enough to make anyone into two different people. I never got her name, but I knew her scent. I knew the feel of her hair. I knew how her smile filled me up with light. She'd given me the strength to tell Burke to go to hell, and I thank her for it.

I was almost madder at myself than I was at him. Of course Burke had set me up. Of course he'd do that just to avoid answering an easy question. Of course he was trying to swindle a desperate group of mutants. Every cruel thought I'd had about Burke O'Hare had been dead on.

I squealed to a stop in front of Burke's office just as the sun vanished under the lip of the world. Yellow dust was now blue, edging to black. My vision, though, was nearly entirely green. I wanted to let loose, to tear my way into the office and take Burke apart piece by piece, just like the mutants had promised to do to me.

I marched to the front door without even a coherent fantasy of what I was going to do. There was just the sense of churning violence. The compelling desire to give over to the part of me that was ready to tear the world limb from limb. The part that broke things and people. Turn it loose on Burke and see how much he liked his creation then. How well he'd stitched me together.

I pulled the door off its hinges. I wasn't really trying. The world is a muddy place, and sometimes things break. The metal of the hinges stretched like taffy, and then they gave with a shriek. I threw the door into the sand. The chains on the ant rattled as it lunged, mandibles wide. The chain didn't have enough give for it to get to me; the insect was for show only. Lucky for it; I would have ripped it apart along its seams.

Frances burst out of the back apartment. She was dressed in a shift that was too small for her, and her face was a mask of panic.

"Jane! Please!"

I stalked forward, eyes glued on the door behind her. Burke was in there. I was hissing now, not even meaning to. The one sound I could make, that any meat golem woman could, a rasp of rage and disgust. Frances caught me about halfway to the stairs. Her fingers, weak human fingers, wrapped around my arms. I could have thrown her through a wall with a shrug. I nearly did. She was no one. Her face, once pretty, was cut to pieces by the lines of stitches, rendering her expression ghastly.

She called my name again. I hissed at her. The intent was clear.

"He's not here!" she lied.

So easy to throw her. Right into the wall. Of course, with the green edging into my vision, with the burning stench of Wichita in my nose, if I threw her, she'd break. Just like that, her lights would go out. I didn't owe her a thing, but I saw Nick. Eyes wide in terror, but worse, the glint of betrayal beneath. Holding up his lighter like a talisman. Frightening away the woman he'd been sleeping next to for months. I couldn't hurt her. I tore my gaze from her face to the open door beyond and hissed again. He'd hear that. He'd know, the coward. He'd know that I had been here, that I'd survived his little setup, that he was too scared to face me.

I shrugged myself out of Frances's grip. She yelped and cradled her hands, watching me with round, frightened eyes. Nick's eyes.

I turned and left just as quickly. I didn't trust myself. If the green took me there, Frances was dead. I was out in the cool night, going...I didn't know. Away. The train was calling me, the way it started as soon as I stepped off it.

Ahead, the neon sign of the Sugar Shack gleamed in the dark. Maybe a drink was what I needed. Maybe that would calm me down. I was going over the desert dust between streets before I stepped onto the boardwalk at the side of the paved road. The street wasn't deserted, even though it was Sunday night. A few pedestrians went to and fro, mostly ghouls going about their errands.

Across the street loitered three headless horsemen. Three I knew. They had been at the bar the night before with Tod, though I didn't see their Napoleonic leader. Their rides were parked perpendicular to the sidewalk: two spectral chargers, one black, one ghostly white, and the third, a pickup truck, its red paint job faded from countless hours in the sun. Two of them, Morgan and the one with the wood axe, leaned against the cab of the truck. The other one paced up and down the boardwalk, spinning his noose like a lariat. When a ghoul passed close, he followed with taunts, his two friends laughing. Plain glass bottles sat on the wheel wells of the truck, a layer of brown liquid at the bottom with thick smoke rising from the top.

I could have walked right into the Sugar Shack. I had to cross the street to go past them. And I crossed the street.

The green was on me now, closing over my head in hungry waves. The thunder of the roiling tide, or maybe it was the rush of the industrial chemicals I called blood. I was walking fast, not quite as fast as when I pulled Burke's door off the hinges, but fast. The horsemen didn't see me until I was nearly on top of them. One of the chargers pawed the ground, and the truck's headlights flicked off and on, fire belching from the exhaust. I flinched from that, but it wasn't enough to stop me.

"Looky here," said the one with the wood axe. "It's the boss's pal from last night."

"Whatcha gonna say, Shreve?" asked Morgan.

"I'm gonna say..." said the one with the wood axe. Whatever he was gonna say, I didn't hear it, because I surrendered to the green. I dropped beneath the water to hide in someone else's memories. The chubby hand reaching for the orange. Wichita in flames, spidery shadows stalking through the night. I gave myself to them until I could smell the little girl held close to me. Until I knew I was finished with whatever I was going to do.

I came to I don't know how much later, breaching above the waves for a shuddering breath. The back ends of two horses and a pickup truck burned hell down the street, fleeing the mad skin-dolly. A shape slumped in the saddle of the black horse, while the other two horsemen cowered in the bed of the truck. The white horse was riderless. Then they were gone, off into the night.

I looked myself over. No new wounds. No buckshot in my skin, no gashes from an axe, no burns from a hangman's noose. Just the stitches coming loose on my right fist. More now, unraveling all the way down to my wrist on either side. Though the flesh was raw, it didn't hurt. Just an itch that no amount of scratching would help. I picked at the stitches all the way back to my bungalow.

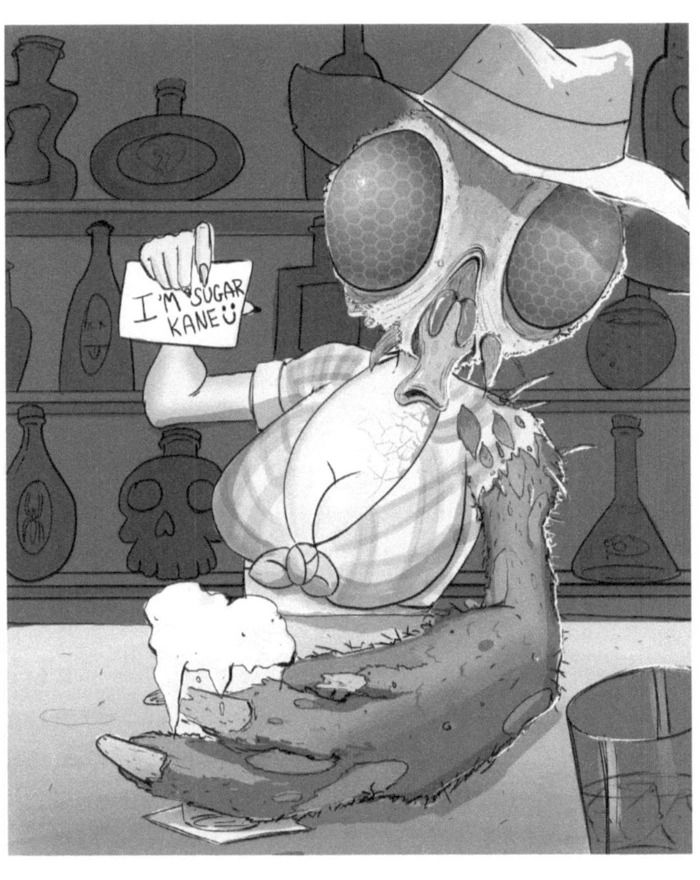

Sugar Kane

TEN

Not that I slept a wink. I tried, really I did. Meat golem endurance could be a real pain. I showered the dust off my body and hoped the day would disappear down the drain with it. Combed out my long hair with its twin skunk stripes. Then I lay down on the bed and waited for the sun.

I could have used Nick's soft snoring next to me. To watch him until I could take a little of the peace he felt and ride that into sleep. Deep into the night I pulled the picture out of my wallet. I could only see the vague outline of him. I tried to trace him with my finger, but I couldn't. It was too dark, and I couldn't turn on the light. Don't know why, but I couldn't.

When the sun peeked up into the eastern sky, I was sitting on my bungalow's little porch, knitting. Just something my hands liked to do. Making garments, didn't matter the kind, helped push the sea back from my lonely rock. I sat there, in the chill morning, waiting for the September sun to get to work cooking us up.

I saw the wolf coming from a good distance off. Working at the Nocturnist, I was one of the few people who dealt with real wolves on the regular. They were on the big edge of dog-sized, and they acted like animals. They sniffed, they wandered, they did things that didn't quite make sense. This one, though, was the size of a pony, and the way he was padding over the desert on a beeline to me said he was perfectly conscious of what he was doing.

As the wolf got a little closer, I took in the details. His white coat, which I'd taken for snow white far off, looked now more thin and silvery. His eyes were rheumy, red tears forming at the inner edge. Even his teeth were blunted with wear.

When he got close, he changed, the fur mostly disappearing, a disturbing elasticity of his limbs reforming to human proportions. He stood up relatively straight, one hand going to the small of his back, which straightened with an audible pop. The werewolf was an older man, white-haired and leather-skinned. Snowy hair formed an impressive pelt over skin, and a soft paunch overhung his belt line. Not that he had a belt. He was completely naked. A gold star was tattooed over his breast, nearly swallowed by cottony hair. His face wasn't cruel or kind; it was just bone weary. He regarded me with what might have been a gunfighter's squint in his younger days, but now was just the myopic gaze of a man with a perpetual headache.

"Don't have to ask if it's you I'm after," he said. "Ain't no other new meat golem in town that'd be at the motel."

I watched him, then held up a finger and stood. He tensed. I shook my head. *I'm not any danger,* I thought at him. I pointed at my throat, then I mimed writing something and pointed to the open door behind me. My slate was in full view, sitting on the rumpled bed.

"Get it," he said. "But don't you get anything else, or this visit turns a lot less friendly."

I fetched the slate but didn't bother to hang it around my neck. *What can I do for you, Sheriff?*

He chuckled, and it felt like it was about a joke I wasn't in on. "Name's Peter Wolff, ma'am."

Jane Stitch.

"Pleased to make your acquaintance, Jane, but I'm sad to say this ain't a social call." Wasn't hard to figure what brought him here, but I was going to make him say it. I shrugged at him.

"Got me a report of a meat golem beatin' the tar out of a couple locals. Now, I hear meat golem, I think of the doc, but they say this one was a lady. Now here you are, a stranger in town, and you fit the description of this meat golem."

Am I under arrest?

He chuckled again. That sound was really getting tiresome. "You tell me." I frowned in confusion. "Y'see, Jane, it's like this. I could arrest you. Throw you in the little jail I got, then bus you up to Parker—that's the county seat—and try you for assault and battery. I could do that, but it's a lotta work, especially for someone ain't fixin' to do it again. Or I could just let you quietly leave town and not come back."

Why?

"Well, like I said, I ain't asking if you done it, and you ain't tellin' me, so that's good. But whether you end up gone back to where you came from or in a cell up in Parker, the effect is the same."

You would do that for assault?

Wolff shrugged. "Them Dullahan boys give as good as they get. This time, someone got one over on them, and maybe that's not so bad, all things considered."

I watched Wolff. I didn't quite know what to make of him.

"The thing is, if someone roughs up a Dullahan, they gotta know that reprisals ain't far off. A body doin' that kind of thing, and sticking around, would find out pretty quick that just because the Dullahans ain't got heads don't mean they forget. Hell, they got memories like an elephant."

I nodded, slowly.

"Glad you're gettin' what I'm puttin' down. Gotta admit, when I heard it was one of your kind, I thought for certain this thing between us gets ugly. But I can see you're a reasonable woman. Now, the only question is: How reasonable?"

I chewed my lip. This was the way out, the way I'd been looking for from the beginning. Wolff was showing me the exit, and it was inviting. I glanced through the open motel room door. Nick's picture lay on the nightstand, the folds curling up at the end. Calling to me. The real Nick was at home. Maybe I could go back there. Find him, make everything all right again. I'd tried, but my creator couldn't be talked to. The mystery would stay unsolved and I could find a way to live as whatever I was.

"So, whaddya say?" Wolff asked. "You going to the train station or the sheriff's station?"

Train, I wrote, and felt my belly give.

"Good girl," he said. "Hope you enjoyed your little vacation."

With that, Peter Wolff took his wolf shape and loped back the way he came. Not too long after that, I shoved my things in my bag. When I picked Nick's picture off the nightstand, I couldn't look at it, even though it was bright enough now to see.

Eleven

With my bag over my shoulder, I walked to the train station. This was a failed experiment if ever there was one. I had expected a lot of endings, but being chased out by the law after one day wasn't on the list. It wasn't even for beating O'Hare, just a couple bastards who decided they wanted to try me.

I reflexively examined the back of my fist. The skin had flayed open past my middle knuckles, revealing rubbery tendons and white bone. It looked like nothing more than a zipper undone. It would have been nice if all I had to do was pull it back up.

The day was a hot one. Wouldn't miss the Arizona heat. It was Monday morning. Weird thought; out here, it felt like the days of the week stopped existing. Every day was simply today, with yesterday and tomorrow kept only for the pain.

I'd be back at work by the time the Nocturnist opened. Wasn't sure if I'd tell any of them where I'd been. I guess that was the nice thing of being a meat golem: I didn't have to tell anyone anything. I could just be silent. Go back to what I was doing and wait for the next time the green closed over me. The next time I hurt someone.

Quartzsite didn't know I'd been there, and it didn't much care. The truth was, the only mark I'd truly made was the hole in my wall, and once it swallowed me up, that would be the end. As soon as I went home with none of the answers I'd wanted. The hole would take me, this unraveling thread of a woman. This ersatz being made of cast-offs. And worst of all, I didn't even know what it would be taking.

As I walked, I didn't bother to follow the streets and dirt roads. I cut across the lots that were almost indistinguishable from the deep desert. Lizards scurried away from my long shadow as it stretched out west, where home had been for five years. It didn't feel like home. That feeling had been the first thing the hole had swallowed up. This place wasn't home either. I had an apartment, but I didn't have a home. I was nobody. Six bodies, no soul.

The spot where the fight had taken place, across the street from the Sugar Shack, was out of my way, but I passed it anyway. Wasn't sure why. Not like there would be a chalk outline of my questions there, dead the second I'd given over to the green.

Just a normal street going about its normal business; mostly zombies and ghouls shuffling to work. No humans here. I wondered about the specifics of Arizona's version of the Fair Game Law, but I don't know how much it mattered. Judging by Fort Meatstick, the humans of Quartzsite might not have any expectation of being protected by the law no matter when they were taken. Not something I would have given any thought to without Nick's stories of how often he was pulled over by the wolves.

I stopped at the patch of sidewalk where I'd done it. I didn't know exactly what happened, but I could figure the broad strokes. I lost control, plunged into that roiling green place we meat golems go. We talked about it from time to time, in furtive signed conversation, but I never knew if it was as bad for others as it was for me. For all I knew, I was crazy even for a meat golem. Or, even worse, I might be one of the stable ones.

"Morning." The voice was soft, cautious. I looked up into the shyly smiling faces of a pair of ghoul women who were passing. I was too surprised to do much of anything, let alone write them a message. They kept moving down the street. I blinked, looking around.

"Brains," said a zombie, touching the bill of a old stained baseball cap as he shambled by.

I mouthed something that might have been a greeting and gave him a nervous smile. Then I saw what the street was trying to tell me. Everywhere I looked were the people of Quartzsite, and they were watching me. Some smiles, others only keeping tabs out of the corner of their eyes. No hostility at all. Amazement. Welcome. Maybe even gratitude. A whole town that was glad I was there.

I stood there, watching them watching me. And I was there and nowhere else. There was no sensation of those other memories surfacing from the green to drag me under. No, it was me and only me under the hot sun, wondering what was so damn great about beating up a couple headless horsemen.

Didn't have the heart to tell these people I was leaving. Those same horsemen I had sent yipping away had sicced the law on me. I wondered if that would puncture the aura the Dullahan boys seemed to have in this town, or if it would only reinforce the idea that there was no fighting them.

My borrowed heart shrank back to its original size as I made my way to the train station. Just a taste of victory before an inevitable defeat. Only thing waiting for me was a couple hours on a train and then a jump into the hole. I wondered if I'd ever see Nick again, and if I did, what I would write to him. Dumb question. I'd shown that the best thing I could ever do for him was vanish from his life. It fit, since I was vanishing from my own.

"Bzzz!"

I couldn't tell where the sound was coming from until I looked up. Sugar fluttered down from somewhere in the sky, setting down on the sidewalk in front of me as graceful as you please. Her wings shivered as they came to a rest against her back. In the sunlight, her wings and eyes reflected rainbows. Sugar wore a pair of cowgirl jeans and a western shirt open to show off her assets. She fumbled with her collection of cards, and showed me *{What will you have?}* She punctuated this by pointing at my bag. I read between the lines. She wasn't asking me what I wanted, but what I was doing.

I pointed in the direction of the train station, but there was a lot of town between me and it, so I gave up. *Leaving town.* Sugar pointed to the question mark on the card. I erased the message and wrote another. *Sheriff told me to get out.*

Sugar made that buzzing sound and shook. She was laughing. She turned and headed for the Sugar Shack, waving me over to come with her. Might as well. I had an hour or so, and nothing said I had to leave town sober. Sugar opened up the front door and gestured to her bar with a flourish. If the Nocturnist looked sad in the daytime, the Sugar Shack was downright funereal. The scent of spilled beer and worse now had none of the new stuff to drown it out. The neon was off, and all that was left were the dank shadows stretched over the exhausted wood. The morning heat hadn't quite gotten in yet, but I knew by afternoon, it would be a sweatbox, for those who still sweated.

Sugar went behind the battered bar and gestured to a stool. She retrieved a pad from under the bar and wrote on it. *{He's not the sheriff.}*

I frowned at her. *He said he was.*

{Then he was lying. He's just a deputy. County seat is Parker. Sheriff's there. Wolff is the only law we got in this town.}

Only law the Dullahans will allow?

Sugar touched her mouthparts like a regular person might touch their nose. *{Dullahans own Peter Wolff lock stock and barrel.}* Sugar tore that piece of paper up, and threw it into some fragrant garbage.

He was awful nice for someone bought. Gave me the choice between arrest or leaving.

{He's not nice. He's lazy. Knows what you did last night & doesn't want the same.}

You know about what happened? I wrote.

{You beating the holy hell out of Morgan, Mal, and Shreve Dullahan? Nope, I ain't heard a thing.}

I laughed. It was soundless. *They called Wolff on me.*

{& you picked leaving town.} I nodded. She shook her head. *{Didn't you have something to do?}*

I did.

{What happened?}

O'Hare isn't going to tell me anything. Had me do some dirty work for him. Sent me out to get killed.

{Doc did that?} I gave her an emphatic nod. *{Like I said, I don't really know him, but he is the doc. Always figured he was at least a little good.}*

Worst person I know.

{What did you want to know from him?}

I took a deep breath. I didn't know Sugar, but she was the only person here who had treated me like a person. She didn't want anything, wasn't serving an agenda. She'd saved my bacon that first night from Tod. Sugar had proven herself. *I want to know who made me.*

{Thought you said the doc made you.}

No. Who made me. I gestured at my left eye, then my right. They were mismatched, one nearly black, the other silver, no clearer evidence than I was born of different people. Then I pointed at the patchy parts of me, the way nothing quite lined up. I was a quilt of dead girls in human form.

{I never thought of that before.}

Most people don't.

{Most of us monsters, we remember who we were, back when we had a human head and before we could fly. Got whole lives up here.} She tapped her monstrous head. I nodded. *{What do you have?}* she wrote.

Someone else's memories.

{And you don't know whose?} I shook my head. *{Guess I can understand why you might want to. What are you hoping the answer will be?}*

I shrugged. I hadn't really gotten that far. When your hopes depended on Burke O'Hare, it wasn't the best idea to get to thinking what particular shape you'd like those pipe dreams to be in. They were going to stay dreams unless some kind of miracle occurred. *I just have to know. It's a piece missing from a jigsaw puzzle.*

Sugar made a low buzzing sound. I imagined it was almost a whistle. She put her pen to her pad and was about to write, but stopped, then wrote anyway. {*Do you know why you were made?*}

I nodded. *He wanted a*—I thought of half a dozen words, but settled on *bride.*

Sugar shuddered. {*Same story all over.*}

That's what happened to you?

Sugar gave an emphatic nod. {*When you're a human fly, you've got a face only a mother can love. Just not your mother, not anymore, right? So we can get a little lonely from time to time. My creator, he's out in Phoenix, thought the same thing and figured even if he changed me, I'd still have certain assets.*} Sugar gestured to her chest. They indeed remained uncovered by chitin.

I nodded and winced. *I guess Burke is more of a leg man.*

{*I'll say.*} Sugar buzzed in obvious amusement. {*I wasn't interested and I told him so. He figured beggars couldn't be choosers. He was right, only I wasn't begging. I went west until I could find a place to buy that I could afford. I didn't want to stay where I was from, looking like this.*}

I wrote a *?*

{*People I used to know. I'm a monster now, and ugly as sin. Didn't want to feel them looking.*}

I don't know what it's like having people from before.

Sugar nodded. {*It's nice to know they're there, but it hurts if you have to see them.*}

I thought it over, then went back to an earlier point. *I went west too.* I suppose we were still Americans in that, even after everything. When things got bad, we went west. Not a lot of west left when you were already in Arizona, but we'd tried.

{*Only now you're back.*}

I have to know. Six women were used to make me.

{*You think he killed them? Or you think he dug them up?*}

I shivered. The first option was always in the back of my mind. I wanted to deny it. Burke was a scavenger, first and foremost. He didn't seem like a killer. Of course, neither did Nick, and he had practically given me an itemized list. I always told him there was a difference between a murderer and a killer. He agreed, but also said there wasn't enough of a difference to make him comfortable. Nick was brave enough to face that truth about himself; Burke wasn't. I had to believe he robbed graves to get at my parts. Put together a meat golem the old-fashioned way. Because the other way was too terrible to consider.

{*I take it he hasn't told you.*}

He put me on that errand and said he'd tell me, only it sure seemed like he didn't plan on me coming back. When I did, he hid out.

Sugar shook her head. {*Yellow too.*}

I nodded. *That's what got my blood up. Why I beat those three Dullahans. Why Wolff's running me off, I guess.*

Sugar twirled the pen she was using between her human fingers. She looked like she was thinking over a response. Finally: {*So you're just going to let the doc get away with it?*}

I shrugged. *What can I do?*

{*Wolff has no teeth. If you stick around, the Dullahans will be out for blood, but Wolff is too old and too lazy to do anything to you. If you're willing to brave the Dullahans, you can stay.*}

And then what?

{*Get those answers you want.*} Sugar regarded me with her giant red compound eyes. {*So what's it gonna be, Jane?*}

I thought about it. The sun streamed through the leaves as the chubby hand reached for the orange. *Guess I'm sticking around.*

TWELVE

The office felt like it should have leeched some kind of grandeur from its place in my journey since the previous day, but it was just as shabby as it had always been. The truck was parked outside where I had left it. The only evidence that I had been there was the busted door. A cursory effort had been made to fix it up, put it back on ruined hinges, but I had done more damage than Burke's or Frances's skills at repair could address. So it was just leaning against the doorframe, giving up like the rest of the town.

As I came to the door, it opened awkwardly, and would have tumbled into the dust had I not caught it. A man, his skin ghastly white, with bandages wreathing his face, stumbled out. I took him for a vampire at first, but though he winced at the sun, he didn't catch fire. That was a dead giveaway.

"Excuse me," he muttered, as he passed, the words mushy.

I squinted after him as he staggered across the desert. Then I went inside, my anger momentarily mollified. I pulled the door mostly shut, but it would never fit flush over the frame again. I wondered if Burke would actually go through the trouble to fix it, or if he would just let the desert swallow this place inch by inch.

The clink of chains signaled the reanimated ant attempting to get friendly, but I ignored it. That cat odor hung in the still air. Rattling of tools and some kind of crinkling cloth came from the back of the office. Frances wobbled out on her meat golem heels to meet me. The fear on her face was almost a scream, but she approached anyway.

"Jane, are you straight?"

I nodded. *Where is Burke?*

"He just finished up with a patient."

I glanced at the door, but all I could see was a faint border of light; the new "vampire" was gone. Frances shifted uncomfortably. "That's what Burke does now," she said without prompting. When I frowned, she kept spilling. "Pay him enough and he'll give you surgery to look like a monster."

Monsters can see through that.

"Not all of them, right?" she asked, desperate for it to be true.

I shrugged and nodded, and she took my meaning: *Why?*

"You look like a vampire or a meat golem, the zombies and ghouls leave you alone."

I had trouble looking at Frances. That kind of despair was hard to live with. It ate into someone, made them a thing rather than a person. Nick told me a lot of awful things about what it meant to be a human these days, but he never told me anything like this. I thought of the poor, mutilated man stumbling over the desert, and I couldn't tell if I wanted to cry or put my fist through something. Maybe both.

The ring of a curtain on runners echoed, and Burke stepped out. A tray of bloody surgical instruments sat by a bed, a few more bloodstains on the old towels littering the surface. My stomach wanted to turn inside out and I reflexively turned away, one hand going to my mouth. I watched him out of the corner of my eye, stepping back into the waiting area where I couldn't see so much of the carnage. As he slapped eyes on me, he grinned. A superior, gloating grin.

"Jane good?" he asked. I nodded, and the fact that I didn't charge across his office and intimately acquaint his skull with the floor was a good enough testimony that I was serious.

He wiped bloody hands on a filthy rag, not doing much more than move the gore around them. He wasn't wearing any kind of gloves. Didn't know if he even owned surgical gloves. He jerked his head in the direction of the grisly table and Frances wobbled off, setting about cleaning up. Really, she was just carting stuff over to the deep, rusty sink set into the far wall, but it was better than letting it marinate. My stomach was doing a rhumba now, and I desperately tried to find anything else to concentrate on that wasn't the persistent butchery of this place.

Burke lurched over to the blackboard and hauled it out so I could see. The remnants of our last conversation were partly visible. Echoes we were never going to be truly free of.

«*You're calm?*» he wrote.

I nodded, but the way he was looking at me, all sanctimony, wasn't helping. *Are you going to answer my questions?*

Burke's shoulders slumped, and he shook his head sadly. «*Is that all you're going to say to me?*»

What else should I say?

«*Thank you would be nice.*»

The green threatened to take me right there. The stench of Wichita being burned to glass in front of me filled my senses, a pungent stink carried over two lifetimes. Finally, my fingers quivering, I wrote, *You sent me to those mutants to be killed.*

"Jane no!" he roared, then wrote, «*Is that what you think?*»

You tried to swindle them. Sold them some skull you dug up and decorated, and told them it was Tod Dullahan's.

Burke spread his hands. "Jane gone." «*You don't understand the realities of this place.*» he wrote.

I know the Dullahans were fighting some kind of war against Phobos and them.

Burke nodded. "Jane yes." «*Phobos owned the valley. Good rantching land here. Then the Dullahans came, and the war started. Mutants and headless horsemen at each other's throats.*» He rasped, and Frances joined in, breaking into a brittle laugh. She looked to Burke, a puppylike need for approval stamped on her stitched-up face, but Burke ignored her. She deflated and went back to rinsing the tools under the yellowy water. I didn't laugh at Burke's little joke.

Bet that was good for business. Two monster clans fighting and the only law a broken-down old wolf, I wrote.

«*You've met Peter. Dullahans own him now, but there was a bidding war. Don't know why they bothered. Wolff just wants to be left alone. As for business, yes and no. Made getting my formic acid harder, but there was never a shortage of people who needed stitching up.*»

Acid?

He gestured at the glass jugs against the back wall. The source of the cat-stink. «*Milked from ants. Lots of uses, scientifically speaking.*»

None of this changes the fact that you sent me to be killed.

"Jane calm," he admonished, and I wanted to belt him. «*Dullahans won their war. Took this land, and you know what happened?*»

You had fewer patients and more acid.

"Jane good." «*A lot fewer. Nobody wants to cross the Dullahans anymore. So I'm stuck helping meatsticks pass and paying whatever Ambrose asks for my acid. He's getting me from both sides.*»

How is conning his competition helping that?

Burke shook his head, emitting a chuckle that sounded like two condescending rocks. «*I'm not fighting any war. I'm just putting a stake together on the back of some meatstick business no one wants.*»

They let you do that?

«*Who's going to stop me?*»

He was right about that. *So what about sending me to the mutants?*

«*Phobos doesn't know she lost. If she could get her hands on the skulls of the Dullahans, she'd win the whole thing—only as near as I can figure, Ambrose Dullahan keeps all the skulls somewhere in his place. Big old manor in the middle of his rantch. Impossible to get there. But mutants are dumb.*»

So you're making money off of them.

«Ambrose will wipe them out soon enough, and their money won't do anyone any good when they're dead.»

You sent me to die.

"No!" Burke roared. *«I sent you because I knew they wouldn't hurt you. You had nothing to do with it, and I was right. You're fine.»*

I hissed. *They had antprods!*

Burke held up a hand. "Jane calm." *«I'm not going to talk to you if you're going to be unreasonable.»*

The green wrapped me up in its tendrils, calling me to stamp Burke's head into the earth. I felt the little girl in my arms, her sweet weight as I bore her up to the orange. I closed my eyes and breathed, my left hand playing over the frayed stitches on my right. Then I opened them. *I'm reasonable.*

«You were never in any danger. You're here now, fine. And those mutants will be dead as soon as the Dullahans find them, which won't take long. All I'm doing is getting a little bit of money before it happens, and keeping the mutants from extinguishing the greatest medical genius of this modern age.»

I wanted to dismiss the last seven words, but I couldn't quite. Burke wasn't going to let me, anyway. I could see it in the fire dancing behind his eyes. He wanted me to ask. He was baiting me.

Instead, I wrote, *So you're more valuable than I am.*

For the first time, he blanched. I caught him off guard. I saw it in his misshapen face: he wanted to say yes. He couldn't, because the instant he did, I would walk out the door, and he would lose the bride he'd made to his specifications. *«They wouldn't hurt you. They didn't hurt you.»*

I sighed. Close as I was going to get. *Do you think this is smart? Sticking yourself in the middle of this war? If the Dullahans figure out you know where Phobos is, you're dead. Same if Phobos comes to collect.*

Burke held up a hand. "Ready," he growled. He shambled over to one wall and beckoned me over. An electrical box was there, breaking up the cinderblock. He fished a key from the pocket of his lab coat and fitted it into the lock. The door opened with a soft creak, revealing two weapons, secured on hooks.

The first was almost a hammer. A baton about a yard in length, it was tipped with a wedge of steel. The perfect tool to crack a skull. The second looked a bit like a flamethrower, with a gun-like tool at one end connected to a backpack with a length of hose. I recognized it: two of the mutants had been carrying something almost identical. The first was a great weapon against mutants; the second, filled with water, would kill headless horsemen.

"They come. They die," Burke said, and for a moment, those flames in his eyes blazed. He wasn't just ready for Phobos and the Dullahans, he was eager for it. Was he spoiling for a fight that bad, or was he desperate to prove something?

Burke went back to the blackboard. «*You see now? You understand? This could have been your life if you'd stayed.*»

I looked around at the dingy doctor's office. My stomach turned again as I beheld the blood, and I moved my eyes off it as quick as I could. The connectors of every pipe were ringed in rust. This place was a rotting charnel house in a corner of hell so pointless even the devil forgot it was there.

Finally I sighed, silently as I did everything but hiss. Burke wasn't going to let me ignore this. If he was going to answer my questions, I had to keep playing his games. He had to know that there was a limit to what I'd take, and I hadn't seen an antprod in that weapons cabinet.

Why are you a genius?

"Jane good." «*Glad you asked. Going to show you something. First I need a friend of mine.*»

THIRTEEN

urke sent Frances out. I couldn't help but notice she was dressed like me now: high-waisted shorts, plaid shirt, scarf in her hair, cheap sunglasses. The only difference was she clomped about on her meat golem heels while I was getting around in my flats. She left, and a moment later I heard the truck cough and sputter and disappear, leaving me with Burke.

He grinned at me, and it was a grin I saw a lot in my job. Just because we're showing off our tops and tails, the clientele thinks we're joy girls. Burke had thought he was making his own joy girl, and found out she had thoughts of her own. His jaundiced eyes flicked over to the apartment he shared with Frances. An offer.

If I went, he might answer everything I had and more. That'd be a hell of a thing. Learn who I was only to find out I couldn't look at her in the mirror anymore. I turned away, going back to the waiting area and using it as intended. Burke rumbled, then busied himself. I couldn't see what he was accomplishing, and I didn't want to find out, not with so much of his job swimming in gore. Whenever I glanced over, he looked to be moving things from one side of the office to the other. He certainly wasn't cleaning. I had the impression that any real work fell to Frances.

It was nearly two hours, charted on a bland and water-stained clock on the wall, before she came back. I had my legs stretched out across the waiting area, my arms behind my head. Every now and again, I heard a vehicle outside, all of them sounding sick and tired, ready to give up like everything else in this town. In the distance, a train's whistle was a banshee's death call.

Then I heard the ice cream truck's now-familiar cough pulling up outside. I thought about getting up, but I didn't. I had taken the seat in the corner, my legs, long as they were, claiming the center of this space. Taking as much of it as I could. Playing at comfort I didn't feel.

The door shifted and groaned. "Your door certainly has seen brighter days," said a voice like wind through a tumbleweed. A voice I knew. "What on earth transpired to make it thus?"

"The one I told you about," Frances said.

"Oh. Oh, yes." The words had bacon grease on them.

The door opened, flooding the front with the strident light of day and illuminating the thick, swirling motes of dust dancing in the air. Frances stepped inside, taking her sunglasses off. She spotted me by the door and blushed, apparently realizing that I'd heard their conversation and probably wondering how much. A spidery shape followed her in. It was a small town, sure, but this was proof the Devil had a sense of humor.

"Well, hello there," Barrow White said. "When Frances said a lady was visiting, I hoped it was you."

"You know each other?" Frances asked.

"Made Jane's acquaintance when she was shopping outside Fort Meatstick the other day."

Frances jumped, flashing me a look of stark terror. I shook it off. Wasn't what I was doing, but I didn't know how to explain. Even to myself.

"White good!" Burke called, shambling out of the back.

"Dr. O'Hare! Capital to see you again!" said the ghoul with a grin. He sucked on the end of the cigarette holder. "So what prompted you to summon me in the midst of my repast?"

"Jane show," Burke said, like this explained everything.

"Sorry, old man, I'm going to need visual aids." He turned to me, flashing his smile again. "Jane, seeing as we're both intimates of this great man, we should be introduced properly. I serve as the doc's aide-de-camp for certain subterranean acquisitions." He reached out a hand that didn't have an ounce of meat on it. I took it, finding it warm and dry, like desert sands. His grin, though, was as moist as a freshly dug grave. "My dear, it is my distinct pleasure. You're as toothsome as a newly-buried bride."

I gave his hand a light squeeze, just to remind him what I'd done to that door, and it, unlike him, was at least partly metal. He grimaced and got the point. When I let the hand go, he shook out the pain I'd pressed into it.

"White done?" Burke demanded.

"Apologies and salutations, old man. I found myself compelled to make an introduction as, when Zeus gave you life, he extracted your manners in payment." White's gaze lingered on my legs, and while some of it was the same kind of ogling I was regrettably used to, there was something else in the tiny frown that creased his narrow brow. Something I couldn't quite put a name to.

"Show Jane."

"Show Jane what?" Barrow raised his thin eyebrows. They looked plucked and sculpted, but I couldn't tell if that was just an impression or not.

Burke sighed and returned to the blackboard. *«Show her the work we've been doing.»*

"Oh! Your discoveries!" Barrow said.

I have to admit, I was a little surprised there really were discoveries to show off. Burke O'Hare was my creator, but any meat golem with access to corpses and a little stitching skill could make another one. That he apparently had something else going made me reassess his intelligence a bit.

Burke nodded and pointed at me. Barrow frowned, then brightened. "I see. You want to demonstrate what we do to Jane." His fingers wormed under his hat to scratch his head. "Why?"

"Jane know!" Burke roared.

Barrow looked to me, just as confused about what Burke was trying to say as I was. Finally, he shrugged. "If we're to add a member to our merry band, as such disclosure implies, I suppose I should be pleased that it is one so ravishing." He showed me his teeth as though to demonstrate.

Burke nodded. "White get!" he pointed, then pointed at Frances, and gestured to one of the walls. I suppose Frances didn't warrant a verbal order.

"Come now, my dear," Barrow said. "If our fate is to be manual labor, at least it be with friendship in our hearts."

The two of them went through the broken door. Burke was grinning ear to ear. When he looked like that, it was easy to forget he was a doctor, and that he was apparently a good enough one to have discovered something. He looked merely stupid and cruel, a bully trying to cement his superiority over me.

"You see," he growled. "You see."

I hissed, but my heart wasn't in it. Instead, I nudged the door aside and squeezed through the narrow gap. The sun was cruel that day, desiccating the wash. Barrow emerged from a tiny shed nestled among the piles of junk demarcating Burke's property. He held a shovel in one hand and a pick in the other. A moment later, Frances followed, tottering under the weight of two shovels and two picks. I took them from her; they were light as toys. The exhausted Frances gave me a grateful look quickly smothered by a glare.

"Oh, if you're inclined to assist our labors, I offer my gratitude as well as my burden," Barrow said, handing me both pick and shovel. He brushed his hands off. "It's a gift to be of assistance to anyone."

Burke shambled out of the office, squinting suspiciously at the sun. He climbed into the cab of the truck without any word to us. Frances ran as quickly as she could on her heels, opening up the back. Barrow sat behind the wheel. I sighed and followed Frances. The back was a narrow aisle with a freezer on one side and the wall on the other. Frances knelt between and just behind the front two seats. I looked around, and seeing nowhere to put anything, set the tools down on the floor, closed the doors, and sat down, my back against them.

"Everyone found their seats?" Barrow called out. "Any who choose not to speak cannot be saved!"

The truck uttered its smoker's cough, chewing on the hard-packed dirt before finding the road. It snaked through Quartzsite, heading for the northwest end of town. I caught glimpses through the windshield from time to time, or when I half-stood to peek out of the filthy rear windows. The former ice cream truck was, ironically, sweltering. I didn't sweat, but Frances did, putting the lie to her surgical modifications. All of that, to be undone by the place she chose to live. She should think of moving north. All the way to Canada, leaving Burke far behind.

Supposedly I was the whole reason for this trip, but I might as well have not been there. Barrow drove, Burke sat, one elbow propped on the edge of the rolled-down window. Frances stared resolutely forward, never so much as glancing back at me. The excavating tools were at my feet. To my left, a freezer. I opened it experimentally. It was still cold.

"Jane shut!" Burke roared back without even looking. Frances did look at me finally, her eyes wide and disbelieving. I shut the freezer.

And I knew, instantly, one thing: I'd been in there. It wasn't a big leap to make. A meat golem and a ghoul. What else would they do together other than dig up corpses? They had the tools, and here they had the freezer to keep the parts cold. I ran my finger over the rough and dented surface of the icebox. I'd been in there, back when I was six women instead of one. Six bodies, unearthed, and ready to be stitched together into a new form.

I narrowed my eyes, as though I could look through the wall of the freezer and time itself and see those bodies, stacked like cordwood. What had Burke and Barrow seen that they liked? The legs of one, the hand of another. But not the whole hand. Something wrong with the middle finger, accounting for that line of stitches now coming undone. An imperfect canvas.

Six bodies, combined into one. Was I one of them? All of them? None of them? Some combination of the same? Or was I someone entirely new, created rather than born? A true person using only dead flesh the world was done with.

The back of Barrow's head was shiny. Sweat ran from beneath his hat into the wispy hair below. Had he eaten what Burke had left behind? I shook my head, having to physically refute that thought. No, Burke was too arrogant. He wouldn't let a ghoul pick over the parts of his bride. I was supposed to stay with Burke forever. No way any of me would line a ghoul's stomach.

And now, Frances was the one staying with Burke. I'd left, and so he found Frances. I didn't know what to do with that. Humans didn't have a lot of options. In this relationship, had she found salvation in a hard world? Or had I doomed her to mutilation and abuse? I knew it wasn't really my fault, that it was a decision made by the two of them. But that didn't stop the shard of guilt, picking at my stitches, ready to unravel me piece by piece.

The truck stopped a short time later. Frances turned to me. "Well? Time to go."

I nearly hissed at her, but I was going to save my rage for those who deserved it. I wasn't going to hurt another human, even if they were obnoxious. I opened up the back and climbed out, grateful to be stretching my legs. We were parked on top of a short hill. In one direction, the hills rose up into the Dome Rock Mountains, crowned by the semi-translucent corpse of the Springfield Shape. A flat place at the top of the hill was half enclosed with the sagging remnants of a wooden fence. An arch of wood spanned the entrance, faded paint marking this place as BOOT HILL. It was a graveyard in the middle of the desert, punctuated with crude wooden crosses.

A human family mourning at one of the graves spotted us and scurried away in fear. I hung my head. They had been remembering the dead, and now the best hope they had was that one part of their loved one would be a meat golem. More likely, he was to be a meal for a ghoul.

"Jane tools," Burke said. I did my best not to scowl and picked up the shovels and picks. The others shambled over the uneven ground.

"Might as well go to the place we know for certain has a fresh body," Barrow said, indicating where the family had only just been. My heart sank even further.

I looked around, wondering if I'd ever seen this place before. Nothing sparked, but that didn't necessarily mean the women whose eyes I had hadn't seen it. The graveyard—and that's what this was, a term like "cemetery" implied at the very least stones for markers—had been partly reclaimed by the desert. I got the impression that any clearing of encroaching brush would be done by the mourners, should they be so inclined. This place wasn't precisely remote, but it was far from the center of town. I turned and could see the bulk of Quartzsite, quietly simmering in the September air. Outside of town, the shapes of giant ants crawled over the desert, kicking up clouds of dust. From this distance, they looked as small as their normal-sized cousins.

"Jane here," Burke called.

They had stopped around the grave, Frances lingering close to Burke, while Barrow paced off the dimensions. I walked over and dropped the tools at Burke's feet with a puff of dust, even if I knew he would never use them. I wrote on my slate, *Did you dig me up here?*

Barrow frowned, trying to remember. Burke's brow similarly furrowed, but only briefly, and he shook it away. "Jane dig." I shook my head and pointed at the question on the slate.

The ghoul glanced at Burke, then, "My dear, your origins are hardly germane to the incredible abilities with which we hope to acquaint you."

I erased the last message with the heel of my hand, but I didn't get the edges of the words. *I know you rob graves.*

"Rob graves?" Barrow looked offended. "Jane, darling, we're researchers, voyagers into the stygian wilds at the fringes of life itself. We are..." he straightened up, looking ridiculous in his patchwork clothes out here in this makeshift desert graveyard. "Necronauts."

Burke shook his head in disgust, pointing at the grave. "Jane dig."

I looked from Barrow to Burke and back again. This was just more of Burke wasting my time. Trying to keep from answering the questions I'd posed. Anything to stay away from those, but whether it was malice or simple contempt, I couldn't know. Playing along burned in me, brought the green up at the fringes of my sight, but I listened. I lifted a pick, light as a toy, and started to dig.

Barrow soon joined me, and though his limbs were little more than sinew, he was able to move the dirt quickly. Frances pitched in as well, but she wasn't much help at all. Burke watched us, standing at the edge of the grave, never once putting a hand on any of the tools we'd brought. When I looked up at him, he would merely smile, an arrogant, gloating grin. We were all exactly where he wanted us to be.

It was a relief when my pick hit something hard. I picked up a shovel and used it to scrape away some of the dirt and found the wooden lid to a coffin. It was little more than a pine box, a throwback to the kinds of caskets that would have been buried in this place a hundred years earlier, when some hapless farmer caught an outlaw's bullet. I tapped it again, looking at the others.

"Oh, well done, Jane. Your excavation prowess is certainly something remarkable to behold," Barrow said, joining me. "Now, let's clear out a bit more."

Frances, exhausted, clambered out of the grave. Her arms were noodles, and she only barely made it up. Burke never moved to assist her. I dug away some of the soil, and Barrow nodded. "Open it if you would, Jane?"

I frowned at him and pointed to the rest of the grave, still covered in dirt and with us standing on it. Barrow laughed. "It's all right, my dear. We only need the top part open, and with your prodigious strength, it shouldn't be much of a chore."

He was right. Opening this thing was as difficult as tearing wet cardboard. I hooked my fingers around the edge and yanked, ripping a decent chunk of the lid off, tossing it up to the surface. Now, through that hole, I could see the dead man. His skin had turned as gray as Barrow's. He was old, with wisps of white hair clinging to a liverspotted skull. His features were craggy but round, a friendly face that proceeded even into death.

"White catch," Burke said, tossing down a coil of rope.

"Thanks, old man," Barrow said. The ghoul crouched over the hole, threading the rope down under the body's back and arms, then tying it at his chest. "Pull."

"Jane pull," Burke said.

My hatred had claws now, and it held on. I had to remind myself that he had answers that I would never get if I hurt him. I climbed out of the grave, picked up the rope, and hauled. The old man was so light, death taking the parts of him with weight. I pulled him out through the hole, then up onto the lip. He was dressed in a suit, dirty and patched, but still a suit. I stopped and marveled. Somehow this old man had made it through the Night War as a human, and he had died in peace. That had to be a one in a million chance. Only now, when he thought he was home free, when he was finally resting, we were disturbing him.

"You know, time marches on in a most disagreeable fashion," Barrow said philosophically. "As recently as only a year or two ago, bodies positively littered cemeteries. Whatever one had a taste for was available. A buffet of endless flavor and texture. Now? We're stuck with this. The leftovers." I never should have expected a graverobber to have any respect for the dead, but Barrow's comment begged for my fist.

"Jane truck," Burke said.

I took the meaning well enough. I hefted the old man up onto my shoulders and carried him over to the truck, where Frances opened up first the back door and then the freezer, showing an interior crusted with old ice. I laid the body down in the icebox with as much dignity as I could muster, the old man in my old temporary resting place.

The others boarded the truck, taking their old spaces. Barrow and Frances carried the tools as best they could, Frances squeezing past me to sit right behind the others. I tapped on the back window and pointed to the open grave. Were we really just going to leave it like that?

"What's the matter, Jane?"

I pointed again, then scrawled a note on my slate, disturbing the desert dust that now covered it in a thin sheen. *Leaving it?*

Barrow laughed. "Oh, those people knew as soon as they set eyes on us. They'll be pleased their grandfather is still useful to someone, even in death." He started the truck. "As I was saying, there's much less variety now than there used to be. It's unfortunate. But you have to think, with so many humans being turned, there are fewer humans to die. And many are turned at that moment of perfect youth, to be beautiful forever. Or, put another way, before they make any more humans. You know, we're looking at quite the bottleneck in the next few years. One wonders what's to be done."

I swallowed, but my throat was dry. Barrow was right. I hadn't even thought of it. Monsters were steadily hunting humans to extinction, and it was all legal. No humans, though, meant no monsters. Would that necessarily be so bad? Leave the world to the lesser creatures, who knew what to do with it.

Barrow drove us back, and I stared at the icebox the whole way. It was tight enough that the body didn't rattle around much, but I knew it was in there. The stink of decay clung to me where I'd touched him. I knew that I would be scrubbing myself that night, and I also knew I wasn't going to get all of it. There was no way. One collection of corpses holding another.

It was sunset when we got back to the office. The sky was pink and purple, and the land had turned a deep night blue. I stopped and stared, my silver eye squinting in the bright rays. Burke shambled out of the truck without a preemptory order, I suppose trusting us to know what to do.

We did. Barrow and Frances took the tools back to the shed while I gingerly lifted the old man's body out of the icebox. I carried him through the door like a bride. Burke gestured to the table where I had been brought to life. I frowned, wondering if he was really planning on dissecting the body there.

This was a terrible price already. All I could tell myself was that they would have robbed this grave anyway. They would be despoiling the body no matter what I had chosen. All I was doing was carrying. But I knew it was a little worse than that. I couldn't get near Burke without a bit of my soul getting dirty. If I even had one of those, or if it was as patchwork as the rest of me. Or simply gone with the six women who had it originally.

I obeyed, setting the old man down and shuffling away, the stink of death clinging to me no matter how far I got from it. Frances and Barrow came in next.

Barrow sidled up next to me. "This is the kind of show you're not like to forget. You're a lucky one, Jane, sprang from the doc's own brilliance like Athena herself. Touched by the hand of, well, not god. The next best thing."

I tried not to look at Barrow like he was completely insane while he stared at Burke with adoring eyes. Burke had turned his attention to the mountain of machinery next to the table. He checked gauges and flipped switches, pausing to watch the needles jump and dance. Frances fitted the corpse's limp wrists and ankles into the metal restraints, buckling them in.

My frown was getting deep enough to be another set of scars. This looked like the tail end of meat golem creation, only he hadn't bothered to build the body first. This was just a dead man. I wasn't too clear on how other monsters went about reproducing, but unless Burke and Barrow were in the process of creating an entirely new kind of monster, this didn't make any sense. Especially as one of the new creatures should be wandering around if they had.

Frances brought Burke a thick syringe. My creator took it without a word of thanks and slipped the big needle up and under the old man's breastbone. I guessed he was hunting for the heart. Then he hit the plunger. The liquid, cloudy and dark in the gloom of the lab, filled the man's body. Burke took the needle out and set the brutal device aside.

Burke flipped a breaker on the side of the machine. The tone was deep, rattling into my very bones. The air filled with static electricity, crackling over my skin. I took a superstitious step back. Lightning crawled up exposed wires, popping and snarling. Burke turned, and gave me his lopsided grin. In the flashing blue light of the machine, he looked insane. This might have been the most honest impression I'd gotten yet.

"Jane see."

Barrow nodded happily, then murmured, "The machine was purchased from a local mad scientist. Same man who created the giant ants. Brilliant fellow." I frowned at him. I knew all that. Knew the machine, even, but none of this made any sense. "You'll see," he promised.

Frances began to pull on the chains, elevating the tray holding the man up to the ceiling. Once, it had been me on that tray. A dark night five years ago, when the lightning put the life into my body. Frances pulled another switch, and the skylight opened. Night had fallen, but only recently. The sky hadn't yet taken on the deep vein blue of evening. Burke turned his attentions back to the machine, adjusting a dial, flipping a switch. Then he looked up once more.

Lightning spidered across the sky. I blinked, shuddering as thunder roared right on its heels.

Barrow was grinning, his big, flat teeth glowing in the olympian light of the machine. The gauges were all lit now like jack-o'-lanterns, the lights on the buttons flickering as well. A rope of killing electricity climbed both towers and stabbed the sky. The room filled with the bite of ozone.

Frances hauled the clanking chains, the metal tray rising higher and higher as she did. Above, another bolt crawled through the ether, unleashing an apocalyptic boom. No rain fell. The unnatural storm was eerie in its sudden anger.

The machine was quiet when I'd been lowered into the room, its task finished. I couldn't summon the memory of it clearly, though. I hadn't been there long, and it was simply a mound of quiet machinery while a stitched-together man tried to make me love him. Though it was my memory, it would never be as strong or as stable as the ones brought through the veil of death. I could change my recollections if I tried hard enough, turn this machine into a bare spot on the floor and an old rusty drain. Or I could light it up again, bringing the ersatz storm from the sky. These were the memories I had been present for, and they were mutable. But the others, I couldn't bend them even if I tried. Every detail of them was hammered into a stone tablet, and given to me to read.

Frances gave one last yank, then wrapped the chain around a section of pipe sticking from the wall, locking the tray in place. She took a step back, glancing up superstitiously at the sky. Maybe she had been pretending to be a meat golem long enough that she had taken on our fears. I couldn't blame her. I stepped back too, as did Barrow.

The only one who wasn't at all frightened was Burke. Now his attention was on the hole in the ceiling. The underside of the tray, black from our vantage, framed by the depthless sky. When lightning raked the velvet night, it came into sharp relief, then vanished into blinking afterimage, the chains rattling with the roll of thunder.

I found myself jittery, the electricity of the air inside me now. The lightning that had given me life wanting to jump out of my skin to join its friends in the storm. I was a little piece of it. Not just the six women who had made my life, but of the storm itself. That bit of heaven, made to kill, but pregnant with life and soul, shot into me. If the body was my mother, the storm was my father.

I wanted to pray, but I didn't know who to pray to. I wanted that machine to not have been there. I wanted the storm, my father, to be sent by God, or by nature, or by whatever else. I wanted that little bit of poetry. I wanted to know that, like a human being, there was an element of divine in me. Not just some clanking beast made by the same madman who had infested the desert with giant ants.

My body was quivering now. There was no one to send those thoughts to. No one who would listen. Wasn't like I had a voice to give to them, either. Only a hiss, to let the world know I was angry, or that I hated. But as much as the storm he had summoned would kill me, as much as my father storm would have done the same had it not bled out, I loved it. I loved its terrible beauty.

And I understood why Burke was grinning up at the sky. Perhaps not every reason behind his misshapen eyes, but one of them. I was grinning, too, I realized, nearly exulting in the power. I had forgotten what we were doing. Forgotten there was a man up there, swinging from the rattling cables.

At least until the lightning stabbed down. The spear burned my vision white. I think I hissed, but I wasn't sure. Burke roared and Frances screamed. Barrow clapped his hands and whooped. I almost threw my arm up over my eyes, but I fought the urge, because I had to see. The thunder was inside now, hammering at us. Something glass shattered in the office, that cat scent growing sharper. A shower of sparks fell from the cradle above.

Burke ran to the machine and threw the breaker once again. Instantly, the storm subsided. The wind died. No more lightning stalked through the sky. I felt my heart sinking. Artificial though it was, the storm had been beautiful in its way. Brief and glorious. The chains started clanking and I found Frances, now wearing heavy rubber gloves that reached her shoulders, gradually bringing the tray down.

The old man lay in the middle. A hole had been burned into his suit, haloed in black. The body, otherwise, looked the same. And then it started to move.

My eyes widened. The old man groaned. I turned to Burke, disbelieving. He nodded. This wasn't possible. A body hit by lightning, no matter what else you did with it, was still just a body. To get a meat golem, you needed to construct a new form. It was as though God, or Zeus, or whoever, wouldn't reincarnate the same person. They needed someone new, or looking new enough to fool them. But the old man was, against all logic and reason, stirring.

"Your eyes aren't fooling you, lovely Jane," Barrow said. He was close to me. Closer than I'd remembered. My senses were still flooded from the storm. My hand struck without my meaning to and grabbed the ghoul around the neck and lifted him off the ground. He was as light as a doll.

He sputtered and struggled. I forced myself to put him down and open my steely grip. The hand still reached for him, and it took me a moment to get it under control. I flexed my hand to prove it was mine again, cradling it with the other.

"Apologies," Barrow said. "I should have known you would be overwhelmed by such a sight." I pointed at the old man and raised my eyebrows. It was the best I could do to ask. I didn't trust myself to write until my skin stopped buzzing.

"Alive," Burke said.

Barrow nodded. "Dr. O'Hare has conquered death itself."

Relief flooded into me. Maybe I'd misjudged him. We'd only dug up the old man to return him to life. A living man was no good to a meat golem or a ghoul. We could take him back to those mourners and let them know that he would be okay. The smile fighting to my lips was tentative, almost frightened.

"Jane see," Burke said.

I nodded, and this time it was genuine. Burke really had created something remarkable. It put one of Barrow's comments in sharper relief as well. Complaining about the lack of people dying. He had found a way to keep that from happening.

I approached the old man. He was struggling as though waking up from an exceptionally deep sleep. Though his skin still had the gray of death on it, his limbs had regained a bit of solidity.

"There is, of course, only one minor problem."

"White bad!" Burke said.

Barrow held up a hand. "The lovely Jane has recognized your brilliance. Honesty would behoove us. We are not thieves in the night, are we? We are not charlatans. We are explorers, researchers. Your skills are still incredible, regardless of their limitations." I turned to Barrow, frowning. "You're wondering what I mean."

"White bad!" Burke roared.

Barrow shook his head. "Old man, the cat is at least partly out of the bag, and we're not going to leave it half in and half out, are we? No, we're not." He turned to me. "The process isn't permanent." Barrow watched my hands warily. His words were cautious. "They are brought back for one hour. Then they return to the embrace of death."

I whirled on Burke, pointed at the old man, and hissed. Burke laughed. "Jane see."

Oh, Jane see all right. I saw it in my own handwriting, on the slate, but I didn't write it. I wanted to lunge at Burke, but then, words pinned me in place.

"Hello? Can someone help me? I think I'm trapped."

It was the old man. He was still cuffed to the tray. I took a step toward him. Barrow reached out, but kept from touching, as though I were a hot stove. "Jane, don't. It's best to just let them return to death. Peacefully, quietly. Like waking in the middle of the night."

I turned and unleashed a hiss at Barrow. The ghoul cowered. "I'll not argue with a woman so hell bent!" I returned to the old man. The waves washed in my hearing. Behind me, the others spoke quietly, but not quietly enough.

"She's bugs," Frances said.

"Indeed," said Barrow. "I can understand why Burke threw her out."

Vanity nearly made me turn around, but the old man consumed my attention. I stood by his makeshift deathbed. "Hello?" His voice was small, pathetic. Childlike, even with all those years behind him. I leaned over him. He blinked, squinting. "Help me. I think I'm tied to something."

I put a light hand on his shoulder. He felt so weak, like a bird. If I squeezed, I would break everything from his collarbone to his shoulder blade. Just crumple it up like paper. I took it away just as the thought poisoned me and turned one of the lights on. Barrow, Burke, and Frances had gone to the other side of the lab, the two monsters engrossed in conversation, Frances lingering next to my creator and casting the occasional unreadable look at me.

I returned to the old man and gave him my best motherly smile. I imagined Wyeth Wyrd and put her gentle and forgiving expression on my face.

The old man yelped. "Meat golem! Miss, please don't turn me. I'm an old man, I..."

So much for motherly, I thought. I shook my head, touching his shoulder again, thinking that might be a better comfort. He calmed a little bit, now just watching me warily. I turned my attention to the cuffs. They sprang open easily with the press of a button. Impossible for someone pinned down, simple for the person imprisoning them. As soon as they were open, the old man brought his wrists up and rubbed them.

"Why am I here?" he asked.

I wanted to tell him I'd been asking the same thing myself. I didn't know what else to say, so I offered him a hand. He took it, rising gingerly into a sitting position, wincing as his back made this turn or that. He swung his legs over the side of the table with difficulty, then rested, partly slumped. He looked up when he heard the faint scratch of chalk on slate.

I'm Jane.

"Harry," he said. "Harry Jenkins."

Nice to meet you.

"What's the matter, Jane? Cat got your tongue?"

I pointed at my mouth. *Meat golem.*

"I've heard meat golems talk. Not too well, but they talk."

Lady meat golems don't. Harry frowned, watching me like I was putting him on.

"How'd I get here?" he asked me finally. I wasn't sure how to explain that. He glanced around. "Where is here?"

Burke O'Hare's office in Quartzsite.

He watched me, his body still tense. "You gonna tell me what I'm doing here or not?"

What do you remember?

Harry's eyes narrowed, then relaxed as he summoned his memories. "I was at home. In bed. Not much of a bed, mind, but it's mine. I live over in...well, your people call it Fort Meatstick." I felt my cheeks growing hot. I couldn't meet his gaze. "Yeah. We think it's got to be cancer, but we don't have any doctors there, and no doctor is gonna see us. Oh, we know Doc O'Hare will fix you up to look like a vampire or something if that's what you've a mind to be, but looking after us? No, he don't do that."

Harry was watching me keenly now. His eyes, a faded green, had stone behind them. I nodded, confirming what he had said.

"All's I knew was my body was shutting down, a piece at a time. Barely even hurt anymore. That was the good part. Last thing I remember, the sickness, whatever it was, had turned out the lights, and I was just there, on my cot, working hard at breathing. Rattle in, rattle out. I knew it'd stop eventually, and then I could rest. Made it all the way through the Night War with my skin intact, and this was what was going to take me. Some disease.

"I wondered if it had really been worth it, fighting to stay human. Figured it was. I was dying on my own terms. Not from something silly, like being doused with water or getting a suntan. I was dying like a man was supposed to, and that sounded like the best thing I could hope for. Dot, that's my daughter-in-law, she was crying, quietly, I think so she wouldn't upset me. I wanted to tell her it was okay. This was how it was supposed to be. Only I couldn't talk anymore. I could just breathe. Rattle in, rattle out. Soon I was gonna stop, and I wouldn't even know it. I'd just be gone, somewhere better than here."

I turned away. A hot tear ran down my cheek. I knew that if I gave in, they'd start falling and that would be the end of me. I clamped down on that swelling of sadness, clenched it in my fist.

"Only now I open my eyes, and my suit's burned and I feel better than I have in a long time."

You feel good? I blinked away as much of the moisture as I could.

He nodded. "Good's a relative thing when you're my age, and you've got as many miles under your feet as I do. I still have the aches and pains. My back hasn't been good since I was young, and I can still feel some of the arthritis in my knees. But I can breathe and I can talk, and that's a damn sight better than I was. Did you give me something?" He smiled. "Thank you. Look, you say you don't want to change me, then...are you letting me go?"

I didn't say anything. I couldn't.

"Because I'd like to go home. Tell Dot not to cry anymore. Her boy, Jim, he's gonna be a man soon. I was looking forward to seeing that. I figure I can help the boy navigate this world a bit. I made it through the Night War, so maybe the rest is a bit easier." I closed my eyes, freeing the tears to fall down my cheeks. "Jane? Why are you crying?"

I'm sorry.

"Feels like you cured me. Why are you sorry?"

We didn't cure you. You're dead. We dug you up.

"You brought me back to life?" I nodded. "You turned me?" There was disbelief in his voice, and rage. Boundless rage. I shook my head, wiping at my eyes. "Far as I can tell, other than the fact that my only suit is ruined, I don't look any different either. Well, this skin's a little gray, but that's not so bad. I always thought if I was turned, I'd know it. I'd feel the new limbs, the new way of getting around. I'd know my new fears in my gut."

You're not turned.

"I don't understand."

O'Hare found a way to bring people back to life.

"Why'd he use it on me? I don't know him from Adam."

He wanted to show me he could. You were just convenient.

Harry smiled. "Guess I should thank him then. Or thank you. Got a whole life of luck passing me over for the next guy, but when I really need it, suddenly the world gives me a break. Last one I expected."

I shook my head. I turned to Burke and the others, and they were watching, amusement in Burke's eyes. I met Frances's gaze and she turned away, staring at the ground. I was going to have to tell this man.

It's not permanent.

"Life isn't."

No, you don't understand. You're alive for one hour. That's it.

He squinted at me. "An hour? That's it?" I nodded. He thought about it. "I don't think that's long enough to go home and explain what happened. What am I supposed to tell them?" I shook my head. I didn't know. I didn't even know how I would begin to know something like that.

He pushed himself off the table, stumbling a bit as he hit the floor. I caught and steadied him. "I suppose I want to see what the night looks like. Been a long time since I've seen the night. Really seen it." He stuck out an arm. "Now, my wife's been gone for years, so there's no harm. Would you allow me to escort you, Jane?"

I nodded, taking his arm. I had to let it go when we got to the door, opening what I had damaged and closing it again. The desert had turned cold, the few lights from the town desolate in the dark.

"That's a beautiful thing, Jane," he said. I had to agree. It was, in a way.

He shuffled out onto the street, then gingerly sat down on the slumping curb that was more dirt than asphalt. "Wish I was about twenty years younger. I could move then. Had to be able to. Though I wouldn't get a better view." Now he was looking up. The sky was infinite, the stars forever. I sat down next to him.

"When I was a boy, I thought that when you died, you went up there," he said. "Now? Not so sure. I don't remember being dead, Jane. I just remember the minutes before. Maybe the memories are stuck there. Maybe there is no there." He sighed. "I wish it was the sky, though. Something more comforting about that. Something sweet and warm up there, no matter how cold it gets. I could keep looking after Dot and Jim." He coughed. "I had a son. Hank. Night War."

I nodded, and I couldn't look at the sky anymore. It was for him, for as long as he had.

"That's why Dot and Jim were my responsibility. My boy couldn't do it anymore, so it had to be me. Now...Dot's tough. I gotta hope she'll be okay. Only if I was up there, I'd know for sure. It's a hard thing, knowing the world keeps turning without you. Most people think it does, but I suppose I'm the only one knows it for damn sure."

We waited in silence, and after a time I was able to look up again, and be in the blanket of stars over the valley. He was right. There was something wonderful there. But it wasn't for me. Not for the women who made me, either. They were still in my limbs and in my head, their lives reaching into mine. If the sky was their reward, they hadn't gotten it, at least not entirely. I wanted Harry to be right. I wanted it so badly it hurt.

"Jane? Is it getting cloudy?" The night was completely clear. "Clouds rolling in, I suppose. That's more like my luck. Last hour on earth and it'll rain. When it does, don't take me back inside. I want to feel the rain on my face."

I put a hand on his shoulder. It was still as delicate as always, but I never thought of breaking anything. He covered it with his. His palm was cold.

"Jane. I think I'm going." I held his hand. "I don't think I want to go anymore. I think I want to stay here." I held him a little tighter.

He said one other thing, but I didn't hear. The words were just gone, like the stars from his sight. He slumped against me. His breath was shallow, irregular. Then it stopped. I held him for a little while longer, wishing he was up there with the stars, but knowing he wasn't.

FOURTEEN

I came back to the office as the sun was beginning to peek over the mountains. I'd buried Harry Jenkins where Burke or Barrow couldn't ever find him. A last little favor. I knew I should find a way to tell Dot and Jim where he was. To let them know that his thoughts were always with them, and that he went into the ground whole. He'd died again, and with someone who had been, for a short time, something close to a friend. But I had another thing to do first.

I plucked the door from the frame and hurled it away. The green wasn't on me. I was cold and rational in my rage. Icy as the freezer in the truck. Grave dirt blackened my nails, and the stink of Harry's first death permeated my skin, marking me.

"Jane back."

Burke sat in the middle of the office, leering at me. Of Barrow and Frances, there was no sign. Burke had been sitting there, waiting for me, the blackboard next to him, remnants of our conversations clouded on its surface, soundless echoes. On his left, the ant crouched next to him. He stroked its head while its mandibles worked.

I took two steps toward him before catching myself. No matter how satisfying it would have been to pummel him, I couldn't. He still had the information I needed.

"Jane see," Burke said, his grin going wider.

My fingers were shaking as I wrote. *What did I see?*

Burke got up and scrawled on the board. "Jane see." *«Now you know how brilliant I am.»*

I shook my head. *It was cruel!*

Burke chuckled. *«You wouldn't see any other way. If it was cruel, it was your cruelty.»* I took another step before stopping myself. Burke's lip peeled back from his teeth.

I didn't know, I wrote.

«You wouldn't have believed. Now do you see what you left when you walked out of this place? You could have been here when I conquered death. When I became the greatest mind the world has ever known.»

I hissed at him. *«Hiss all you want, but you know it's true,»* he wrote.

You're a monster.

«We're all monsters. I'm just the only one who is good at it.»

I seethed, feeling the green encroaching on all sides of me. I couldn't think of a single thing to say to him to make him understand what he'd done was awful. That he'd used Harry Jenkins like a plaything, and that Harry, that anyone, deserved more than that.

«Now you know I'm a genius,» Burke wrote.

Will you answer my question? Who was I? Where did you find the bodies to make me?

Burke shook his head. "Jane say."

Say what?

«Say what I am.»

You're Burke O'Hare. You're a meat golem.

«I'm a genius. You say it.»

I was shaking. I wanted to throw him through a wall. Wanted to scream all the awful things he was in his face, but I couldn't scream. Couldn't even write it. He held my identity hostage, and would continue to do so unless I danced exactly how he wanted me to.

You're a genius, I wrote. My fingers nearly snapped the chalk in two, but I made the words. I showed him the slate.

He chuckled again. "Jane know."

Now tell me who I was!

Burke shrugged. "Not know."

I hissed. *You don't know?*

«*It was a long time ago,*» he wrote. «*There are graveyards all over this place.*»

The scream inside me was boiling, but I couldn't let out the steam. *Why did you do this to me if you were never going to answer my questions?*

«*Because you needed to know! You needed to see! I'm the greatest genius this world has ever known, and I'm unknown! No one sees me! No one knows what I've done! I made you! You were nothing. Just some cut-up dead girls, and I gave you life! And what did you do? You left! There was nothing out there for you, and you thought that was better than living with me! You needed to understand what you lost!*»

The words came off his chalk with squeals of pain. When he turned to regard me, he was breathing heavily, his lopsided mouth hanging open. In his eyes, I saw no affection at all. There was just the anger of ownership. A disbelief that the world could treat him this way, and I was the world.

I hissed at him, but it was disgust rather than anger. Burke was pathetic. Even his discovery was petty, no matter how world-shaping he seemed to think it was. Conquer death for an hour, then die all over again. I went into the sun that refused to warm me even as it scorched the wash.

"Jane know!" Burke roared after me. "Jane know!"

FIFTEEN

urke's voice continued pounding into my mind long after he was out of earshot. The bastard didn't even know. He'd made me jump through hoops, set me up to be killed, tortured Harry Jenkins…and I had let him do it. Everything I'd hoped to get out of it was gone. And that was the worst part. He hadn't been holding out on me because he wanted something from me. He had been holding out because I wasn't important enough to remember. My life, my entire existence had slipped his mind.

Sunlight flooded into the wash, and for a time, it was beautiful. The deep shadows of the evening still lingered between the gold. I walked quickly, to put Burke behind me, like I should have the instant I left Quartzsite the first time. I found myself on the northern edges of town faster than I thought possible, the sun inexorably climbing. The giant ants had been released from their hills, marching over the horizon in their endless columns. From that distance, I couldn't see any of the horsemen looking after the swarm. There was only the bizarre beauty of the insects themselves.

Furtive movement turned my head. I stood on an abandoned piece of property, a nearby adobe house steadily crumbling in the face of the weather. A single piece of fence, nearly entirely collapsed, was all that remained of any kind of border. The movement came around the corner of the house, then, as I turned, it ducked back.

I took a few steps, peering around the corner. Huddled against the wall was a child, tiny and filthy. I'd seen her before, on my first trip to Fort Meatstick. She was barefoot, wearing only grimy rags. Foolishly, I thought she was related to Harry, but she couldn't be either Dot or Jim. I wondered if she knew them.

She stared at me with frightened brown eyes. Her skin was deeply brown, a combination of genetics and the sun. Her hair was probably meant to be straight, but it was a rat's nest. She shivered as she waited for the monster to hurt her. I held a hand out to comfort her, but I was gone. Maybe it was Burke, maybe it was the girl. But I was gone so quickly.

My reaching arm was no longer patchwork. It was small and chubby, unlined by age. It wasn't mine. It belonged to a little girl, reaching for the orange, enchanted perhaps by color or shape. I wanted to give her that color, to suck it out of the fruit and show it to her in pure, gorgeous form, to have her experience the flawless orange so I could see the wonder in her face. I knew I couldn't, and I knew that every day, that orange would be a little duller until there was nothing special in it at all.

I blinked. I was by the adobe house again, and the girl was gone. The sun was higher in the sky now, and I had lost her to the memories.

Sixteen

I returned to my motel. Maybe Wolff would come by again and tell me to leave. I didn't know what I'd do then, but I was too frustrated to think at all clearly. I washed the dirt and grave stink off of me in the shower, but I couldn't get it all. I ate a meal of potato chips from a vending machine and coffee from the pot in the motel office. The advantage of staying in that fleabag was that my room was still available, and the ghoul gave it to me without conversation. I was pretty sure he was happy for the money.

Seething, I tried to imagine my next step. This couldn't be the end. If it was, I was on the next train out to Los Angeles, just like Wolff wanted, albeit a day later. I'd be coming back with just as many questions, but at least I had tried. Maybe that would be enough to forget the feel of Harry Jenkins slumping against me as frightened life left him for the second time.

I managed to sleep for a few minutes that morning. Too much was running through my mind for proper sleep. I'd rest when this was over. When I knew for certain what my names had been.

When I woke up, I knew what I had been missing. I moved quickly, not wanting to be caught outside by either Wolff or the Dullahans. I saw neither on the trip across town. Just the occasional ghoul or zombie, shuffling between their origin and destination. They watched as I passed, some nodding, others merely checking my passage. It was hard to believe this entire town had been so hungry for someone to do something about the Dullahans that a hotheaded cocktail waitress had become some kind of local celebrity.

I found Barrow sitting in his chair outside Fort Meatstick under a ragged parasol, watching his chosen human hungrily. He drank from a jelly jar filled with a crimson liquid, topped with a tiny umbrella. My stomach turned as I realized it was old blood. He tipped it up and it poured sluggishly into his mouth, more solid than liquid. I turned away, putting a hand over my mouth. I didn't have much to throw up, but I would if he kept it up.

"Jane?" Barrow asked. "What a lovely surprise. Here to look for your chosen?" I peeked to see that he'd at least stopped sipping at his meaty drink and he had. I gave him a queasy wave and did my best not to look at the cup drinking in my attention.

"Can I get you something to drink?" He lifted a stained bottle from here it had been sitting by his chair. A heave wracked my body. I shook my head no. "I've other beverages, perhaps to your liking. Bile, barely a week old." He gestured to an old pickup truck parked not far away. I shook my head more violently, the gorge inexorably rising.

"I'd hate for my reputation as a careful and courteous host to suffer. Perhaps if you would tell me what your libation of choice is, I shall keep some stocked so as to encourage your presence."

The last thing I wanted to think about was a drink, and I certainly wasn't going to put my mouth on anything that had been in Barrow's icebox. *You recognized me.*

"Of course, dear Jane. We met not long ago, and craftsmanship of the kind that created you isn't soon forgotten."

I shook my head and pointed at the words again. Then rubbed one out and wrote, showing him the new sentence. *You recognized pieces of me.*

Barrow's features rippled. The flapping, diaphanous shadows of his umbrella turned suddenly sinister. He set his jelly jar down on a dented metal end table. "I don't follow," he said, but his eyes dipped down to my legs. A lie he couldn't quite fight.

I took a step. Maybe it was the difference in perspective. Maybe it was fear. But his expression was no longer intimidating. He was frightened, and he was trying to hide it. I pointed at the message on my slate. The twine was raspy on my neck.

"I must apologize, Jane."

Tap tap, went the chalk against the slate. What I was seeing wasn't imagination, either. I saw it in a bolt in his moldy green eyes.

He broke into a big-toothed grin, but it was brittle, ready to crumble at any second. "Jane, be reasonable."

Tap tap.

I was almost within arm's reach of him. I could see him thinking about the moment I grabbed him. He could probably feel my fingers, like steel, constricting his windpipe as I lifted him off the ground. He even coughed, his own fluttery hands reaching for his throat, as though he could fend me off if I lunged. I thought I saw bruises on his neck, but it could have been shadows.

"All right, yes. I'd never forget a pair of stems like yours, Jane. They were art. It's why we picked her. Burke had to cobble a bit together from the other girls. Counteract a little bit of decay and if I'm to be honest, freezer burn, but yes, I recall them."

Where?

"Where? Where did we find them?" He looked across the desert in the direction of Burke's office, as though he could see my creator looking disapprovingly. I nodded.

"Ehrenberg," Barrow said finally. "Little town west of here on the Colorado River. There was a human cemetery there. We dug up some of you there."

What about the rest of me?

"I don't know." He held up his hands. "There's no more lies in me! It was the Night War. There were lots of graves then. Lots of digging. I can't remember where we got the rest of your parts. But the legs, yes, they were from that cemetery in Ehrenberg."

A thought occurred to me, and I had to ask him. *I was just dead, right?*

"I'm afraid I don't quite follow."

You only dug me up. You didn't kill anybody to make me.

"Goodness no!" Barrow said, sounding genuinely horrified. "I exclusively disinter. I don't inter, if you understand my meaning." I walked away. "Jane!" I stopped, but didn't turn. "Don't tell him what I told you."

Why doesn't he want me to know?

Barrow shook his head, his shoulders slumping. "I don't know. I don't even know that he doesn't want you to know. I'm telling you the truth. It was a long time ago, and the Night War was a crazy time for all of us." He squinted in the direction of Burke's office. "I don't think he remembers you. I know that must smart, but the truth is a salve of sorts."

If he doesn't remember, why are you scared of telling me?

The ghoul didn't answer. He didn't have to. We both knew Burke's mind, maybe better than he did. Barrow was trapped in the world Burke made for some reason, but I wasn't. I could leave it all behind. Once I knew what I needed to.

Seventeen

Ehrenberg wasn't hard to find. A ghoul, after shyly shaking my hand, told me it was a short drive west. Just had to take the road out of town. No train went there. Nothing went there. Except for me.

I didn't want to see Burke, but he had the only car I knew I could get. I hoped he would be too much of a coward to deal with me when he knew my blood was up. The door of the office was on the ground, a short distance from the doorway, the desert steadily swallowing it up. The empty space was black, like a missing tooth. I imagined that door was going to be gone until Frances or Barrow fixed it. If they ever did.

The door of Burke's truck gave a throaty creak as I opened it. I climbed inside, and a flicker of pale movement drew my eye. Frances stood in the doorway now, her skin ghostly white, her needless stitches angry red. She watched me, and I maybe I was imagining it, but I saw sadness and pity in her eyes, rather than the sullen hostility I found earlier. She made no movement to stop me, merely watched as I grabbed the keys from the floor of the cab and started the truck. She was still watching when I drove away, leaving her behind me. I wondered if she stayed there, standing just out of the sunlight, watching the lonely road and thinking about driving it herself. Or if she thought I was a fool for taking it.

Ehrenberg wasn't too far away, which was fortunate, as the indifferently paved road was hell to travel. A tiny town pressed up against the Colorado River, it managed to make Quartzsite look metropolitan. I peered out over the searing desert and thought about all the towns out there. Places that had been settled because someone found metal in the hills, or a group of white settlers decided this was as far as they could get and no farther, chasing off whoever had been here first. Ehrenberg bled desperation, but it was a desperation for those who had forgotten need. The river was the only blue, and it listlessly wound south, leaving town without ever actually going anywhere.

I caught glimpses of a few giant ants as I went, but they were always in the distance, scuttling over the hills in their endless search for food. There was no sign of any rantches around Ehrenberg. This place had been passed by even with the new industries. Ehrenberg was the kind of place that existed out of pure stubbornness.

There wasn't much town to check, and what there was looked a lot like Quartzite. There was what passed for a main drag, where the bulk of the shops were, and then houses of adobe and clapboard bleeding out into the desert until they simply stopped. I found the church quickly, near the center of town, then realized that wasn't what I was looking for.

The sign said FIRST CHURCH OF CHRIST, REMAKER. A monster church. There were a couple of different monster brands of Christianity making the rounds, once enough people were turned who started worrying about their immortal souls. The truth was, I didn't know a whole lot about them. Sure, there was this scarecrow back home that sometimes liked to proselytize at me and the girls, thinking we were selling the goods rather than just showing them off. He told us all about our souls. I always tuned him out.

Now, because I was here, because I was finally doing this, I thought he was insane. A soul for a skin-dolly. Good one. He had a soul, because he used to be a man. I wasn't a woman; I was six. He was from one of those

Remaker churches, preaching that Jesus was the first monster, turned by God, killed by humans. Making it easy for the monsters to look on humans as deserving, or even needing, what monsters thought to give. This wasn't the church I needed. It had no answers for me.

So I kept looking. The church I wanted was on the southern end of town, away from nearly everything else. The main building was scarred from battle, old wounds whose jagged edges had been smoothed by time and indifference. A cemetery, only barely better maintained than the one that had briefly held the remains of Harry Jenkins, stretched out into the desert behind it. This place said it was Baptist, and that would do for me. I parked on the dirt road in front.

The church was undeniably shabby, but it was just as undeniably important. To the people here, those few humans hanging on wherever the local version of Fort Meatstick was. I hoped it was a better place than that, but somehow, I didn't much think so. My stomach tangled; this was a place that would have sent me running. This was, of course, where the humans stayed, protected by wards and treaties, and they could strike. That's what I thought before I knew Nick, before I understood just how thoroughly the humans had been terrorized. This place, though, played on all those old fears. I imagined the pastor inside with his killing tools, just waiting for some hapless monster to enter.

I took a deep breath in stolen lungs and tried to get my stomach to loosen. It stubbornly refused. I hadn't eaten much, but it wanted to spill every last bit into the dirt. I walked up carefully, peering into the eaves for waiting hunters. There was nothing, just a lonely breeze, trying to find somewhere better than here.

I opened the door. The inside of the church was cool and echoey. The building was big, probably bigger than it needed to be, built back when there were the humans to support it. Less and less now, especially if Barrow was to be believed. That was the way of things. What would happen when the last human died or was turned? In my mind, that last person became Nick and my stomach tied up even tighter.

The windows in the church had long since broken, letting in the air and the dust. The pews were scarred as well, some from bullets or fire, some partly dissolved. My steps were as soft as I could make them, but I was a meat golem. I clomped wherever I went, just a little piece of grace I never brought back through the veil.

I realized at that moment that I had been there. Nothing in my mind, no memory sparked of my surroundings, but something about the way my feet trod on the old planks, the way my hands reached for the pews. The roughness of the wood, the tiny pits and scars, was familiar. It wasn't home, but pieces knew it.

A door in the back opened and a man emerged. He was white, with a craggy, desert-tanned face, and iron-gray hair in a military cut. He wore a black western-style shirt, patched and repaired, along with faded blue jeans and boots. His horn-rimmed glasses reflected the light from the broken windows, making his eyes impossible to read.

"Can I help you?" he asked, then stopped moving, his body tensing.

I held up my hands. Nothing in them, but we both knew that didn't matter when it came to meat golems. I took the slate up and showed it to him, then the chalk. He nodded. "Go ahead."

I'm sorry to bother you.

"No bother," he told me. "It's just...I think you're lost. The Remaker Church is over on Comber Boulevard. I can give you directions if you like."

I was looking for the human church.

His expression turned to stone. "Don't know who you're looking for, but you won't find him here."

I shook my head. *I'm looking for me.*

Now he frowned. "I'm sorry, miss. I thought I had this figured out, but you've lost me. What's going on?" He shook his head. "No, I apologize. I'm Sherman Dukes, the pastor here."

Jane Stitch.

"Miss Stitch, all right. You ain't here to hurt anybody." I shook my head. He gestured to a pew. "Have a seat and tell me what you're after."

I sat down, traced a scar in the wooden floor with my toe. Pastor Dukes sat down a row in front of me and turned to talk. His gaze fell on my hand, where the skin sagged away from the cut.

"You're hurt?"

I touched the wound reflexively. It didn't hurt, just an itch, like bugs tracing the path of the skin. I shook my head, then stuck my hand out and wobbled it. *A little*, was the message.

"Can I do anything?" he asked, but the voice was stony. He didn't want to help, but needed to ask. I shook my head, putting my hand in my lap, suddenly self-conscious that the pastor should see me coming undone.

He looked around the church, probably as a way to let me have my embarrassment. "Sorry about the state of this place. Don't get as much from the collection plate as we used to." His gaze fell to the pew next to me, where a section of wood looked to have liquified and then solidified. Bubbles had formed in it, now as hard as oak. "Back during the war, before Ehrenberg fell, a bunch of us were holed up here. Used the pews as barricades. Turns out pews ain't much against a martian's death ray."

I nodded in sympathy. *I'm sorry.*

"You weren't there. Unless..."

I gave my head a vehement shake. *I've never been here before.* Only that was a lie. Some of me had. I shook my head. My frustration must have shown on my face.

"Miss Stitch, you're gonna have to forgive me. We don't get a lot of monsters here anymore. We don't exactly have a bustling population of humans, so nothing to attract too many monsters. So I'm bum puzzled about your errand here." I nodded, trying to show him I agreed. The slate was heavy in my hand, and I couldn't see any of the words I wanted to say in the cloudy surface. "Is this a spiritual question?"

I wobbled my hand. *A little.* The skin flapped about, and once again, I hid it in my lap.

"If you're asking me about your soul..." he shook his head, then started a new thought. "In this congregation, I have Catholics, Baptists, a couple

Mormons even. I keep to the good book in services, and then I figure no one can really take issue. We all believe in the same thing, or so they say." He sighed, casting a guilty look at me. "The Bible doesn't say anything about monsters. Well, nothing good anyway. If you want a more satisfactory answer, like I said, there's a monster church across town. They can afford to fix the windows there."

I shook my head. *I'm not religious.*

"Mind me asking why? Normally I wouldn't, but when someone looking like you walks into a church and says they're not religious, it gets a body to thinking."

Dukes had a point. *I'm looking for pieces of me.*

He frowned, then understanding dawned horribly on his face. "Is...is that something you people normally do?"

You people, he'd said. Even he referred to me in the plural. I shrugged.

"You don't know either? I suppose there ain't much of a roadmap for the world we have, is there? So you're looking for who...who was the source for your body, and your search led here."

I nodded. *September 15, 1951. That was the day I was reborn.*

"Kind of a recent birthday."

I saw the hole in my wall, sucking in every last bit of my life. *Were any graves robbed around then?*

"Oh, of course." I felt myself frowning, and caught it. He didn't seem to notice. "That was right about when the last of Ehrenberg fell. You might have seen how many ghouls we have around these parts. When human communities were taken, it was like ringing a dinner bell. I couldn't stop them, either. Not once we had our own wolf making sure the monsters could do whatever they wanted and to the devil with the rest of us."

I'm sorry.

"Don't be. You come here asking about graves then, and I can tell you that was when it happened."

Can I look?

"Look where?"

In the cemetery. The graves are still out there?

"I leave the markers. We have so few humans left, it's important to remember those who didn't make it as far as we did. The war took a lot." He watched me, and I followed his eyes. They didn't dip to my legs, the way most did. No, his gaze was tracing the lines of my stitches. Then, something in the look died, as though he had made a decision about what I was. When he spoke again, a blade was hiding just beneath the words. "Yeah, you can look. I'll be going out with you, just in case this is some kind of way to steal the last couple of people who are still resting."

I nodded, looking away. I couldn't stand to see the set of his jaw anymore. I got up and went out the door, the pastor trailing me. His steps were nearly entirely silent, like someone used to stalking. I shuddered, abruptly back to the image of the human monster lurking in his impenetrable castle. He didn't seem to have an antprod on him, but my imagination put it in his hands all the same, buzzing just behind my neck, ready to end me with a single jolt. Green fought to drown me, but I denied it. I was a monster in body, but not in behavior. Still, I felt the orange breeze on that day, my fingers dimpling chubby flesh.

The hot sun on my shoulders was nearly a relief. I stepped out onto the path circling the church. Dukes paused at the threshold. For a flash, I saw Frances instead, stitches over white limbs. But it was the pastor, watching me with open suspicion now, his hands empty.

The cemetery in the back looked to have been there a long while. The earliest graves were marked from the 1860s, though the lettering on those had been scoured by the desert sand. I picked my way through them, reading the names of the dead, thinking of the years of their lives. At first, there were the years before the monsters lived in the open, when people would have led relatively normal lives.

Nick once asked me why everyone pretends that monsters suddenly started existing in 1945. I didn't know the answer then and I don't know it now. No one explains it. No one talks about it. It's just something we all say, a transparent lie that everyone pretends to believe. Like identity.

Then I started seeing the dates I wanted. A scorpion scuttled away from my shoe, finding its burrow beneath the baking sand. The cemetery had gone in a cycle: the oldest graves were marked with planks of wood, then there was a brief window when they had used stone, then back to wood. Modern names on graves that would have been recognizable in the Old West.

Then I saw her name. RACHEL PRAGER, 1925-1951. A Star of David had been etched into the wood. I stopped in my tracks and knelt in front of the marker. My hand reached out to it unbidden, my fingers tracing the lettering in the wood. Now the electricity playing over my skin was familiar. It was real.

Rachel Prager. I stared at the name, feeling the syllables running over pieces of my patchwork flesh. This name meant something. This name was right. Some of me had been named Rachel Prager.

I blinked, and, like a magnet, my eyes went to another name. LORENA QUINTANILLA, 1926-1951, a cross under that one. I got up, epiphany making me coltish, and fell to my knees in front of that grave. That name mattered too. It was a different feeling, a thrill but a more subtle one. My body knew these two names. Knew them better than any.

I got up, hunting for more. It made sense. Burke had been looking to make a meat golem. If he could harvest from one place, it saved on time. I shuddered, briefly torn from the ecstasy of discovery. That had been a concern. I was made from convenience.

Another name drew me back. HASAYA. I went to it cautiously. Unlike the others, it wasn't perfect. The letters felt strange under my fingers. Not quite right, but close to it. No last name, either. No birthdate or symbol of a religion. Just the date, 1951, inscribed on the wood.

I got up, hunting through the remainder of the markers. I found myself praying that Burke had been lazier than I thought he was, but I still had no one to pray to. The pastor's god would ignore me, and I wasn't going to speak to the Remaker. No other names sprang to me, even though 1951 was far and away the most popular time to die.

Rachel Prager, Lorena Quintanilla, Hasaya. Three names. Half of me.

I turned, and found Pastor Dukes only fifteen feet away. In the harsh sunlight, he looked like a shadow.

"You found something." I nodded, and I pointed to the three graves. "A lot of people died that night. Died here. I didn't know most of them. There were too many, all coming to what they prayed was safety."

I listed the three names on the slate and showed it to him. As he read, a tiny flicker came over his features. Perhaps recognition. "I will say this: I buried everyone here. I made the markers."

How did you know their names?

"Everyone had people. In those days, there were little packs of survivors. Like makeshift tribes. They knew names, even if they didn't know you before the Night War. They could tell me enough to put a name down, maybe a date. I buried a lot of people that day. Men, women." He paused. "Children."

The little girl reached for the orange.

Can you tell me anything about these 3?

His expression softened. No longer stone. He was clay, a golem himself. "More about some than others. I don't know as much as I think you want."

Anything.

"Rachel Prager...she was Jewish. We don't have many Jews out here, so she and her husband stuck out. I'm sorry, I don't recall his name. She came in with a group and holed up here. After she died, her husband slipped away. I don't know what happened to him. I buried her and I have to hope whatever God is up there will understand that I did the best I could and it shouldn't reflect on her."

He glanced over at Hasaya's grave.

"I can tell you the least about her. She was with Rachel's group, but no one knew her. Really knew her, I mean. She was an Indian, but we got several different kinds out here. She could have been any one of them and she wasn't talking. She was also dying. They said a vampire got to her and she was running on empty. She was nearly bled white. Maybe if we'd had a doctor, she would've lived, but I don't think so. She died right before the monsters broke in. Just too much pain for her."

And Lorena Quintanilla?

"I knew her a bit. Sweet girl. Died saving someone else." He shook his head. "I don't know what they loved or who they really were. None of them came to this church back then to worship. The war kind of threw us all together. The most we had in common was the worst night of our lives."

You said they had people.

"Some people aren't people anymore. Others are buried around here."

I looked at the ground, as though the bodies would suddenly pull themselves free of the dirt and tell me who they were. Who I had been. Only the bodies weren't there; only their names had been left behind. I should have been prepared for this. If the living didn't remember me, how would the dead? I thought about writing to the government, seeing if there were any records of these three women. So much had been destroyed in the Night War. Those days before, most monsters wanted to forget. A lot of them wanted to pretend they had always been as they were now. They had been caterpillars and now were butterflies. They weren't going to listen to one voiceless meat golem.

"I might be able to help." I barely registered the words, then I was looking up, squinting in the sun, my silver eye nearly shut, even behind the sunglasses. Pastor Dukes hadn't moved from his spot. He was still a shadow in this graveyard. "There might be someone around here who knows a bit more."

I gave a hopeful nod. "Yes. I'll ask if he'll see you. If he says no, then he says no. There's no appealing it. You get what you get, understand?" I nodded, this time eagerly. "All right, then. I'll send for you, Miss Stitch."

How will you find me?

"It's a small town. Don't worry."

His words didn't fill me with a sense of safety.

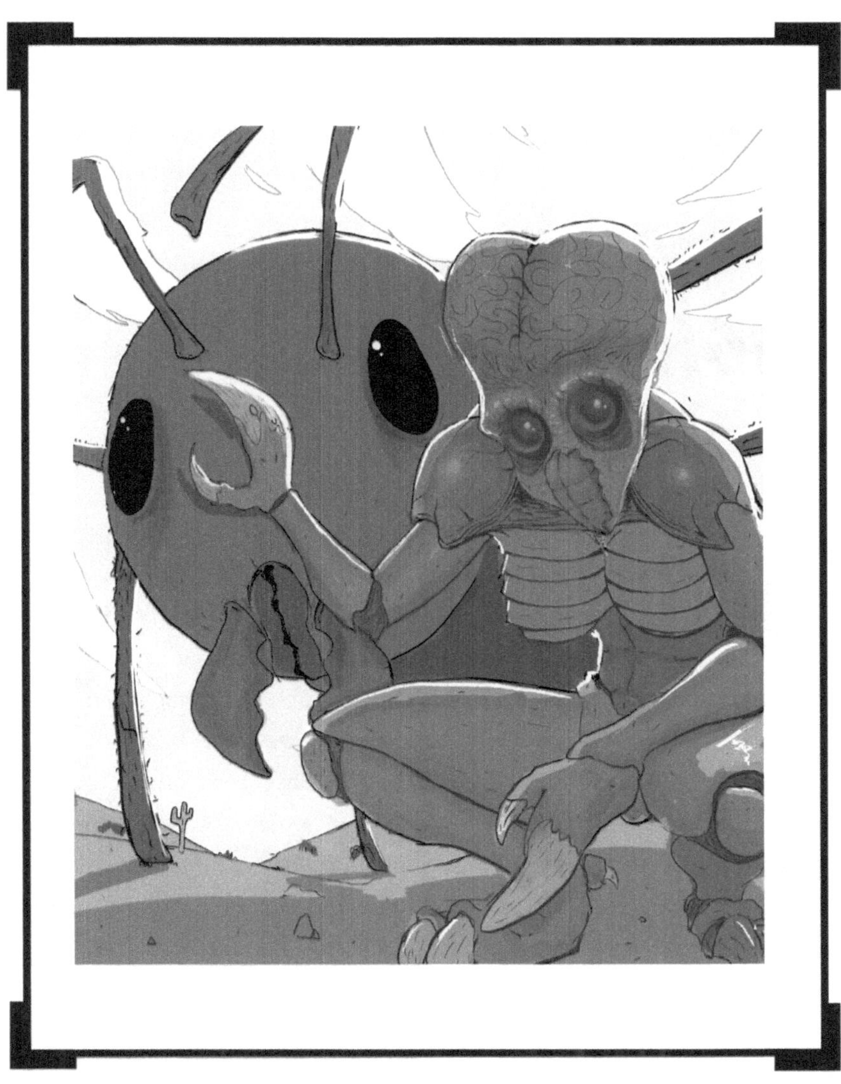

Phobos & Giant Ant

Eighteen

arry Jenkins wasn't up there, and he wasn't looking down on me. No matter how hard I looked, I didn't see any bit of him. I lay on the roof of the ice cream truck, my legs crossed at the ankles, my hands folded on my stomach. It wasn't the most comfortable bed, but it would do. The sky was my blanket and the river was my lullaby.

After I left the church, I walked through Ehrenberg, my thoughts on everything and nothing. I found the human settlement huddled on the banks of the river. That was queasily familiar. Their wards were out, the same type as those at Fort Meatstick. Here at least there wasn't a ghoul peering through the barrier hungrily. Maybe he was home that day. The humans I saw were just as sullen and shellshocked as the ones in Quartzsite, but their limbs weren't quite as heavy.

Their homes were a combination of shacks and tents. Fishing lines dipped into the lazy river. I stood up on the banks and looked in, and soon, more than one of the humans were staring back, defiant. My stolen heart tied into knots. As far as they knew, I was looking to cut them into pieces and sew them into a new one of me. There was no such thing as innocence anymore.

I left them behind, the grass and reeds of the riverbank fading back into parched desert. From time to time, I saw a local, but here I was unknown and so they ignored me. They didn't have Dullahans here, or didn't know about the dizzy dolly who had gone ape on a couple rantchers. I felt more kinship with the lizards and the dragonflies anyway.

I found myself in the center of town not long after. A few shops stood open, windows dusty. I stopped in front of one. A small, vacant storefront. Abandoned maybe. My reflection off the blurry glass was little more than a silhouette. I could almost be a human woman, if not for the small asymmetries only I noticed. The illusion was ruined when an itch brought my right hand up. The stitches were fraying even worse now. My skin had unzipped straight down to my wrist, where the line ran in a spiral up my arm. If I were human, I'd have been in crippling agony. For me, it was a nagging itch, made worse when I paid attention. The feel of thousands of ants crawling over the exposed flesh.

I could see a bit of Burke's handiwork as well. The stitches over the skin get the lion's share of the attention, but meat golems are assembled from the bones out. More stitches secured muscle to tendon to bone. A way to make me a complete and functional person. At least physically.

I turned my attention back to the silhouette. If one of the others, Rachael Prager, or Lorena Quintanilla, or Hasaya, were standing in my place, would someone mistake me for them? Or would they notice that my fingers were just slightly the wrong length, or that my left arm was a tiny bit longer than my right? Or that I was just a pile of stitched-up dead flesh playing at being a person?

I cupped my hands around my eyes and peered into the gloom of the empty shop beyond. I found a small room with an old wooden floor that probably had felt the tread of real cowboys. A wooden counter blocked off the back, and I could dimly make out an open door beyond. The shop had a second story, probably going to an apartment for whoever owned it. The emptiness tugged at the free-floating sadness that had been my coat since I came here. No humans to operate that shop, no monsters to care. Another place hollowed out for no good reason. I touched the window, leaving my irregular handprint behind in the dust.

I found a place to eat at the end of the block. Dead flesh doesn't need as much food as living, but it does need some. It was an old, western-style building with one room divided into a dining area and a kitchen, and both almost big enough to move around in. I sat outside, under a tattered awning that looked out over the desert. In the distance, a strip of diamonds marked the river. A zombie took my order and brought it to the zombie in the kitchen.

The sandwiches were ant brisket and weren't bad for it. Only the term everyone used for ant meat was *fourmi*, the way cows were actually beef and deer was venison. They brought it out barbecue style, with burned tips, drenched in pepper sauce, and covered in onions. I ate and watched the river, wishing it would carry my memories to me.

I stayed at the table as long as I could excuse it, watching the occasional passerby in the scorching heat. My fingers searched for the source of the itching, but they never found it. I had to consciously stop myself, worried that I would expand the hurt. Flay myself with fidgeting. Eventually, my skin would come unraveled and I would just be a collection of muscle and tendon. Wouldn't be much to look at then.

I picked up the truck later in the day. It gave me some small pleasure that Burke was without it. I'd stolen it, basically. I wouldn't be hard to find, but I hoped he wouldn't even try. That he would just be annoyed and powerless.

I stared at the church when I arrived, wondering if Pastor Dukes had found whoever it was he was looking for, if the person was inside at that moment, hearing about me. It struck me then that I had no idea how Dukes was finding the person. Judging from the human enclaves I'd seen, telephones weren't common, or even present. Dukes would have some other way of getting his message out. I stayed there, hoping to catch him sneaking out or back, but I knew it was a stupid impulse. Even if I did catch him, it would destroy whatever small trust I had built.

Before I left, I returned to my graves. I needed to read the names again, to feel the letters under my fingers. No reason behind it, at least nothing rational. I needed the names close to me, even the one that wasn't quite right. The names were really just words, but they were the words of me, words I carried with my heart before I knew what they were.

I took the truck then, repeating the names in my head. Rachel Prager, Lorena Quintanilla, Hasaya. Not quite my names, or the names of my mothers. They were someone the world had never bothered to define.

I drove to the river. There was nowhere else I wanted to be. The uneven ground jostled me as I pulled off the road and parked. I got out and stepped to the river's edge. I was on the bank, but it was relatively low here, going from sand to mud. A few ruts scarred the ground here, as though pioneers had crossed more than once. It would do for a single night, I guessed. With the sun starting to get low, I climbed up onto the roof. I thought I'd get down later and sleep in the back, but I didn't. Some of it was the blanket of stars. Some of it was I didn't want to be back there, where my parts had once been. Here, at least, I was above them.

I don't know when I slept, but I woke up with the sun. It shone over behind me, turning the river gold. I blinked, not quite certain I could handle this kind of beauty. It would have been nice to stay there. Never move again. If I did, maybe the sunrise would never end, and I could be a piece of it forever.

A crash inside the truck told me how stupid it was to start hoping willy-nilly. I slid off the back, dew along the dusty top making the trip a quick one. I dropped to the ground on the other side, the grass soft and wet under my fingertips. Then I threw open the door, ready to confront whatever was in there.

The icebox that once housed my body was now open, and the green and scaly legs of a gremlin stuck out, waving this way and that. From the inside, the little monster was cursing in his bizarre patois. I'd had a bad experience with a gremlin in the past, and though it's easy to say you're not going to tar them all with the same brush, it's tougher in practice. They always had inventions that even they seemed not to truly understand, and each one could cause the kind of pain I didn't even want to imagine.

I hissed. The gremlin froze, then the struggles grew more frantic. One arm, overly long, tripped with three talons, appeared momentarily, and just as quickly disappeared into the freezer.

I reached for his ankles, shied, then gripped. The gremlin's swearing grew louder and angrier. I yanked, and the little monster came free, knocking against the lip of the icebox. I dropped him onto the center of the truck, like I was a terrified housewife with a stray mouse. The gremlin, partly dazed, pushed himself to his feet. A thread of green blood ran from his temple into the fluffy whiskers on his reptilian cheeks. The monster's huge ears went back as he hissed at me, his red eyes narrowing. I hissed right back.

"Ice cream!" he insisted. I shook my head. "Ice cream!" he rasped at me again.

I shook my head more violently, then grabbed my slate and wrote, *No ice cream here!* I held it up in front of his face and pointed at it with an emphatic finger.

His hiss turned into a low, confused growl. His expression went from angry to betrayed. "Why?" I shrugged. I didn't know why I didn't have ice cream. I just didn't. One talon went up into the impressive sideburns. He scratched them absently, watching me. "Fight?" he asked.

I shook my head and took a step back. Watching me, he reached down to the floor and picked up a parasol. I tensed, ready for it to turn into a machine gun. He loped to the back exit and opened the umbrella. It was decorated in Chinese cranes and looked like a dressing gown I owned. He peered out suspiciously, as though I was going to redirect the sun.

"Bright light," he confided, then hopped out. He checked the shadows on the ground, angling the parasol to the rising sun. Then he hobbled away across the desert, in the direction of town.

I watched him go before looking around in the truck. The crash had come from a shelf over the icebox. A collection of Burke's tools, from thick suturing needles to blades, had come free and showered the interior. I put them back where they looked like they belonged and closed the doors. The more time I spent away from the freezer, the more unbearable it became to be close. I'd sat next to it all the way out to the graveyard without worrying too much, but now it was intolerable.

A gill-man surfaced briefly from the river, soon disappearing back under the listless current. Probably just passing through and wondering what he was doing in this horrible and dry place. He looked at Ehrenberg the way most people seemed to: a place to pass through on the way to somewhere else and then forget. Only those who were trapped stayed.

I stayed out there for a long time, watching the river move past me. The border between Arizona and California was right out there in the middle of the water, an invisible spine trailing all the way down to Mexico. My past on one side of the line, and my past on the other side. No idea where my future might be. The three women I'd found in this place had come here thinking they would survive the Night War. They thought they would have a future. They'd been wrong. I could just as easily be mistaken.

"Excuse me?"

Judging by her size, the girl was twelve. By the look in her eyes, she was pushing forty. She was human, painfully thin, and pretty in that way that never really lasts. Her hair was blonde and wavy, and reminded me a bit of the river when the sun hit it. Her eyes were a cloudy, haunted gray. Her cheekbones were high, and her lips thin. Twenty years earlier, and she would have looked like she stepped out of the dustbowl. Here and now, she had even less direction, even fewer places to go. She wore a threadbare jacket over a dress, and a pair of shoes that looked to have only a few steps left in them.

"Pastor Sherman told me to bring you to the church."

I left the truck there. A walk would be better. I followed the girl, even though I didn't really need to. The church would be my landmark in Ehrenberg no matter what. The girl was silent, never even looking at me. I would have asked her name, but she'd need to see the slate, so I didn't.

I watched the tension in her neck as we walked, the preemptory flinch whenever my foot scratched on the sand. She was a wounded bird, and I wasn't going to spook her if I could help it.

When the church was in sight, the girl peeled off, scurrying back in the direction of the river. I pitied her, because there wasn't a thing else I could do for her. She was going to return to the little shanty on the banks of the river and keep finding new ways to survive. One day she would come up empty, and that would be the end. No monster would remember her.

I opened the front door and found Pastor Dukes sitting on a pew next to another man. This man was small, his skin brown. He wore a narrow mustache, patchy stubble speaking to how little he was actually able to shave. He wore blue jeans and an old work shirt, both torn and mended. His hands and forearms, revealed by rolled-up sleeves, were scarred with hard work. His face was deeply lined, but that didn't mean much for someone with a hard life. He could have been thirty or he could have been fifty.

"Miss Stitch, thank you for coming," Pastor Dukes said. I nodded with a hint of a curtsy. The other man watched me with wary eyes. "This is Richard Quintanilla."

My eyes widened, and before I could stop myself, I took two quick steps to him, one hand reaching on its own. The man flinched, and I forced myself to stop. I had to remind myself that I was a meat golem. To these men, I was a terrifying monster.

Jane Stitch, I wrote, though I wanted to write Lorena. I wanted the part of me that had been Lorena to run to him, but all of me was buzzing with the echoes of the lightning that brought me to life. *Were you Lorena's husband?*

"Uncle," he said. "I was Lorena's uncle." His accent was Mexican, but not the kind I heard back in Los Angeles. This was another kind, a mystery to me.

I realized then I didn't know what to say to him. From the look in his eyes, he didn't know what to say to me. I didn't know what parts of me were Lorena. What he would be looking at with the depressing sheen of recognition.

Pastor Dukes looked from me to Richard and back again. "Jane. You wanted to talk to someone who knew you. Richard is the only person left who did."

That was it. An entire life reduced to one person. An uncle. I wondered how common this was, how many families had been winnowed to one. I nodded to Dukes, then gave Richard a stuttering wave. I went to a pew and sat so I wouldn't loom over them. Questions had run through my mind since the beginning, but now that I was here, in the presence of someone, the words were hard to write. Lorena was too big a concept; I didn't think she could fit out of my chalk. I kept starting a word, then rubbing the words away, then starting again. Finally, I had something. It felt silly and small, but it was something. I turned the slate around and held it up for Richard.

Who was Lorena?

Richard read it, his eyes going soft and distant. "She was from here," he said. "All the Quintanillas are from here, from when this used to be Mexico. She grew up in Yuma. She was my brother's second daughter. He had five children. Do you remember them?"

I shook my head. *I don't remember anything about Lorena. I know her name.*

"That's too bad. I think I'm the only one who remembers any of them now. My brother and his wife, all of their children...none of them lasted the Night War. I had hope for Lorena, though. We came up here, thinking we could find a safe place in the mountains. Those mountains killed the Springfield Shape, maybe they can kill any other kind of monster."

My hands played over the pew in front of me. I didn't even notice it happening. The roughness of the scarred wood was a pleasant tickle under my fingertips.

"I was wrong." He swallowed, then shook his head, shuddering. He turned to Dukes. "I ain't talking about that night."

Pastor Dukes put a hand on Richard's shoulder. "I know."

Now I swallowed, looking away. I couldn't watch these two men, caught in the grips of memory. When that happened to me, I became a raging beast. These two were worn down by it, breaking anew even though it happened a long time ago.

"I thought, once Sherman gave her the rites, even though he isn't a good Catholic, she could rest. But no." Richard's eyes were suddenly clear, a tear falling from one of them. "When he told me there was a meat golem thinking she was part of Lorena, I didn't believe it. I wanted to tell him that when I came and found out, but..." He gestured helplessly at my hands. I noticed what they were doing, almost like I was playing a piano that wasn't there. I did that from time to time when I was uncomfortable.

"That's Lorena. We had an old piano. Broken down, but she kept it playing. She'd play whenever she could. Broke her heart when we had to leave it behind when the monsters came. But she always did that, what you're doing with your hands. I don't want you to be Lorena, but you are."

My hands were shaking. *I wish I wasn't.*

"I do too."

My vision went wobbly. I wrote again, *Tell me about Lorena. Please.*

"What do you want to know?"

Anything.

"She was a good person. Lost her family one by one until she was the only one left. Didn't break her. By the end, she was the one keeping me going. I think if I lost her, I would be gone too. Then I did lose her, and I wasn't gone. Only because I could think about Lorena, and what she would want from me. So now I'm the only Quintanilla left and I have to find a way to live with it."

Now I felt the Lorena in me. I wanted to go to him. Muscles twitched in my body, likely her muscles, compelling me to cross the short distance between us and hold him, but I knew that would be the most awful thing I could do to the man. I brought up the slate to say something, but even that was inadequate.

I ran from the church, stopping only when the bright sun was on me. The chemicals I called blood rushed through my veins, my stolen heart pounding.

"Did you get what you wanted here?" Pastor Dukes asked, emerging from the church in the shadow of the doorway.

I didn't know what to tell him.

NINETEEN

I sat on the roof of the ice cream truck watching the glittering river. I couldn't quite face Quartzsite yet, not after talking to Richard Quintanilla. All I could do was watch the water wearily rolling past and wishing that could be everything for me. No Los Angeles, no Quartzsite. No Burke. No wondering what I was. The river and I, alone in the world.

"Pardon me?"

I turned, and found the speaker standing by the side of the dirt road, shading her eyes with her hand as she looked up at my perch. She wore a threadbare man's suit, dirty and patched, and her hair was cut short. She had gaunt, hungry features, and a sun squint that likely never went away. At first glance, I could have taken her for a boy, prematurely aged by the war, but under the suit, she had one or two feminine curves. She was white, but her skin was like leather. Her eyes were a pale blue, nearly colorless, like life had washed them out. She looked nervous, but so did every human who talked to me. She was also the first to try it since I'd left the church. I didn't move from my spot on top of the ice cream truck, thinking that if I did, she might bolt like an old alley cat.

"I don't mean to be rude," she said. "I heard there was a meat golem in town asking about..." she cleared her throat. "Lorena Quintanilla?"

I nodded, picking up my slate and considering it before dropping it to dangle around my neck, then I scooted to the edge of the roof. The woman took a cautious step back, and I dropped to the earth. I wrote a quick greeting on the slate and showed her. *Yes, I was. I'm Jane Stitch.*

"Fern Calloway," the woman said. "Why were asking about Lorena?"

What did you hear?

"Sherman Dukes, the pastor, he was asking around, looking for Richard. Mentioned a meat golem. Heard it had to do with Lorena."

You knew her?

Fern nodded. She kept reflexively glancing away, as if my attention was too much, but then she'd quickly snap back to me, remembering I was a monster and not to be taken for granted. I didn't know how much I could make her feel at ease. I towered over her, and though she had a toughness, I was a meat golem. She might as well have been made of wet paper. "What did you want with Lorena?"

It's hard to explain. Even as I wrote, my restless hands kept wanting to go to Fern. To do...I wasn't certain. I kept them under control only with difficulty, forcing them to concentrate on the words.

"Did you know her?" Fern asked.

I am her. Some of me is some of her.

Fern's face fell. Her gaze wandered over me, during the silence, pausing at my hands. "I see it. I see her. Some of her." She swallowed, considering her words. "I'm sorry, I've never talked to a...to a meat golem before. I don't know what it's like. What you're like. Do you remember Lorena?"

I shook my head. *I don't know anything about Lorena really. I came here to find out who the women were who made me.*

"That makes sense. The pastor found Richard. I imagine he didn't mention me."

I shook my head. *He didn't say much. I think I disturbed him.*

"Why?"

Because parts of his niece were stitched into a new woman and brought to life.

Fern blinked in surprise. "I think it's kind of nice."

Haven't heard that before.

"Lorena's dead, but she's not gone. There's a piece of her still alive in you. That's how it works, right?"

I'd like to think so. I think Richard was thinking of her soul. Maybe. Or maybe I was projecting my thoughts on him, since I was thinking of her soul. Of my soul.

Fern snorted. "He would. I don't cotton to that kind of thing. I was pretty sure there wasn't a god even before the monsters came, and now I'm dead certain. If there's no god, then there's no souls. A person dies, they die. I thought Lorena was completely gone, but no. She ain't. So yeah, it's nice."

Never thought of it like that. I wasn't sure I trusted Fern's opinion of things. It was far kinder to me than I had a right to. *How did you know Lorena?*

"Lorena and I were together." Fern looked at me with her clear, colorless eyes.

I mouthed an *Oh.* And suddenly, my hand's reaction made sense. I knew what it wanted.

"Back before the Night War started, although not that much before. Back when that sort of thing was still frowned upon." She snorted. "The monsters might not care about it, but a lot of people still do. People like Richard. This person who used to be Lorena walking around, and he doesn't even bother to tell me. Do you know what he called her when she was still alive? You don't want to. Then she dies in that church, and all of a sudden, she's this angel. Death lets him write whatever eulogy he wants, and he's going to keep writing it until everyone who knew the real Lorena is gone, and it's his story that sticks around."

You don't think I'm erasing Lorena?

"Are you Lorena?"

I don't know.

"Did you remember me?"

My hand seems to.

A bit of color crept into Fern's washed-out cheeks, and she smirked. I felt my cheeks growing hot too once I realized what I'd said. "That's something. But you didn't run to me. You didn't kiss me. After five years gone, Lorena would have done that."

I'm sorry I didn't.

Fern shook her head. "It's all right. I'm not asking for any of that, and if I did, there's a certain young lady in town who would never forgive me. I just heard about you asking around and I had to know why. Glad I did."

I wrote the next message carefully, rubbing it out and starting again several times. Finally, I decided on the simple. *Would you tell me about Lorena?*

Fern offered me a smile. "Sure."

TWENTY

It was evening before Fern stopped talking about Lorena. She wasn't done. I don't think she'll ever be completely finished. She said such beautiful things. I knew her, this piece of me. If nothing else came of this, I knew one part. They had been in love, even planning to find someplace out in the desert where they could be together the way they wanted to. Then the Night War broke out.

Fern's family had already disowned her. "They wanted a daughter and I dressed like a son," she said. So she went with Lorena's family, who similarly hated her. Lorena had died in that final attack on the church, a martian death ray raking across her head. The last thing she had done was push Fern out of the way. Fern was never going to get over that guilt, even if we both knew Lorena wouldn't have wanted to be in a world without Fern any more than Fern wanted to be in a world without Lorena. The Night War made them choose.

The best part was Fern making it clear there was an open door between us now; I could see her again if a question occurred to me. I bought us both some food from the barbecue place and let Fern eat most of it. She put it away like she hadn't had a real meal in a long time. I watched the zombies eye her with disgust over their rotting features, but they knew better than to bother a meat golem's guest. Then she left, hoofing it in the direction of that sad little community on the riverbank.

I took the truck down the road, leaving the river and three of my graves behind. Three names meant something, but I didn't know what. I knew the name that went with most of my hands, and one of two that went with my legs. Didn't know if it mattered. I was carrying them—Rachel, Hasaya, and Lorena—in me, but was I a simple equation? Add them up, with three unknowns, and you get Jane?

Lorena was more than a simple unknown, it was true. She had been a damaged girl, in love with someone the world wouldn't allow. Then, when it was finally possible, she'd been killed. Thrown away. Garbage, collateral damage. Until Burke had her dug up and put part of her into me. As many facts about Lorena as I learned, it was the feelings she evoked in Fern, the rust in her voice, the faraway look in her eyes, that told me far more.

The desert threw on its gloomy cloak. Giant ants scuttled by in the distance, heading for their artificial hills. I bounced and rattled over the terrain, the names repeating over and over in my mind. A new mantra for me. Names and not much more. I knew something about Lorena, but Rachel and Hasaya were mysteries, with Hasaya not even being precisely the correct name. There was little else I could do there. I would know more about Lorena as long as Fern was willing to talk, but the others were lost. Rachel's husband was god knows where, and there likely wasn't a single record of Hasaya anywhere on Earth.

At least I could keep their names close to me. Even if everyone else forgot them, I could remember them. I'd honor them by holding their names. In a little inadequate way.

I found myself wanting to talk to Nick. Seeing him would be hard; the fear on his face was a knife twisting in my gut. I couldn't use a telephone, either. I wanted there to be something between those two extremes, because he was the only one who might kind of understand. He was a detective who found missing people. I'd found the opposite. He would know the thrill of discovery and the skin of satisfaction over the deeper and colder suspicion that none of this mattered. When I felt the ghost of his touch at my temples, brushing my hair away where the skunk stripe streaked through the black, that was my memory. Not the woman who'd once had this brain. This one was made by the reanimated brain in its second life.

By the time I noticed them, they were already all around me. I caught sight of the first out of the corner of my left eye, the sparks of his steed's hooves like sunlight in the deepening night. It was Shreve Dullahan, his double-bladed axe clutched in one white-knuckled hand, the reins of his charger in the other. His torso was half-turned in my direction, giving no doubt of the target of his attention.

Light haloed me from the back. I couldn't see anything through the grimy back windows, but I knew it was Morgan Dullahan following me in her truck. At the same time, Mal Dullahan's black charger thundered into view through the passenger side window. Mal held up his hangman's noose, then whipped it over his head like a lariat. Both he and Shreve were whooping, their voices sharpened to a hateful edge.

Green encroached on my vision. I kept my hands glued to the steering wheel and squinted against the light. They wanted another round, and I was strongly considering giving it to them. Then my headlights lit a figure in the middle of the road like he was a soloist onstage.

Tod Dullahan sat astride his charger. The beast's eyes were red, and as it pawed the ground, its hooves kicked up sparks like a sword at a whetstone. The light from the truck washed all the color out of both figures. They were pallid as death, the both of them. Tod didn't hold up a hand or make any threat. He merely sat there, impassively watching the ice cream truck barreling down on him.

I stomped on the brakes. Wasn't me; it was the urge of whoever had owned my legs first. Rachel maybe, or Hasaya. One of them wouldn't run over a headless horseman, even if it sounded like a good idea to me. The truck hurled dust into the air with its skid, the headlights splashing away from Tod, throwing him into funereal shadow. Now, all I could see of him were his horse's eyes and the kick of sparks.

Behind me, the truck came to a stop, its lights unblinkingly on me. Mal and Shreve took the stop as a chance to ride in circles around all of us, continuing their whooping. If they had six-shooters, they would have been shooting at clouds.

"Plain Jane!" Tod called.

The industrial chemicals in my veins went cold. The tide kept rising, the deep green sea hungrily devouring the outcropping on which I stood. I stepped out of the truck and regarded him. Then, purposefully, I pulled the slate up over my head and tossed it onto the driver's seat. The chalk clacked against it. Wouldn't need to talk.

"You've been trouble since you came to my town," he said.

I watched him. Explaining that I had been no trouble until his palookas hassled me was unlikely to win any debates. Behind me, I heard the creak and yawn of a truck door being opened, and then the scratch of boots over the sand. The door shut after the person had walked away. Their stink, that weird smell of fake rotten fruit, enveloped me.

Mal and Shreve reined in the horses, who whinnied in anger. Tod in front of me, Morgan behind, Shreve to my left, and Mal to my right. My hand flexed on its own. The green washed over my senses, and I saw sunlight. I pushed it back only with effort, and when my eyes were my own again, I found I'd taken some steps toward Tod. The other horsemen had closed in, weapons now at the ready.

Tod laughed. "Got some fight in her! Oh, Jane. It's a damn shame you jumped my boys. We could've made some music together." I felt Morgan closing in on me. The green tide desperately wanted to bring me under. I tried to tell it not yet, but it pounded at me, pulled at me. It wanted to hurt these four, and I wanted to let it.

"You should have listened to Wolff," Shreve called.

"Don't blame you for not," Mal said.

"If she listened to Wolff, she wouldn't be worth a good goddamn," Tod told his men. "Hell, if she listened to Wolff after clobberin' y'all, I'd start wonderin' about you."

The horsemen were silent. I imagined if they'd had heads, they would have been hanging them.

"She caught us by surprise," Morgan said finally.

"She better have," Tod said. "Makes you a bushwhacker, Plain Jane. You like jumpin' folks when they ain't lookin'?"

My mind spun. Tried to think of some scenario where I beat these four. There wasn't one that I could see, but I never planned out my violence beforehand anyway. I was best when I just gave myself over to the green and let it do the work for me.

"We're taking our pound of flesh," Morgan said in her faint Irish lilt.

"Yeah, maybe you think twice about startin' something you don't want to finish," Mal said.

Shreve spun the axe. It was disconcertingly light in his hands.

Tod hopped off his horse, the bowie knife dancing between his fingers. It sizzled where it cut through the air. "I wonder where you thought you were, Plain Jane. This land belongs to the Dullahans, and if you thought just because you knew the doc, we was gonna go easy on ya, you got another thing comin'."

I hissed. Wasn't that a bitter joke, the thought that Burke would bring me anything but misery. I felt Morgan right behind me, her presence electric. I didn't control myself; I didn't let go, either. I merely handed the reins to the green, switching places. It was the horseman now and I was the charger. I whirled, my hand automatically seeking the neck to compress and lift. The most natural feeling in the world.

Only I was reaching for a neck that wasn't there. My hand closed over nothing, and Morgan, though unready for the sudden attack, wasn't going to wait around until I worked out something else to grab. She hit me hard in the belly with the butt of her shotgun. My wind was gone in a flash of white, my chest burning as I fell to my knees. Tod stopped in front of me.

"Shreve." The other horseman tossed him an antprod, which Tod snatched out of the air. Blue death snapped at the edge.

"That was your one move, Plain Jane. I got a lot more than that, but this one is the only one I need." He brought the antprod down. The broken paving and the desert sand were harsh against my elbows and legs. I fought the urge to skitter away. Ironic, that. It was fire that took my will away and made me run, but it was electricity that would kill me. I could force myself to stand against what would kill me, but not a product of my mind.

"Pop her!" Mal crowed. "We'll go string her up by the doc's!"

"No, I ain't gonna pop her," Tod said. "Unless she decides to get stupid. You gonna get stupid, Plain Jane?" The antprod sparked, burning a hole in my vision. I shook my head. "See? She ain't so dumb after all."

Morgan's hands were on me then, hauling me up to a sitting position. I could have stopped her easily, but with the antprod sparking mere inches from my face, I was gentled. She got my weight off my elbows and guided my hands behind my back. Gravel bit into my skin. Manacles clinked into place over my wrists, then Morgan pulled me up by the chain between. I scrambled to my feet, shying away from the lightning humming its deadly song right in my ear.

Tod handed the antprod to Morgan. She held the shotgun indifferently in her left hand, the antprod near my neck in her right.

"You'll want to be walkin' to my truck now," Morgan told me.

The spectral pickup waited, its faded red paintjob like an old bloodstain in the dim light. As we got close, the engine snarled and the tires crinkled against the gravel. It leapt forward, circling once like a hungry shark, before stopping right next to us.

Morgan gestured with the antprod. "Get in."

The back gate of the truck fell open with a creak. I climbed in with difficulty, grateful to Rachel, or possibly Hasaya, for her long legs. I sat down on the flatbed, and the metal was colder than death. Morgan climbed in after me. She sat without looking and the gate rose to meet her, shutting right as her butt made contact with it and the corner of the bed. She sheathed her shotgun in a wide leather holster on her back and clutched the antprod. Every so often, she traced a figure eight with the sparking tip, as though to remind me of the deadly instrument. Not that I needed reminding.

Tod threw himself into the saddle and the pale charger reared up on its hind legs, blowing brimstone out of its nostrils. As it whinnied, Tod unleashed a demonic scream, and then both rocketed out through the fearful town. Shreve and Mal galloped a full revolution around the truck before following Tod's fiery path. Then the truck's tires ground on the gravel and it was moving, too.

On the street, a single ghoul watched. I'd never seen him before and I would have had trouble recognizing him if I saw him again. He was just a ghoul, the generic image of that monster when people said the word: thin, gray-skinned and haunted-eyed. He watched me with sadness and disappointment. Fear, too, which kept him nailed to the spot, lurking in the shadows of an abandoned storefront's doorway. And self-loathing, as he watched the only person to stand up to the Dullahans get taken away, probably to die. Whatever hope he had for his town was leaving with me, shackled just like I was.

I didn't know how to tell him that I wasn't any kind of hope. I was a goddamn cocktail waitress who just wanted an answer or two. It was bad luck that crossed my path with Tod Dullahan's and not a single thing to be done for it. Then the ghoul was gone, the truck's speed turning him into a smear of shadow. That was the only way the Dullahans ever saw him, even when they were standing still.

The Dullahans ignored the road whenever they felt like it. Even the truck didn't need it. It wasn't actually a truck anyway, it was a headless horseman's steed, pulled from wherever those came from. Hell, maybe. It reacted like a living thing, making adjustments around the deeper holes and bigger cacti, the tires throwing unholy flames just like the hooves of the horses. Flames that made me shy away from the sides of the truck's bed.

A glance through the back window showed that the steering wheel and gearshift worked themselves. The truck's driver was itself, or some symbiotic urge between it and Morgan. She perched on the edge of the bed, her left hand curled around the lip, but it didn't look like she needed to hang on. I'd never heard of a headless horseman being thrown from their mount, and I couldn't imagine this was any different.

My heart seized whenever we went over a bump or bottomed out in a hole, because Morgan did move then, the antprod wobbling. If she lost her balance, that thing didn't even have to stab into me to end it. Touch any bit of metal around me and that would probably be it. Take the lightning right into my body. The second bolt that turned out the lights.

I wished I knew what they wanted, but it was probably nothing. I was a threat to their social order. Never mind that I was passing through. Never mind that I didn't want a fight. Bad luck was going to give me one.

Morgan was impossible to read so long as she remained silent. The lack of a head was more and more disconcerting the longer I stayed around them. I'd never had much to do with headless horsemen. No real reason. They were drivers, wanderers, and apparently rantchers. Not too many in Hollywood. I gave them the kind of thought I gave most monsters who rarely crossed my path. Now, looking right through where a head would be, wishing I could see some glint in the eyes or set to the jaw, all I could feel were the heebies crawling up my spine.

"I'd keep in mind what I was lookin' at, if I was you," Morgan said. She had been staring right back at me the whole time.

It was difficult looking anywhere else, what with the antprod hanging over me like a guillotine blade. I forced my head to turn. We were leaving Quartzsite now, dark reclaiming the scattered buildings. Only a few lights twinkled back there, and I knew they would be swarming with moths and locusts. Here, the only light was the little bit still bleeding up over the western horizon, soon to be swallowed up. We traveled out into the desert north of town, trailing dust and sparks in sheets.

The wash steadily began to rise, and before long, lights shone out of the dark ahead of us. I dimly glimpsed conical shapes only where they came in contact with the sky. Hungry voids against a field of stars. The lights barely described a series of buildings. Tough to tell what they were from a distance. As we got closer, I saw more and more of them, some large, but most small. I was on the Dullahan rantch.

The thunder of ants pulled my attention the other way. A pair of horsemen, each wielding crackling antprods, drove a swarm in the direction of one of the artificial anthills. They brought with them that same stink that clung to Tod and his gang. A miasma from the swarm itself. My eyes followed the trail of giant insects to the void in the sky, and there I saw the slender shapes of the ants, making the starry sky ripple with their passing. We left them behind, now traveling up a road that wound into the expansive compound.

Tod still led the way, and he was heading for what I now saw was a weatherbeaten and faded, but relatively new, barn. The wooden walls didn't look to have any gaps, the sodium light out front was working and drawing in every locust in the area with its white hum, and the paint on the whole thing would hold out for another year or two.

Tod's charger whinnied as the horseman reined him in. They all dismounted, Morgan easily sliding over the side of the pickup. I couldn't tell if she'd transferred her attention, as there was no head to turn at all.

"Come on now," Morgan said to me.

I clambered to my feet and hopped off the flatbed. There was nowhere to run. I'd gotten myself good and trapped. There was either open desert, punctuated by thick, electrified fences, or the other cluster of buildings, likely where Ambrose Dullahan and whatever other thugs he had were waiting. I'd managed to put myself entirely at Tod Dullahan's nonexistent mercy. Shreve and Mal opened up the double doors of the barn while Morgan kept me covered with the antprod.

"Well, Plain Jane, here we are," Tod said. "Probably wondering what's going on. Well, we can't have the people of Quartzsite thinking it's open season on Dullahans. We just fought a whole war to prove that wasn't the case, and one angry skin-dolly ain't gonna undo all that hard work. Now march."

I stepped into the barn. It was warmer in here, a little bit of stored-up heat from the day. One side of the barn was given over to stalls, sized for giant ants, though they were all empty now. Some equipment, which I took to be veterinary, was haphazardly scattered by the stalls. The back was dominated by sacks of sugar, helpfully labeled. Right next door were more of the glass jugs filled with formic acid, the cat-stink fighting against the artificial rot clinging to everything else. The other side of the barn was shelving, featuring collections of tools, some beginning to show rust at the edges. A hayloft was above, but it was an easy guess that I wasn't getting anywhere near that.

"Over there," Tod said. I didn't see what he was pointing at, but I didn't have to. Morgan gestured with the antprod to a support beam on the left side of the barn among the shelving. I couldn't help it; my gaze lingered on the various tools, some of them recognizable, others mysterious and likely ant-related, and imagined the lurid torments they could inflict. Among the tools were especially ghoulish mementos: mutant claws, cut off at the wrist, sewn shut and stuffed. Weird place for a trophy. I couldn't help but wonder if Lorena's hands would be next to them soon. The chains rattled with my shivering.

Morgan laughed. "Plain Jane's shakin'!"

"She should be," Tod said. "This ain't gonna be fun for her." Mal and Shreve packed a lifetime of menace into their chuckles.

"Turn 'round," Morgan said. "Back to the beam."

I obeyed, and Morgan quickly undid the shackles and then re-locked them so that the chain was wrapped around the beam. There was a second where she had to have put the antprod down and I was free, but I couldn't seize it. My stomach was in an icy tangle, my hands were shaking too badly. I watched the other three horsemen, three headless figures, each armed with a brutal frontier weapon. There was no compassion or hint of mercy from them. There couldn't be. Their humanity had been taken along with their heads.

"Now, it's important to me you understand this, Plain Jane," Tod said, stepping forward. He skinned his bowie knife and it hissed softly, like a snake waking up. "I ain't hurtin' you because I want to. I'm hurtin' you because you decided to come to my town and go after my people. You know I can't have that. Anyone knows I can't have that. If Phobos or any of those bugbrains heard, we'd look weak."

I wanted to hiss at Tod, but I couldn't. Fear had taken the last sound I could make, balled it up, and threw it away. I was fully mute. Mal tittered. Shreve was whispering "go, go, go" under his breath. Morgan strode out from behind me, tapping the shaft of the antprod in her hand like a baseball bat.

"So when you bushwhacked my boys, you were saying that the Dullahans don't take care of our own. Well, I'm here to tell you that we do. And the way that we do it is scale. You know the Bible, Plain Jane?" That was almost funny. "Well, in the Bible, it says that justice is about an eye for an eye. So you beat on my people here, we let them put a beating on you."

"She bushwhacked us," Mal whined. Tod half-turned to Mal, and though I didn't see or hear any kind of signal, Mal's shoulders slumped, mollified, like he could see Tod's facial expression. Like there was one to see.

Tod stayed in front of me, holding up his knife. I was a full head taller than him, but it didn't matter. I think part of him loved that it didn't matter. The big, bad meat golem was terrified. Whatever had passed between Mal and Tod was over, Tod now speaking to me. "The thing is, I ain't out for justice. I leave that to the good Lord to mete out. So, we take what justice wants, and we add a bit to it, and that shows what needs to be done."

He brought the knife closer. Heat shimmered in the air, coming off the blade.

"So this is it, Plain Jane. If you had listened to Wolff, this wouldn't be happening. When it's done, if you're smart, you're gonna leave town and never come back. You got no rights to be in Quartzsite. None at all."

The blade burned as it sliced into my arm, and I couldn't scream.

TWENTY-ONE

It was hours. Or at least it felt like hours. I guess torture has a way of stretching out the minutes, but I didn't have any experience in the matter. That's what they were up to. Torture.

Tod worked me over with his bowie, cutting little slices into my limbs. To warm me up, he said. Just enough to hurt me, to remind me that his weapon burned with the fires of Hell. That he could put the fear of every meat golem into me.

Then he found the unraveling stitches. He'd laughed, and sliced along them, finding the proper depth. Severing nerves, veins, tendons, the parts Burke had meticulously put back together to give me life. The whole time yammering on about shoddy craftsmanship.

Then he cut the arm off. No warning there. I felt it as a scalding, sun-hot agony that turned to ice. I stared at my arm, lying on the floor of the barn. It had been cut off mid-forearm, at an angle, along the line of stitches that once held it to my body. When Tod cut it off me, the searing agony taking the world away, he had laughed.

"This thing ain't even yours!" he crowed. I cried, but I was crying for Lorena, this last insult from beyond the grave. Her hand, to be treated like garbage once again. The others joined in laughing, then Shreve advanced on me. I shrank from him.

"Where are you going?" Tod demanded.

"Figured she's had enough."

"You think she's had enough?"

Mal tittered. Shreve said, "I don't know, Tod. You cut a piece off her, it's getting kind of late. I mean, we all have to be up early to take the swarm out to the watering hole."

My hand, Lorena's hand, lay on the floor of the barn, the fingers sluggishly waving with false life. The bone had been cut in two, the remains of medical staples showing how the sections had once been connected. The skin where it had split and began to unravel looked like old, discolored rubber. What passed for my blood, a milky greenish liquid, pulsed out onto the floor. Though I can't stand the sight of blood, I didn't mind those chemicals. They were too divorced from humanity, the bleach burn of the scent tasting nothing like the blood I'd had when I was six different women. The slice along the wound alternated between a maddening itch and the white scalding, changing without warning.

"You hearin' this fella?" Tod asked the room.

"I'm hearin', but I don't believe a word," Morgan said.

"Listen to me, hayseed," Tod said, jabbing a finger into Shreve's chest. He still clutched the bowie knife in that hand, held with his ring and pinkie fingers, turning the gesture into a naked threat. "This woman right here showed you to be yellow. She beat you 'til you ran. All three of you. Now you want me to let her go?"

"Um," Shreve said thoughtfully.

"No, I'm gonna take every little bit of her that I can. I'm gonna show this town what happens when you mess with a Dullahan."

"This is gonna be fun," Mal said.

"It ain't about fun," Tod spat. "This is about who we are in this place, you understand?" Then he paused. "It being fun is a nice bonus."

"I could use a drink," Morgan said.

"Think we all could. Mal, check the shackles."

The horseman moved around behind me. He yanked my mutilated arm up, pulling a hiss out of me, a hiss that sounded like flesh being pressed to a skillet. He reshackled me above my elbow on the ruined arm.

"She's good." Mal laughed. "Hey Tod, you keep cuttin', we're gonna run outta places to shackle her!"

"After the next round, she ain't gonna be runnin' anywhere." The horsemen turned to leave.

"Where do you think you're going?" Tod asked, one shoulder cocked slightly in Shreve's direction.

"To get a drink with you," Shreve said.

"Unh-uh. You're stayin' here. You think we're gonna leave her unguarded?"

"Mal shackled her!"

"So Mal gets a drink. You think about that the next time you try to gainsay me."

Tod, Mal, and Morgan sauntered out of the barn. I'd say Shreve watched them morosely, but he had no head to have an expression on. The slump of his shoulders implied some disappointment. He wandered after them for a step or two, then stopped and turned.

"She ain't goin' nowhere," he muttered.

Whatever disobedience Shreve had in him wasn't enough to send him out the door. It merely pushed him to meander around the place, peppering the air with resentful mumbling, twirling his axe like a lazy drum major. I watched him, my eyes pain-hooded. This was probably as good as it was going to get. One horseman instead of all four. And I wasn't going to let them dishonor Lorena any more. I kept thinking of Fern, the way her gaze fell to my hands whenever she talked. Lorena Quintanilla mattered to someone. She mattered to me.

In my agony, I had done a lot of thrashing around. I'd even greened out a few times, though it wasn't a plunge into the deep water. The pain kept me weak, and the green needed to be strong. In any case, none of my struggles had done a single thing to either the shackles or the beam. The wood might as well have been stone.

The problem was, there wasn't another option. I kept my eyes on Shreve and pulled the chain taut against the beam. I felt no weakness in it, but that was in my drained state. If I was going to do something about it, I needed the kind of strength meat golems were feared for. The stuff that only came out when I was lost.

Though it was impossible to be certain, it didn't look like Shreve was paying any attention to me at all. I shut my eyes and took the first steps onto Not My Memory Lane. I knew it so well, better even than some of those memories I'd made as myself. I could bring them to the fore without any effort. Taste them on my tongue. As I was doing it, I felt Lorena's hand against the beam, her agile fingers teasing out a tattoo from the wood.

The baby was in my arms, her chubby hand reaching for the orange. The sun was so bright between the leaves, bright enough to blind. The sun didn't shine like that anymore, or if it did, I never felt it. The breeze heavy with citrus. The baby was everything in my world, showing her what an orange was, seeing her face teetering between confusion and wonder. She wanted the orange, but she didn't know why.

My hands had never felt that baby, but the softness of her skin, the warmth of her little body, were as powerful a sensation as any I had ever experienced. It was a struggle even holding her out as far as I was; I wanted to bring her close, nuzzle her neck and shower her with kisses.

The green began to close over my head, the seething ocean bringing me down into its bosom. Didn't want to give me air. Only the inexorable strength of the tides.

The memory was always a distinct one, living in its own little box. There was no context. It was like a dream, but far too vivid to be anything but reality. I pushed at it, drawing the angry waters around me, willing the green with its sticky tendrils. The heat of Tod's bowie knife had nearly been enough to send me there already. Burning would always be Wichita.

Fire, hungry and close, sent me right back to that time, and so it needed only the barest of nudges to send me there now. I was on the precipice. And now, the orange trees weren't trees anymore. They were martian tripods, striding over the burning buildings, through the oily columns of smoke. Their death rays shimmered in the hellish haze, first igniting, then melting whatever they touched. I'd seen the photos afterwards. We all had; they were famous. The prime example of what happened to any human who would dare stand against the monsters.

They had brought hell to earth that night in Wichita. Fire slithered over the ground, spreading the glass as it went in shimmery streaks. Greasy pillars of smoke blotted out the moon and stars, turning the earth into the noon sky and the sky into the charred earth. And I was there, somehow. Standing with a little girl. She was older, so much heavier in my arms. I turned her face to mine. Her blonde hair whipped about in the hot wind. Tears cut through the grime. Her eyes were red, nose running freely. She was sobbing, a helpless, wracking cry as she knew now that there was nothing in this world that was safe. Her mother and father were powerless to guard her against the world's rampant cruelty. She had no hope of any kind left. It was burned down and turned to glass by the war machines in front of her.

I held her tight with human strength, but it was meat golem power in my limbs. The waves, green with rage, crashed in on me. The promontory that should be above water was ready to drown. As the water hit, rocked, and hit again, it left its icy fingerprints inside me. Expanding, burrowing, growing. The green had me now, and I wanted it. I stared at the face of the little girl who was not quite my own. I was the helpless one, helpless to comfort the girl across time and death. There was only the anger, once impotent, now terrifying.

The beam at my back gave a crack and shuddered. "Huh?" This came from Shreve, at the other end of the barn. I didn't bother to look at him; he wasn't important. If he wanted to come over, I could show him what was in me.

I felt the little girl shaking as I drew her close to my body. I was seeing two things at once, almost on top of each other. My mismatched eyes working at cross purposes, one seeing through time, the other space. The barn was all around me, but so was Wichita. So was the burning prairie and the stalking tripods, the ground turning to glass beneath my feet. The sobbing shredded my nerves and commanded my muscles. The woman then had no power over the martians, no way to strike back. Neither did I, but I had a beam.

It was humming behind me, wobbling, trying to hold up everything it supported. I pulled my arms forward. The wound ignited along my forearm, and for a moment, I thought I had been hit with a death ray. But no, those weren't here. There were no martian tripods. Just a headless horseman.

"What? What are you doing? Stop!" Shreve commanded. No one was listening. I hissed, bringing the little girl's fear into my limbs. The green almost washed over me entirely. Almost put me under. I kept my head above water, gasping as the green closed in. But I was strong now, too, with the rage permeating my tissues. I yanked again and the beam cracked, cracked again. Splinters bit into my intact wrist and into the searing pain of the stump of my arm. The whole thing vibrated in shrill terror. Shreve screamed something, and then the world was thunder.

I was on the floor, no clear memory of how I got there. I stood, planks and beams of wood sliding off me like rain. That ammonia stink and the sizzle of acid eating away at fallen lumber soft around me. The chill of the desert hit me then, the wind carrying the chemical scent, the almost-rot, of the ants. Off in one direction, the lights of the big house twinkled. In the other, the dark of the desert.

The barn had half-collapsed. One beam had given, and then two more had snapped, the others bowing dangerously. Where I was had turned into little more than a pile of lumber and collapsed shelves, small spires of white smoke where the acid had found a meal. I knelt and, moving some of the shattered wall aside, I found my arm. I picked it up with the good one, the fingers still moving around like they had something to say.

I heard nothing else, but it could have been that my ears were ringing with the fallen structure. Shreve was nowhere to be seen, and I wasn't about to go digging for him. Instead, I struck out for the deep dark, and hoped to be there before the cavalry arrived.

TWENTY-TWO

It didn't take long before they came out of the black. Two of them rode horses, the sparks from the hooves intermittent. The other had the pickup truck, spraying catherine wheels in the night. They spread out over the desert, the truck in the middle and the two horsemen on either side. There was more desert than there was of them, though, the gloom giving me ample cover.

Only one horseman ever got close. It was Tod, of course. The heartless luck of the universe would always put him on my trail. My guts crumbled as he drew near. His charger looked like a ghost in the night, illuminated only when a hoof struck the desert floor, hurling sparks and light upward. Tod was up in the saddle, one hand on the hilt of his bowie knife, riding hard into the night. As he drew near, I crouched into the lee of an outcropping of rock and cactus. He thundered past, and I watched him disappear into the darkness before I went too.

It was a long walk, and the whole time I was clutching my severed arm. The wind tickled the open wounds. I was wet, the caustic chemicals that should have been inside gliding out of me. The jaundiced lights of Quartzsite never looked so sweet. By then, the lambent lines of the hunting horsemen were entirely gone, receded into the nightmare I was leaving.

The sky was getting lighter as I stepped onto the pockmarked streets of Quartzsite. I didn't know how set on catching me the Dullahans were. Whether they'd hunt me to the ends of the earth or just trust that I'd taken the hint when they'd mutilated me. That I would be fleeing on the next train west as quick as possible. Tod didn't seem to get it. Wolff had nearly convinced me, but Tod never would. I kept seeing Tod in front of me, showing me the sizzling blade, and though the dread that image produced nearly suffocated me, it wasn't going to make me leave.

Because I had three names. When Tod's blade filled my consciousness, when it threatened to drown me in the green water, I said their names. Lorena. Rachel. Hasaya. Their names kept the rage at bay.

The ice cream truck was parked out in front of Burke's office. I barely registered it, instead staggering through the front door. The ant lunged at me and I paused, taking the poor beast in, really seeing it through my haze of agony. Meat golems were known for stitching together our pets and bringing them to life the way it had been done to us. From time to time I considered it, though really I would have preferred something like a parrot. Something that could talk when I couldn't.

Now I saw the cruelty in it. That giant ant of Burke's was already the creation of a mad scientist, and from the look of it, the runt of the litter. Burke had killed it, or found it dead, then stitched it back together and applied electricity. Now he kept it chained in his office. There was no reason for it. No point to having the animal here. He barely seemed to acknowledge it. It was there as an affirmation. To show that he was Burke O'Hare, genius.

The door to the apartment opened and Frances poked her head out as she hastily belted a dressing gown. "Jane? Holy...what happened to you?" I stared at her, waiting for her to figure out I didn't have my slate. "Wait there," she said. She disappeared back into the apartment and emerged again a moment later with Burke. He was dressed in a pair of boxer shorts and an old undershirt, both stained from heavy use. When he saw me, his eyes grew big and soft.

"Jane no!" he said, and loped down the stairs. Frances followed slowly, watching me with something almost like concern. She was barefoot, her feet dusty from the desert. Burke reached me and looked me over with naked horror. "Jane what?"

I shook my head. Burke caught it quickly and gestured over his shoulder without looking. He didn't have to; Frances was already crossing the room toward a pile of my things. I saw my purse and my slate waiting for me. She grabbed the slate and sauntered over, taking her time.

Burke, meanwhile, guided me over to one of the hospital beds. I sat at the foot, but I wasn't going to lay down. Burke gingerly took the severed arm from me. I let it go. The fingers were still twitching, though far less often than they had been. He inspected it, then set it on a tray beside him. Frances set the slate next to me, and I thought I saw the tiniest bit of sympathy in her normally sullen gaze. She left, then returned quickly with a pair of bolt cutters, handing them to Burke.

"Jane still," he rumbled. He cut the shackles off me. They clattered to the floor, stained with green. Burke handed the tool to Frances, then reached for the slate to say something. I hissed reflexively, grabbing the slate with my good hand and moving it away. He flinched, his expression filling with stormclouds. He gestured over his shoulder again, and Frances wheeled the blackboard over to him.

"Jane what?" he rumbled again.

Now I wrote, my hand quivering. Between that and writing lefty, the word came out in a jumpy scrawl. *Dullahans.*

«*I heard,*» he wrote.

"Whole town heard," Frances said. Then, softer, "When I got the truck and found your things, we thought, maybe...you know."

"Tod bad," Burke said. «*The bastard hurt you. I'll kill him.*» Then, quickly, he wiped it away with a nervous glance at the door. I shook my head. Even if I thought Burke had the spine to go after the Dullahans, I didn't want him to.

I'll be gone once I find out who I was.

"Jane bad!" Burke said. *«This is stupid. It doesn't matter who you were. Matters who you are now!»*

Matters to me.

Burke rumbled in his throat. Finally, he shook his head and got to work on the arm. It burned as he stapled the bone back in place, then began to reset the connections: vein, tendon, nerve. Burke worked swiftly, instinctually. It was one of those things we all knew how to do. I had never wanted it, but if I had to, I could stitch a bunch of corpses together and give it life. Same way a human knew how to have sex, I knew how to do that. I blinked away a tear, abruptly thinking of Nick. What he would do if he knew I was in this state.

"Jane dumb," Burke said. I heard anger, but there was also a tinge of sadness. Perhaps even grief. He paused in his ministrations. *«The bodies were just raw materials.»*

You know that isn't true. You have memories you don't understand. You have urges you can't control.

Burke looked away. "Jane dumb!" he insisted. Then, *«It's who we are. Vampires drink blood. Werewolves howl at the moon. We remember.»*

I want to know what I remember.

Burke growled, then went back to fixing me. As he connected my tissues, one to the next, sensation began to bleed from my orphaned limb to the rest of my body. The fingers continued to twitch restlessly, then they weren't *the* fingers but *my* fingers. They still moved on their own, though after a point, I could feel them moving. They were originally Lorena's, and so I let them do what they wanted to.

When Burke was finished with the delicate internal stuff, he began to stitch me up. The needle tickled as it passed through my papery skin. He pulled the sutures tight. I watched him the whole time, marveling at how shoddy his stitch work was. Even lefty, I'd have been better off doing this part myself. I wouldn't have trusted Burke to fix a hobo's bindle, and here he was putting the lines on me. Finally, he finished, sitting up straight and groaning as his back stretched out.

I flexed my hand. Mine again, now that it was attached. The sensations were muddy, the fingers heavy and soft. As I moved them, thinking hard about precisely what I wanted out of them, the suture between my middle and ring finger popped. I don't think there was anything Burke could have done, and certainly not with his skills. But it wasn't up to him. It was up to the hole in my apartment back in Lincoln Heights. The hole that turned deeper and darker in my memories. It would open me back up until I had enough names to fill it.

Burke got up. "Jane stay." I was about to angrily rebuff him, but after a second, I nodded. Burke shambled away. A moment later, I heard the door to his apartment shut.

"Who is he?" Frances asked.

I frowned, thinking she was talking about Burke. She wasn't. She was in the far corner of the room, where a cot was pressed against a wall. Two clotheslines had been hung up against either wall, with some thin sheets hung over them. A makeshift room of sorts. Behind her, I could see my purse sitting on the bed; my bag was back in the motel room, though god knew if it was still there. Wasn't like I was paid up. She wasn't looking at my purse, though. She was holding a dogeared photo in her hand.

I hissed, charging over the ground between us. Frances quailed, though she didn't run. I snatched the picture out of her hand, or I tried, but my right hand wasn't listening. My fingers bounced off her wrists. She dropped the photo, leaving it to flutter to the floor like a snowflake. I caught isolated glimpses of Nick, slumbering peacefully on the couch.

"I'm sorry!" Frances wailed. "I didn't mean it!"

I stared at her. She was plainly terrified, and cradling the hand I had inadvertently hit. She watched me with wide eyes, expecting more violence. I shook my head. Then I knelt, picking up the photo and staring at it. Nick's face was slack with sleep. Peaceful. He was safe, the way he so seldom was. The way I showed him he couldn't be when I nearly took his head off. I held out the photo to Frances. She stared at me like I'd gone crazy. I nodded to her, and she cautiously took the picture. Then I returned to where I had been and picked up my slate, hanging it around my neck.

His name is Nick. The words weren't as clear as I would have liked them. The hand felt like I was moving it at a distance, vainly trying to see what was too far.

"Boyfriend?" she asked, though she already knew the answer. "He looks nice." That last wasn't too convincing. Nick was cute in his way, but it was a little ways to get there. I didn't think that much of him at first myself. "What is he?"

Human.

"No kidding?" Frances chuckled, then looked up at me with guilty eyes. I cocked my head and raised my eyebrows. "No, it's just that...both you and Burke are with humans." I glanced at the closed door of the apartment, as though that would explain anything. The fact that we were both with humans hadn't occurred to me, even if I wasn't with anyone. "Why do you think that is?"

I shrugged. *I can only answer for me.*

Frances handed the photo back. "You love him a lot." I took it, and suddenly, I couldn't look at Nick. Not when all I would see would be the hole. The knuckles on my right hand itched.

"Why'd you come here if you have him at home?" Frances asked. There was an edge to her words, an accusation. I had Nick, so why was I trying to steal Burke from her? Only I didn't have Nick and I wasn't trying to steal Burke. It wasn't about them. They were peripheral.

I'm here for me.

"I don't get it."

I need to know who Burke made me from.

"Why?"

I cast about, trying to make her understand. I didn't think I could. I couldn't even make Burke understand, and we shared an experience. I found an analogy; it wasn't perfect, but I thought maybe she would get it. *If you didn't know your parents, you would want to.*

Frances snorted. "Wish I could live a life where I never met my old man." I frowned, and gestured to her to keep going. She shook her head. "It ain't important. I'll never see him again. Even if I do get turned, he's never getting a visit from me."

Is that what you're waiting for? Burke to turn you? Frances shrugged in that way that said yes, but she knew how silly it sounded. *If Burke turns you, you won't be you anymore. You'll be gone, mostly. You'll be memories the monster you were used to make doesn't really understand.*

"Is that what it's like for you?" I nodded. Frances turned away. I watched the tracks winding up her legs. "Maybe that wouldn't be so bad."

I could say nothing Frances would hear until she looked at me. Finally, she did, and I showed her the message. *You think that now, but the monster that isn't you will wonder.* I erased it and went on. *She'll go looking for you.*

"Ain't nothing to find. Hell, even before the war there was nothing. Now, there ain't even footprints."

Same for who I was.

"Can't find anything?"

I found names. Half of the women used to make me. I don't know how to find any more.

"You're a monster," she said simply. I wrote a question mark on the slate. "The world is yours. You want to find more, you'll find more."

The apartment door cracked open. "Fran come!" Burke roared.

Frances flushed, giving me a look that started haughty and triumphant, and then just as quickly deflated. Barefoot, she moved up the stairs silently. Proof she wasn't a meat golem. She disappeared behind the door a moment later. Then the sounds started, and I could have done without those. They were ostentatiously loud and the less said about it the better. I figured I was going to have to stuff something in my ears if I planned to get any sleep, or hope Burke tired out quickly.

Since I couldn't sleep, I wandered around the operating floor. He only had three hospital beds, and all three were in various stages of giving up. Equipment, some in carts, some in heaps by the far wall, spoke to Burke's needs, or maybe just his tendency to hoard what the desert gave him. I ran my hand over the lightning control device where it squatted in the center of the room. Bringer of life and death, that one.

I paused at the ammonia-stinking jars of acid. The concrete floor here was scarred from spills. I wondered how many jars had shattered during Burke's experiments. I never thought of this part of rantching before. I wondered what the use of the acid was, other than the obvious.

Soon, I was snooping. By that time, I was annoyed with both Burke and Frances, but I wasn't going to bang on the walls until they stopped. So I gave myself license to check some of the other doors in this place. One led to a bathroom that was in better shape than the surroundings would indicate. Small wonder, since it would mostly have been Frances's. It was little more than a toilet and a sink, both breeding copious amounts of mold. Old copies of *Look* sat on the toilet tank.

Another door opened into a closet, and stuff spilled out. There was a vacuum cleaner, clothing, bags, cookware, broken medical equipment—anything that could be shoved into a closet and forgotten, was. It fell over my legs and out into the office with a muffled crash. I glanced over at the wall of the apartment. The sounds hadn't even slowed down. I started picking the stuff up, thinking I could put it back neatly, but pretty soon figured out that wasn't a realistic urge. So I just started shoving it in.

Then my hands closed around a scarf. It wasn't especially distinctive, other than being handmade out of faded blue cloth. I pulled it from the tangled pile. My fingers tingled where they touched it. I knew this scarf. I traced the weave, though my right hand was clumsy, reacting a second or two later. I had made this. While I couldn't picture it in my head, some part of me knew every stitch, every pattern. At home, with my right hand still functioning, I could have made a scarf exactly like this without trouble.

I took it to my bag, once again checking the apartment noise—still going—and hid it inside. I searched the closet thoroughly just to make sure there wasn't something else in there to spark me, but there wasn't. The scarf was it. Then I cleaned up.

Afterwards, Burke had finally gotten tired, and the office was quiet. I drifted off to a dreamless sleep.

TWENTY-THREE

Frances came staggering from the apartment in the late morning. She didn't look at me, instead brushing past to go to the bathroom. She walked gingerly, with a bowlegged shuffle. Bruises, in the shape of fingers, decorated her upper arms and cut across her useless stitches. She emerged from the bathroom shortly afterward and blinked in unfocused hostility at me.

Where is the shower? That had been bothering me since last night.

Frances snorted. "No shower. We have a tub out back. If you want, you can use the hotplate over there to boil some water." She pointed to a hotplate sitting on a cart near the wall, which until that point was indistinguishable from the other junk in this place.

What about the witches?

"Witches?"

Every place has witches.

"They ain't gonna give you a shower."

I know. Do you have them?

"We have some. Which ones do you want?"

The best ones.

Now she frowned, apparently realizing I was serious. Her eye makeup had run overnight, making her look like a grouchy raccoon. "You want the Frog Mothers then, I s'pose." I nodded. I hadn't heard the name, but if you asked for the best witches, you just nodded whenever you got a name. "They're up in the Dome Rock Mountains. What do you need a witch for? Looking for a fix?"

I ignored the dig. The truth was, a lot of girls used hexes. I wasn't one of them. Yet. I just nodded at Frances and grabbed my purse.

Frances gave a long and theatrical sigh. "Just watch out. We got ogres all up in the hills, and ain't nobody been able to do nothin' about 'em. You get lost, and even the local wolf ain't gonna do much more than shake his head."

I nodded and gave her a small smile. I could have guessed that last bit, but it was still nice to be warned. I fished a pen out of my purse and found something to write on.

It was a napkin, covered in written messages, ink veined with water spills. Short, but to the point. All in my handwriting. To someone else, it would have looked like a haphazard collection of notes to myself, a conversation where the other half was in my head. Only it wasn't in my head. It was with Nick, him talking and me writing. I'd kept this one because it was our first conversation at work. The first time we were together in a meaningful way. The words had always made me smile, a keepsake warm with his presence. Now, they blurred and wobbled.

"Jane?" Frances asked.

I sniffed, tucking the napkin back in the purse, then finding a pad. I wrote *Directions* on the top and handed it over. She nodded and drew me a map. Nothing complicated. I wasn't going to find any pirate gold, but I should find some witches. And I could keep my mind off Nick.

Frances didn't say anything else when she handed the pad back. I left the office and stole the ice cream truck again. Maybe not the nicest thing to do. I could have pretended it was because Burke had been gross, but the fact was, I just took it. I had no way else to get around. I drove to the motel and found the ghoul grumpy about my cavalier attitude toward paying him. I paid up, retrieved my bag, which he had confiscated, and returned the key. I might be back, or I might not be. I wasn't worried this place was going to suddenly fill up with tourists here to see the wasteland made by Phobos and the Dullahans.

From there, I drove west. The sun, still rising behind me, shone off the quartz-pink tone of the Springfield Shape. Only one decent road led up into the mountains, splitting off from the one that would take me to Ehrenberg, so I followed that, eeling up over the gray-brown rock. Didn't take long before I started seeing evidence of the ogres in the hills. Their shrines, marking this as the domain of one tribe or another, appeared on the roadsides. They were stacks of rocks too big for a human to move, topped with a log driven through the top and then decorated like a Christmas tree at a maniac's house. Bones, some that looked uncomfortably human, hung from them like windchimes. Supposedly, you could read the iconography as readily as a medieval banner, but I never learned. The only ogres I knew were bouncers and nothing in those encounters had inspired me to get any friendlier or learn heraldry.

Ogres were one of those monsters no one knew quite how to deal with. They were useful the way twelve feet of brute force could be, but the bulk of them lived a tribal existence outside of what we would generally call civilization. The wolves were usually content to let the ogres alone until they started bothering non-ogres. Out here, with Peter Wolff as the law? I was pretty sure these ogres could get away with turning a whole family of mummies into tea with nary an objection voiced. That's when I realized that I was driving an ice cream truck on a hot day. I'd better hope the ogres didn't see me. Or that they didn't like ice cream.

I followed the map Frances had given me, navigating the twists and turns of the mountains. Now I could see just how big the Springfield Shape had been. It wasn't the biggest blob in the world. No, I'd seen pictures of the Pink Menace, the one that ate something like half of the Soviet Union before learning what every other invading army learned about Russia in the winter, but this was the biggest one in the US. Now, we all knew better than to let blobs get out of control. There were emergency measures in place, stockpiles of potassium hydroxide, that kind of thing. We let the blobs make themselves useful, eating our garbage, but if they wanted more, they were destroyed. Hell of a thing, because "more" invariably meant the end of the world.

There was something beautiful about the Shape now, the way death had crystallized it. In a hundred years they might be mining it, using it as a new kind of mineral, vital for some mad scientist's invention. Just like the precious metals that had once settled Arizona, the blob would fuel a new boom out in the desert.

As the road switched back, Quartzsite came into view below. From a distance, the buildings looked like water-damaged matchboxes. Beyond, lines of ants busily tracked about their hills, throwing out beige curtains of dirt. If it came down to it, which would survive: the people in those buildings, or the swarms of ants? The answer was uncomfortable, a stubborn stone in my shoe that I wanted to stop thinking about, but couldn't.

I held the steering wheel mostly with my left hand, trying to flex sensation back into my right. It still felt like someone else's limb I was using at a distance, that Lorena had decided to take back. The stitches had broken down to the middle of my hand. Though I wanted to blame my constant fidgeting, I knew it was the hole back in my apartment. It was hungry and I hadn't given it nearly enough to eat. Three names, but it still yawned, ravenous and black.

Frances's map wasn't great, but it did get me there, dipping into a fold in the terrain. The plant life was a little more verdant, the soil more reddish than dun. The Springfield Shape hung overhead, forming a shady lip. On one side of the fold, the living rock of the mountain. On the other, rock and soil, severed to make this road. A few straggly pines sprouted among the cactus and tumbleweeds.

This road looked to be free from the persistent ogre presence. It twisted and turned, then the lip blocking it fell away and the road emerged on a plateau. Pine trees grew up next to the mountain, helping form a natural barrier on one side. The other looked to be more or less a sheer cliff. Three distinct homes formed a semicircle against the far wall of the terrace: a tarnished Airstream trailer, a tent that looked to be made of deerskin, an old Model T that had been turned into a dwelling with the application of canvas and deerskin.

The whole area bore the signs of being a long-term campsite. A firepit, smoldering with old coal-black wood, sat in the shaded space between the tent and the T; a wooden drying rack, decorated with the carcasses of squirrels and rabbits, stood next to the Airstream in the sunlight. The strongest sign I was in the right place came from the brooms, set outside the trailer, the tent, and the Model T. These were old-style, bundles of rushes bound together with a malformed branch in the center. As I pulled into the circle, three entrances opened at once, the doors to a trailer and a car and the flap of a tent, all thrown wide. Three figures emerged.

All three were Indians, and that looked to be about all they had in common. The figure in the center, coming from the tent, was the eldest of them. Her hair was iron gray, her back stooped but her eyes bright. Her cheeks were sunken and furrowed with wrinkles. If she had a tooth in her head, I would be surprised. She wore a deerskin dress and leaned on a crooked staff. At the apex of the staff was a small concave place where a tiny frog perched, watching me with intelligent eyes.

The youngest, on my left emerging from the Airstream, couldn't have been much older than twenty, her hair sliced in a short and brutal mohawk. She dressed in western gear, like the people in Quartzsite, but hers was in better shape, if more used. She wore a bone choker around her neck and earrings made of silver and some kind of pinkish stone. Her figure was thin and boyish, her rolled-up sleeves showing off ropy forearms. A hummingbird flitted around her head.

The last, coming from the Model T, made me double-take. It wasn't the coyote that came out first, its red tongue lolling, but the witch. Wearing a knit dress with a pattern of triangles and silver jewelry accented with pink stones, the figure appeared to be a man. Despite the brooms and apparent familiars, I was ready to assume I'd gotten to the wrong place. After all, everyone knew men couldn't be witches. His hair was long, braided in the back, and he had a nice, moon-shaped face with keen eyes.

I stepped out of the truck. "Looking for something?" the young one asked. *The Frog Mothers. I'm lost.*

The young one smirked, and exchanged a look with the one I thought was a man, who smiled and said, "You found us." My eyes widened and I stared. "I confuse some white people. I'm Ooljee Hanyi, mother of the Frog Mothers. This is Sonseearray, our maiden, and Gouyen, our crone." Sonseearray nodded. Gouyen merely chewed on nothing.

Jane Stitch. It's nice to meet you.

"What'd you come here for, Jane?" Sonseearray asked, coming closer, but staying out of arm's reach. The hummingbird orbited her like a buzzing moon. "Don't get many of your kind up here."

I reached into the truck and pulled out the scarf and showed it to them. "It's a nice scarf," Ooljee said.

I need to know who made it.

"You should have asked the person you bought it from."

"She didn't buy it," Sonseearray said. "She's a thief."

"Is that true?"

The stab of guilt at Ooljee's question showed on my face. It was in a closet. *I think I made it.* I erased it. Then, *Kind of.*

Ooljee and Sonseearray frowned. then Gouyen spoke in a voice like an old screen door. "A piece of her made it." Understanding dawned in the others.

"I see," Ooljee said.

"I don't," Sonseearray grumped.

"Jane wants to know who made the scarf. Who that part of her name was. Isn't that right, Jane?"

I nodded eagerly. *I can pay.*

"We don't want money," Gouyen said. "Got more'n enough of that."

I frowned, and wrote *?*

"Your blood. We want a pint of that. Whatever it is you have for blood," Gouyen said.

Sonseearray nodded. "A pint would do nicely."

"We can make sure it won't hurt," Ooljee said. I brought my hand up, where the skin was coming loose from the knuckles. None of them so much as winced in sympathy.

"You heard. Is it a yes or no? Dangerous calling the spirits for one of your kind," Gouyen said. "Most people are just one. A couple are two." This last was said with a glance at Ooljee. "They come down, get confused, no telling what will happen."

But you're willing.

"Wouldn't make the offer if we weren't willing. Is it a yes or a no?" Wasn't a question on that. I nodded. "Good. Otherwise you'd be wasting our time, and ain't nothing good about wasting a witch's time. You two, get her ready. I'm going up to the table rock." The frog opened its mouth, and for a second, I thought it was going to say something, but it just shut it again. The crone shuffled out of the campsite, disappearing on the other side of the Model T.

Sonseearray went into her trailer, the hummingbird whirring behind her. Ooljee approached me, smiling. I felt the same thing I did with Wyeth, the sense of effortless comfort, like I could tell this stranger anything. Ooljee hooked her hands into the belt at her waist. It was covered in beaded suns.

"So tell me, were you looking for this thing, or did it happen?"
Looking.

"Quite a quest you found for yourself. You from Quartzsite, Jane?"
I nodded. *I live in Los Angeles.*

"Hollywood is far away from here. Come on now." We began to walk to the Model T. The coyote padded along next to us. We were heading for a fold in the rock near the back of the camp that was nearly invisible from the wrong angle.

The door to the Airstream opened and Sonseearray came out, twirling a buck knife in her hand. I quailed from it, Tod's bowie flashing in front of me. In a second, the green crashed in, and I felt the weight of the girl in my arms. It was a physical effort to surface from it, gasping as I freed myself from its cold clutches. The world came back, and I was only a few steps from Sonseearray, hissing. The witch had knelt, blade in one hand, other one in the dirt, ready to scoop some up. I shook it off, backing up, hands out.

"What the hell was that?" Sonseearray demanded.

The knife. Sorry.

"Are you gonna go bugs every time you see the knife?" I shrugged. "You watch it."

"Calm down," Ooljee said to the maiden. "Jane? Are you okay?"

I nodded, pulling my eyes from the knife only with difficulty. I tried to concentrate on the ways it was different. The handle made from a deer antler. The blade, significantly smaller. It wasn't hissing with hellish heat as it moved through the air. It was just a knife. Tod couldn't touch me here.

"Jane," Ooljee said. I followed her gaze and saw that I had picked another stitch clean out of my hand. The skin looked like an old glove ready to give up the ghost. I pulled my fingers away from the wound. My face grew hot unevenly over its patchy surface.

"Doesn't that hurt?" the mother asked. I shrugged, then shook my head. The mother's thick fingers went to the unraveling skin, bringing it up for inspection. "I'm beginning to see why you came here."

"Who cares, so long as we get our blood," Sonseearray said, passing us and disappearing down the path.

"I'm sorry. She's young."

I shook it off. We started walking again. Ooljee was slow, but I couldn't tell if it was because she was a naturally slow walker or if she just wanted to take her time. The coyote took the lead, occasionally stopping and looking back at us. If I didn't know better, I would say the creature was impatient.

"Have you found any parts of you?"

3 names. Rachel Prager. Lorena Quintanilla. Hasaya.

"Hasaya?" Ooljee frowned. "Are you sure you don't mean Haseya?"

Do you know her?

"I've known one or two. It's a Diné name." I frowned. "Navajo," Ooljee clarified.

I broke into a grin as a piece of me fell into place. *She died in 1951.*

"I'm sorry, I don't know her. I was turned in '48. Spent the war up here. When the Shape came through, I thought I was going to have to move, but Gouyen had another idea. One blizzard later and we were frozen, but so was it."

Haseya was Navajo.

"Diné," Ooljee corrected.

Would the others know her?

"I doubt it. They're Yavapai. And yes, before you ask, it would have been nice to be in a Diné coven, but it was a messy time, and we don't always get our first choices. For Yavapai, they ain't bad."

I laughed silently, mostly to show my appreciation. Haseya was Diné. I didn't know what any of that meant, not really. *What does it mean to be deeneh?*

Ooljee frowned, then chuckled. "It's spelled D-I-N-E. Accent over the last. In English, I expect. In the language, it's...well, it's some squiggly lines. I'll show you." She reached for my slate and I hissed. She quailed. "Sorry. Didn't know that was bad."

It's my voice. I can't give it away.

"Oh. Now that makes sense. Well, I'll show you what it looks like good and proper when we're done here." She thought it over. "As to what it means, well, it means a lot of things and not much. Meant more before the Night War, I'll tell you that. Now, most of us are turned that could be and what do you know, suddenly we're all part of the family. Couple holdouts say that if we all turn, there's no tribe left."

What do you think?

"Don't really know one way or the other. I'm a witch, but I'm also Diné, and frankly, both matter to me. You...you're part Diné. Kind of like a child, I guess. How old are you?"

I was born in 1951.

Ooljee snapped her fingers. "Of course. Haseya died in '51, so you were put together in the same year, before she turned. Not like a monster—like, well...you know." I nodded. It was the meat golem version of the birds and the bees. Or, well, the corpses and the bees.

"I wish I could tell you I knew this part of you, Jane. When we're finished, I can show you a few things. Be a shame for you not to know where you came from. And the white parts, well, I expect you know all about what white people are like."

My face grew hot and I nodded. Ooljee raised her eyebrows. "Got yourself a man, then? I had a white man once. Confused and angry. What's yours like?"

Brave and sweet.

"Sounds a lot better than mine."

Looks like a weasel.

Ooljee laughed. "Mine looked like Errol Flynn, but that's no excuse. I suppose a white man is as nice as his face forces him to be." I grinned. Out here, for some reason, it felt fine to talk about Nick with Ooljee. As though she would keep the hole away. "Tell me, where'd you get these names?"

Cemetery in Ehrenberg.

"This Haseya was buried there?"

I nodded. *Until she was dug up.* I finished with a shrug.

"Shame, that. I should go. Pay my respects."

Human cemetery. They can be jumpy.

"That is true."

I started to hear something I couldn't quite process. It sounded wrong out here in the searing desert heat. But as we moved farther along the path it grew louder and louder, and when we emerged, I saw what I had thought was true. A creek ran down the slope, collecting in a pond. This clearing was a secluded bite taken out of the rock, overlooking the desert on one side where a flat rock, long enough for a person to lay down on, sat on the edge of the cliff. Trees grew tall here, sheltering the inner part of this clearing.

Sonseearray knelt by the pond, bathing the knife in it. Gouyen shuffled away from the water, but her frog leapt from his perch on the staff to land with a splash, and soon he was swimming with wide, lazy strokes. Gouyen gave the frog a baleful look and stopped next to the rock.

"Lay down here," the crone said. She opened a canteen, upending it over the earth. The thirsty soil drank what it could. I obeyed. The rock was as hot as the air around it. The knife whispered through the air.

Tod Dullahan

TWENTY-FOUR

The sun shone on half of my face. The other glittered with the pink refraction of the Springfield Shape. The three witches gathered around me, their faces mere shadows.

"Gonna want to relax," Gouyen said. I nodded. My silver eye was completely closed, but even then I could see the sun, dyed green by my eyelid.

Ooljee picked up my left hand, bringing the arm out straight. She held me gently; no doubt I could have taken my limb back, and however much of the witch along with it, whenever I liked. The blade alighted on my wrist, light as the hummingbird buzzing around my head. It felt nothing like Tod's bowie, and I kept that in the forefront of my mind. Kept the green from swallowing me. The knife whispered over the skin, a searing line. Then, the caustic warmth of my blood flowed up and out.

"It's full," Sonseearray said after longer than I would have liked.

I felt a cloth closing over my wrist, then pulled tight with the echo of the burn. Ooljee released my hand and I brought it up to cradle it over the slate resting on my chest. Ooljee put her hand over my forehead, brushing a bit of hair away. "Are you all right?" I nodded.

"Now don't you get up," Gouyen said. "You stay right where you are. Don't matter what you hear or you think you hear. You stay there. This hex ain't what you'd call safe, you understand me?" I gave another nod. "Now—"

"She understands," Ooljee said.

"I don't think she does," Sonseearray said, "but she gave us what we want, so it ain't my problem."

"Stop flapping your gums and get to work," Gouyen grumped.

The witches spoke to each other in low tones, and it wasn't all in English. They spoke some kind of shorthand with one another, weaving between languages, one of which held the crackle of lightning. I heard the clack of more wood, the scrape of metal on metal, and then I smelled something else. A more natural scent, like the desert refined. I stayed as motionless as I could, the new wound throbbing on my wrist. The sun kept beating down on me. My head was light, the heat of the day drawing me up into the sky. I think I drifted off, because suddenly, Ooljee's hand was on the back of my neck, lifting it.

"Drink," she whispered. I felt metal against my lips and opened them. The liquid was molten desert. The sharp, green taste of cactus, and the tart poison of berries mingled somewhere in there as it rushed down my throat. It was coming too fast to stop, and I just gulped it as quickly as I could. It vanished down my throat in an incandescent stream. I could feel its light igniting me as it went. The river hit my spine, my stolen nerves blazing. I felt like I must be shining, the world around gone to gloom. I was one of Harry Jenkins's stars, fallen to earth.

Pain wracked me, from stomach to crown. I felt myself, far away, pulled into an agonized rictus. And then I was gone.

The sky was still there. The one I watched with Harry, that wouldn't hold any of us when it was over. So much bigger and more beautiful than the one in LA. I was deep in the desert somewhere. I knew only by the persistent smell in my nose and the taste coating my tongue. The landscape was shadow, as surely as if there had been blackout curtains thrown over it. It left only the sky and its stars. More than I could ever count, but far away. Unknowable. I watched it, spinning above me, the clouds of light brighter than they had ever been. Faster and faster, as though I was caught in a cylinder of night. Spinning through the years.

I wasn't walking, but I was moving. Or the world around me was while I was standing still. Shapes loomed up out of the desert and vanished just as quickly. The click of chitin and persistent tread of thousands of legs came from the dark. The desert wasn't moving. It was the ants, all around me now, their rotten insect scent overpowering everything else. They marched around me and away, and the sky went with them. I tried to turn, to see where the swarm was headed, but I couldn't. I was stuck where I was, in the dark.

Until I wasn't. I was in the contours of the Springfield Shape. Biology turned geography by infinite hunger and the insanity of the world. The blob capped the mountain, transformed to crystal by the cold, and never brought out of it. Pockets of soil held a few trees and bushes, but mostly, the Shape was exposed to sun and elements. I knelt on the plasticky surface and put my hand on it. The hand that Tod had sliced from my body. My fingers tingled with the memory of acid. The air was brighter here, but there was still no sun. It was the illumination of the stars and the moon, a witch light to guide me.

"Hello there, Plain Jane," Tod said.

Tod Dullahan was here, his nightmare charger strolling from a stand of trees that was much too small to hide horse and rider. His hand rested on the hilt of the bowie. As the horse moved from the stand of trees, I saw now that Tod had a head. Not a head, but a grinning skull. A swirling pattern like wind-washed ribbons surrounded his eyes, and slices ran down his jawline.

"Fancy meeting you here," he said, the skull's jaw flapping with his words.

I was going to hiss, but then words came out. "Go to hell." I blinked. "Can I talk? Did you hear me talk?"

"I heard you, Plain Jane. Didn't know you had it in you."

I was cognizant enough to briefly regret that my first words as a meat golem were "Go to hell." I suppose it was true enough to the core of me. "What do you want?"

"What I've always wanted, I suppose. You. I could be with you like a man or like a murderer. Figure out which later."

My mind wasn't quite working. It was never really working like it should be, the way other people take for granted. But normally, I'd be fighting the green. It wasn't where I left it. Not precisely gone; I could hear it crashing distantly, but it couldn't touch me. I never wondered how Tod had found me, or how I'd gotten here from the plateau of the Frog Mothers. I was simply there, in the new reality of this place.

I reached to my belt and found something wet. "I wouldn't do that," Tod warned.

I looked to see what I wouldn't do. It was a severed head, hollowed out and filled with water. A tiny frog paddled through the depths of the skull. I recoiled, but there was no blood. The edges of the neck were ragged, broken surgical sutures poking up over the side. A leather thong threaded through the neck skin and hooked into my belt loop.

Which was how I realized I was wearing my work uniform: a halter top, some satin shorts, fishnets, and meat golem heels. Not really desert wear. Tod was still, hand lightly resting on the bowie. The skull wasn't any easier to read than the former headless version.

"Do what?" I asked him. My hands closed around the head and I brought it up. The knots writhed undone, like living things. It was Burke's, cut from his neck. Water sloshed around behind his lips and spilled down over his milky eyes. The water wasn't running now, but throw it and it would be. Running water, the one thing that could reliably kill a headless horseman. The charger took a few nervous steps backward. "Leave me alone," I said.

"You know I won't do that."

"Why the hell not?"

"Quartzsite is my town."

"I thought it belonged to Ambrose Dullahan."

"You seen him? 'Course not. Only reason the old man has power is because I say he does. You and me, Plain Jane, only one way this thing with us ends."

"Then let's end it."

I threw the water from the head. Tod screamed, and it was drowned by the pounding of water. There wasn't a Tod anymore, wasn't the Shape, wasn't this place I was standing. Instead, the water I threw had become a river, lazily flowing south, the reeds collecting all along the shore. I stood next to the ice cream truck, watching gill-men and sirens cavorting in the shallows. Fern was in there with them, kneeling between the thighs of a fat siren, as naturally a part of them as any of the true aquatics. Richard Quintanilla was there too, passionately making love with a gill-man. Not far away, I saw Pastor Dukes's church, in the middle of an expanding cemetery.

Three shapes stood among the markers. I saw them as I'd seen the witches, as shadows against the thirsty desert sun. They were uniformly tall and lean, and I'd almost mistake them for mirror images of myself. But they weren't. There were differences, or else it was in the searing shimmer. I started toward them. This wasn't quite Ehrenberg. It was close, close enough that I never thought to question it. Not until later did I realize that everything looked like a dollhouse in larger size, the proportions ever so slightly off, and Pastor Dukes's church was nowhere near the river.

I crossed the distance, going from the reeds by the river to the dust of the desert, and the figures in the graveyard only got a little bit bigger. Then I was among the markers, and they were only a mite closer. I picked up speed, first jogging, then running past the broken markers with the Old West names. My breath burned as caustic as my blood. My limbs grew heavy. The distance stretched and stretched, getting closer, but then I would look at my feet, or around the graveyard, and they would be almost as far as they had been before.

It was forever before I was close enough to speak. Three of them stood in the graveyard, their backs to me, gazing south, along the flow of the river. The first I saw was tall and thin, brown hair piled up on her head, strands escaping the bun. She wore a tattered floral print dress, something that had traveled with her across the country. As I took her in, she turned, showing corpse white skin. I knew her face. Especially the prominent nose that took up so much of her face. I saw that nose in the mirror.

The other shape was a bit shorter, and even from the distance I was standing, I knew those hands. Most of the hands anyway; some of my fingers bore stitches, attesting to their being assembled from several sources. She wore a skirt and blouse, almost in as sorry shape as the other one's clothing. She turned, and she was a sunburnt olive, her face unfamiliar, but one I'd known all my life.

The last of the women wore khaki pants like someone in the army, and an old western shirt. She wore jewelry with similar designs as Ooljee's, though much less of it and with none of the pinkish rock. I knew her black hair well; I combed it every day, though now it sported a pair of white streaks reaching from my temples. Her face was that of a stranger, all except her right eye, so dark as to be black. That eye was mine.

"Rachel?" I said to the white woman. "Lorena?" to the olive-skinned one. "Haseya?" to the last, trying to mimic how Ooljee had said it, and knowing my pronunciation was slightly off. They nodded as they heard their voices, their faces soft as they watched me. None of them spoke; I don't know if they could. They felt like shadows, intangible until this hex had brought them to a form of half life. I caught a glimpse of a shape in the heat shimmer. Squinting, I peered into the desert.

Three more shapes stretched out into the distance, far beyond the borders of the cemetery. The closest stood in the wreckage of a building. The farther ones were in the deep desert. Giant ants scuttled around them, going about their insect errands. The shapes were mere silhouettes, details vanished in the distance. They looked as Rachel, Lorena, and Haseya had, before becoming somewhat solid.

I took a step toward the others and then paused, trying to commit every piece of each woman to memory. I knew they would fade, but there were parts—Rachel's nose, Lorena's hand, Haseya's hair—that I would never forget. That I couldn't forget. I reached for them, and they were abruptly out of arm's reach, their faces sad.

"Thank you," I told them, and they nodded.

Then I started into the desert. I was exhausted. This was a marathon, one that enervated body and mind. When the three women were out of view, I never looked back. Not that I was scared to see them watching me, but scared they'd be gone forever, banished to whatever place they existed now in their half-death.

There were those who said that life after death had been solved, now that we had monsters like ghosts, vampires, and meat golems. It wasn't true, though. We were a different kind of life. This, the existence of these women, was closer to what Harry Jenkins had talked about. Were these spirits torn from rest, or memories stored in the parts of me that they used to be? I hoped it was the latter, or at least that these three didn't suffer when I had them pulled back through the veil.

I ran, the nearest shadow drawing closer slowly but inexorably. She came into view first, a figure like the others, tall and willowy like me. Her hair was light brown, long and fluttering in the hot wind. Her dress was in bad shape like the others', but that's not what I concentrated on. No, it was the faded blue scarf around her neck. The scarf she'd made.

She stood in a ruin from a dream. The front was Burke's office, though the walls had been chewed away either by artillery or the desert. It was more the suggestion of Burke's office, an acknowledgement of its existence. The closet was open, the objects once stuffed inside now in an avalanche. The woman stood in front of this tongue of junk, her back to me, peering over the broken wall and into the desert. Out to the ants.

I ran to her, covering the distance only after I was nearly spent. Nothing could have kept me away. As I neared, she too turned, and her face spun and stuttered like a bad TV screen. I reached out, and this time she didn't shy away. I touched the scarf and her face came into perfect view. She was impossibly fragile, with bright blue eyes that were almost white. I realized that this was the source of my own silver; death had changed the color of it as it had with my patchy skin.

"Who are you?" I asked, and she gestured to the desert. "What is your name?"

"Sadie," she whispered. "Sadie Schroeder." I kept the name close, enshrining it next to the others. The names I once was. The names of my parts.

Then the desert was gone, replaced by prairie. Endless and flat, stretching around me like death. I knew what it was without needing to guess. Texas. I was in Texas. Sadie's old home. Her house was small, on the edge of a tiny town whose name I didn't remember and which might have been erased from mind and planet after the war. I watched her, with her family. That was a blade through my chest. Her family. Her husband, a man with lean eyes and braided muscles. Her children, an infant and a boy of five who looked more like him than her. They were piling into an old truck, the back heavy with their possessions. Absurdly, there was an old rocking chair among them, but maybe then they thought they would go to a place where you might need a rocker. Where you would lose days to it, instead of what was left.

They were fleeing. In the distance, martian tripods stalked over the land. The armor of the monster horde. I wondered if these were the same ones who burned Wichita. Maybe they were. Maybe these beasts had, at different times, hunted every piece of me, their pursuit the reason each part had found its way inexorably to Quartzsite.

The Schroeders left their house behind. None of them would ever see it again. They cried, and I knew that this scene had played out a hundred thousand times all over the world when the monsters came. It was how all these stories went. The death of home before the long night.

Sadie faded, like the dream the office had suggested, and I saw other things. Tent cities erected on the prairies, surrounded by guards and vehicles. Later, the guards grew more and more ragged, the uniforms less and less present. Soon, she and her family were under the stars. But they were together. Somehow Sadie and her husband had kept both kids alive and unturned. Somehow they were all still human. I knew it didn't end that way, but I let myself believe it did, if only for a short time.

I was with them, but they were small, like dolls, and no one reacted to the giant watching them. I watched as Sadie knitted first blankets and then, when the materials ran short, scarves to keep people warm. Through all of this, she had the scarf I had found, growing more ragged, more faded, as she huddled into it for warmth. Just as often, she wrapped her sons up in it, holding them close as their bodies wasted away through the years of the Night War. The boys matured with Dust Bowl stares and hollow cheeks.

One night, the older boy was gone. Sadie and her husband searched, but he had simply vanished. Food or turned, I didn't know.

Then the day had dawned. The camps were gone. I saw a town, out in the desert, apparently built around an old Spanish mission. I watched the Schroeders arrive, welcomed by the people who lived there. I moved past them now, into the desert. The Dome Rock Mountains, crowned with the Springfield Shape, greeted me. I could see my body on the flat rock. My hands clutched at my guts. My back was arched, my face locked in a rictus. The slate, my voice, all askew.

I tried to turn. There were still two out there. Two people I didn't know. I'd seen them in the distance. Far beyond Sadie Schroeder. They had been mere shapes, but so had the others. But the hex had other ideas, and brought me closer and closer to my body. I fought it. There was more to know, more to be revealed. But it wasn't to be. The hex was over, and I was returned to the body I didn't know.

Twenty-Five

I opened my eyes to the early morning. Dew clung to me and worked its way into my bones, dragging a chill along with it. The sun was up, but being on the west side of the mountain, I saw instead a shadow consuming the desert floor. I sat up, blinking. The night gnawed at my creaking joints every time I moved. I turned away from the sheer cliff to the plateau where the witches had been. They were gone, no real evidence they had been there at all.

My mouth felt like I had been licking the rock all night. A dry mouth was pretty normal for me, but this went beyond. Someone could have sanded some splintery lumber butter-smooth with my tongue. I got up, my legs wobbly underneath me as I made my unsteady way to the pond. When I didn't go ass over teakettle, I sped up, then fell to my knees and drank.

The water was sweetly metallic, and I gulped it, ignoring the fact that I'd seen a frog doing the breaststroke in it the previous day. I drank until my mouth was only as dry as usual, then sat back on my haunches. My limbs quivered with exhaustion as I contemplated the pathway out of the hidden plateau.

I got up with difficulty and limped down the passage. It was longer than I remembered it being, and I had to stop and lean on the rock walls more than a few times. Whenever I did, I repeated the names in my head, correcting Haseya's and adding Sadie's to the litany. Sadie wasn't out there anymore, but her family might be, in that Spanish mission out in the desert.

Smells snaked down the passage. Fire, definitely, and something being charred. And coffee. I approached with caution. Even hunger wasn't going to get me to run at flames. I emerged on the far side of the Model T. The Frog Mothers were active, Gouyen tending the fire, while the other two cooked. A metal pot hung over the burning logs, as did a skillet where some kind of meat sizzled. I kept my distance from the fire even as I savored the aroma coming from the food. The presence of the mother helped calm me a little.

"She's alive," Gouyen said. Sonseearray scowled, fished in her pocket, and flipped a silver dollar to the crone. The old woman's hands were quick, snatching the coin right out of the air.

"I imagine you're hungry," Ooljee said. I opened my mouth to speak, but nothing came out. Then I remembered: just a dream. In the real world, I couldn't talk. Would never talk. I closed my mouth and nodded.

"Oh, now we're feeding her?" Gouyen asked.

"She had a rough night."

"So did we, hexing one of her kind."

I can pay for it.

"Don't need your money," Gouyen said. "You can work it off."

As exhausted as I was, I nodded eagerly. Something about the prospect of working for the Frog Mothers appealed. Ooljee patted a flat rock next to her. I shook my head and pointed to the fire. Understanding dawned on Ooljee's face. "Sit where you like then. I'll bring it to you."

I made my way to the edge of the clearing to a large rock that didn't have too many sharp edges. Didn't so much sit down as have my legs collapse under me. Sonseearray pulled the dented metal pitcher of coffee off the fire and poured some into old camping cups. She made a show of not having one for me, until Ooljee marched over and gave me hers. After that, Sonseearray managed to find a fourth cup, which she gave to the mother.

"You probably want this," Ooljee said, tossing the scarf to me.

I took it with a new sense of wonder. I'd seen where it had been. It had warmed Sadie and her children, been a vital part of her survival through the worst years. I kept catching myself thinking of Sadie as alive, because I'd seen her moving and breathing. But she was dead, parts of her becoming parts of me. I clutched the scarf, then wrapped it loosely around my neck. It did ward off the chill from the dew.

"Did you find what you were after?" Ooljee asked. I hesitated, but then nodded. "Not everything?"

I shrugged. *1 more name.*

"Names matter," Ooljee said. "Why do you think monsters change theirs?"

I named myself. Didn't have another.

Ooljee watched me, eyes softening. "It's very different for meat golems. Still you picked those words out of any others. Why Jane Stitch?"

I shrugged. *I like to sew. Sadie sewed. It's like chain stitch.*

"But what does Jane mean?"

Woman, I guess.

"A woman without a name." I nodded. "Good. We'll get to the rest when I teach you a bit of the language. Help you understand a little more of that one piece of you."

I think I'd like that. Then, I wiped away the message and wrote a new one. *Is there a town nearby? Old Spanish mission? All human?*

Ooljee frowned. "She means Daybreak," Sonseearray said. The maiden shrugged. "It's south of here, off the main road. They ain't friendly."

Daybreak. I turned the word over in my mind. The human town. The next step, but I wasn't certain I could take it yet.

Twenty-Six

On the second day with the Frog Mothers, I was hauling firewood down from the peak of the mountain. Game trails led up from the Frog Mothers' camp. I hiked to the edge of the Shape, where the rolling wave had crested and then crystallized. It was partially transparent, and in places, I could see the indistinct shapes of trees and bushes the blob had been in the process of devouring when it was frozen. It was now covered in a thin sheen of desert dust, blown into the peaks from the wash. In the pits, soil had collected, and the first saplings were reclaiming the monster as part of the mountain sprouted.

I knelt by the Shape, running a hand over its surface. It was smooth, and felt a bit like volcanic glass. This had been a person once. A person, turned by a blob, and become a near natural disaster. It was easy to forget something like the Shape had once been human. Its name, its identity, everything, had been wiped away. Now it was just a thing on top of a mountain.

I picked along the terrain just below the lip of the thing. Gouyen had told me to bring what I found on the ground, and so that's what I was doing. I picked it up, threw it into the leather sack hanging from my shoulder, and kept going. I was no longer weak. A day of rest with the Frog Mothers had put me right, though my mind wasn't resting. Whenever I was still, I turned to thoughts of Sadie Schroeder, and what she'd lived through.

This was really only my second experience with the rigors of the Night War. Nick had told me a few stories in his unguarded moments, but he always clammed up before long. They were hard memories for him, in some ways harder than the ones from the Day War. But it was different actually seeing what the Schroeders had gone through. What they'd suffered.

When the sack was full, I went down the slope, finding the trail that would lead me back to the camp. There was peace out here. Nothing to listen to but the desert. There were times I thought about staying. Maybe not with the Frog Mothers, but somewhere close. Out in a little house in the middle of nowhere. At least out here I wouldn't be a danger to anyone. I wouldn't find anyone like Tod Dullahan, either. And since I didn't eat or drink all that much, it was more of a possibility than a simple dream. The longer I was away from Los Angeles, the more the thought of never going back appealed. There really was only one reason to go back, and I couldn't look at him yet. Not until the hole in my wall was filled with names.

I brought the firewood back and added it to the stack behind Sonseearray's Airstream, frightening a snake when I did. I came out the other side, dusting my hands off on my shorts.

"That should be enough for today. Maybe tomorrow, too, seeing as how much you can carry," Ooljee said. She was sitting sideways in the driver's seat of the Model T, the door open. The coyote was curled up on the hood, regarding me with a sleepily wary expression.

I nodded, picking a canteen off the branch of a tree and taking a swallow. The water was from their little stream, as delicious as it had been the first time I'd tried it. Easy to think that it had some special properties, what with them being witches. It was just as likely we were drinking powdered bits of blob, though, and that was a disturbing thought.

I put the canteen back and sat down on my blankets. Ooljee had made a little camp for me right up against the cliff wall, with the T giving me a comforting barrier against the campfire. It wasn't much, and certainly less than I was used to, but I liked it. Despite the hard ground, I'd gotten the best night of sleep since I'd put my hand into the wall.

A sound grew steadily in my ears. I think I heard it long before I was aware. Soon it was obvious it was a car of some kind, approaching up the winding pass. I stood, walking out into the center of the camp. I didn't realize it until I was standing there, but I had put the three witches protectively behind me.

Soon, the sound was louder and there was no doubt. A cloud of dust peeked up from the slopes, and then an old truck coughed and limped into view. Barrow's truck, and the ghoul was behind the wheel. The passenger door creaked open and Burke stomped out. He wore his soiled labcoat over an old faded blue shirt and a pair of slacks that had seen better days.

"Jane bad!" Burke shouted.

I sighed. *What do you want?*

"Truck mine!" he pointed at the ice cream truck I'd borrowed.

I caught myself wincing. He kind of did have a point about that. *Sorry.*

"Jane sad?" Burke demanded. "Need truck!"

I nodded and gestured to it. *It's all yours.*

Burke paused, taking this all in. "Jane come," he said finally. I shook my head. "Jane. Come."

I'm staying here.

"Jane why?"

This is what I have to do.

Burke shook his head in disgust. He opened his mouth, then growled to himself. I knew the look. It was when you had to say something more complex than you were able. He took a step toward me and I instinctively moved my slate away. He wasn't going to touch my voice.

I'm sorry I took the truck without asking. Take it back. I'm staying. Burke let out a roar.

"I put up with this long enough," Gouyen said testily. "You keep it down or I'll give that tongue of yours to a snake."

Burke started, and was about to yell, when Barrow sprang from the truck. "Come on, now, old man. We have your car, and there's no need to trouble any of these fine ladies any further. Jane, lovely to see you as always. The rest of you...witches...the same, of course."

Burke rumbled, but allowed himself to be led to the ice cream truck. Barrow found the keys under the seat and handed them to the meat golem. Burke stared at me through the dusty windshield, frustration and anger swirling on his misshapen features. Finally, he started the truck and executed a slow and clumsy turn before going out the way he came. Barrow followed him in the other truck.

"Your creator, I take it," Ooljee said. I nodded.

"What an asshole," Sonseearray said, thoughtfully, before leaving the clearing in the direction of the spring.

Twenty-Seven

It was two days later when I finally left. I couldn't stay with the Frog Mothers forever, no matter how much I wanted to. Life with them made far more sense than my former existence, than anything I could imagine, really. The beautiful busy emptiness of the desert was the first thing that had partly drowned out the susurrus in my mind. I spoke mainly with Ooljee. We talked about what I wanted, and without being obvious about it, she reminded me of what I had been doing in the first place. She taught me a little of what it meant to be Diné, as well. I hoped the language would feel familiar, but it didn't; Haseya's brain had died with her. Ooljee explained a little about herself as well, that she was *nadleeh*, a person neither male nor female in a way white people could understand. There was too much for me to learn in my short time, too much for me to wrap my borrowed mind around. Ooljee was persistent and patient.

Daybreak awaited. Sonseearray gave me directions, and I think she was only too happy to have her guest gone. It was a short way, closer to Quartzsite than to this place.

"You can use our car," Ooljee said. I pointed at the Model T and raised an eyebrow. She chuckled. "That thing doesn't move anymore. No, go down the path on the way in and you'll find it. Keys are inside."

Thank you.

"Think nothing of it. You've done more than enough for us over the past couple days."

"She ain't even worked off the hex," Gouyen said.

Ooljee shook her head, then said something in her language. I recognized the sounds, but the words were out of reach for my unpracticed skill. "You'll be fine," the mother said in English.

I steeled myself. I could picture Sadie's husband and their youngest boy as they had been five years ago, when Sadie died and was turned partially into me. They would be changed somewhat, damaged in the time between that one and this. After Richard Quintanilla's reaction to me, I didn't think they would be too happy to find that their loved one had been butchered to make a monster. Although perhaps they could be like Fern Calloway, happy that one part of their beloved wife and mother survived.

I had to know. I had to meet them. Learn what I could of Sadie Schroeder beyond a simple name. Whatever they were willing to tell me. Even if it was merely loathing.

I reached for Ooljee, then my hand faltered. I couldn't quite bridge the gap between us. The touch of a meat golem was a threat, and her throat was so close. If the green crashed in...

Ooljee smiled and took my hand. "You're welcome. If you want to know more about what Haseya knew, I'll be here. Becoming monsters is making so many people forget. It's nice to know there are some who want to remember." I nodded. That was as close as I would get to Haseya. A connection as precious as it was rare. "Now get out of here. Stay any longer and Gouyen will want more of your blood."

I took my things and walked out along the road. Sonseearray watched me go, but she didn't wave. Gouyen stared out over the desert, glancing back only once, then spitting over the cliff when I caught her looking. I turned my attention to the path ahead, imagining the figures on the road, those silhouettes rendered spidery by the shimmering heat. I pictured them resolving, first into Rachel, then Lorena, then Haseya, then Sadie. Two more on the horizon, whose faces remained a mystery.

I touched the scarf around my neck. I didn't need it in the heat, but I wanted it there. It felt right in a way I couldn't explain. Like coming home after a bad day. Like a look from Nick when he didn't think I was watching. The feel of the material under my fingers wasn't quite it. It was something deeper, in the tissues of my arms, the way the yarn made my fingers move, the patterns they made. I knew it. Deeper than a memory.

I found the truck tucked away on a side path. It was in better shape than some of those I'd seen out here, though it was old. The desert had been at it, but belonging to a witch kept it from falling apart. I started it up without trouble and guided it back onto the winding track. From there, I drove out onto the roads circling the mountain, heading down. Wherever the ogres were, I saw no more sign of them than the shrines. They likely gave the Frog Mothers a wide berth. Not even ogres wanted to tangle with witches if they could help it.

The road came out on the wash. Quartzsite simmered in the heat. I ignored it, taking the turn to Daybreak. I watched cacti and tumbleweeds go by outside, and eventually, a series of hills swallowed Quartzsite behind me. That was when, in the distance, I glimpsed the yellowed adobe of a mission. As I got closer, I saw a wall, built up out of old junk, mostly rusted out cars, stretching around the edges of it. Wards covered that, with everything from evil eyes to crosses. The central mission building was surrounded by smaller outbuildings, mostly the kinds of shacks that had been a persistent feature of the human settlements in the area.

Silhouettes dotted the walls and the top of the mission. People, looking out over the desert, watching my approach. Guards. Sentries, like a medieval castle. The village was a scavenger's facsimile of a place that could almost appear safe. Though I had eyes to see the cracks in that façade. No place was truly safe anymore.

I drove through a clay archway, big enough for two trucks to come through side-by-side. Now I was good and surrounded. Rifles, most of them showing evidence of age and jury-rigged repairs, bristled from every hand. But guns didn't worry me: the unlit torches on the various sconces did.

Although perhaps most troubling was a scaffold built in the town square, right next to the well. This looked far newer than anything else here, and lacked the rickety quality as well. Its maintenance spoke to the fact that it had been used. Plenty.

A man stepped out in front of the truck and put his hand up. I couldn't tell if he was white, or Mexican, or Indian. The desert had pruned him, turned him into an inhabitant of it rather than a member of any tribe of human beings. His skin was a deep red-brown, furrowed with cracks rather than wrinkles. A squint erased his eyes. He wore an old battered hat that hardly had a shape anymore, just a wide-enough brim to give him some shade. Iron-gray hair fell to his shoulders in greasy threads. In one gnarled hand, he held a rifle that looked older than the state of Arizona. His blue jeans and western shirt were patched and threadbare.

"Hold there," he said, swallowing nearly all the letters of every word. I obeyed, the truck giving a strangled squeal as it stopped. I turned off the engine and let it shudder in the heat.

A few of the other men drew closer. They had the same look as this one, as though they were steadily undergoing a metamorphosis into the old man in front. They watched me first with fear, then opening into suspicion, and then finally confusion.

"Ain't your day," said the old man. Another man jogged to the first, murmured something in the old man's ear. "Huh?" said the old guy. Then he shook his head. "You in the truck, step out. Nice and slow."

I obeyed, moving as deliberately as I could. The rifles weren't exactly pointed at me, but they weren't pointed away either. It would take quite a few bullets to kill me, but each one would hurt, and there were enough if they all decided to make it a town activity.

"Who are you?" asked the old man. The entire town was silent, waiting for the answer.

I took the slate in one hand and the chalk in the other, holding it up to show them. The old man gave me the ghost of a nod. *My name is Jane Stitch.*

"Don't answer my question."

It's the only answer I've got.

I didn't think the old man could narrow his eyes even more than they already were, but he proved me wrong. "Don't think Dullahan sent her." The name crawled over my spine with shards of glass. I shook my head. "Now there's an answer. Well, here's another'n. You made yourself a turn into Daybreak. This here's a human town. We don't want your kind here and never did. Now you get back in that there truck and you go back to wherever you came from. You forget you ever saw this place."

Wait

"Stop writing. We don't care what you got to say. Go on now!" The call was taken up quickly by the others around, telling me to "Go on now!" Now, all I saw was loathing on these faces. Wouldn't be long before someone threw something. Or one of those rifles went off.

I turned back to the truck, my mind spinning. The green was crashing in now, fear longing to be replaced with rage. No telling what I could do to these people before they scared me off with some fire. Easy to see they didn't have a single volt of electricity in this whole place. It was time for me to get out, regroup, figure out another way.

"Ma'am? Ma'am?" The voice was high, coming out of the chant and getting closer. I turned, and the mob was contracting around me, each man feeding on the anger of the man next to him, each one eating up a little more ground. They weren't who was talking to me. No, it was a boy, maybe eleven or twelve years old. His hair was blond, his skin burned nearly brown. He was desert skinny and dressed in rags, but his face wasn't beaten. He was looking at me with curiosity.

"Kid! Get away from there!" someone yelled.

"Skin-dollies is crazy!" someone else called.

I flinched at the last. I might not want to hurt this kid, but all I could see was Nick, cowering below the hole in the plaster, the lighter held up impotently. The kid took another step forward and I flinched from him, now, as though he could pull the aggression from me.

"Ma'am. Where'd you get that?" The grimy finger leveled at the scarf around my neck.

I touched it, the tendons inside my stolen fingers coming alive with the pattern. The mob had partially paused, the ones in the front gone quiet as they watched, the ones in the back still boldly calling for my exodus. I picked up the slate. *I think I made it.*

"Daddy!" the kid called out. "Daddy, come up here!"

The boy needn't have called, because his father was already pushing through the mob. As he emerged in the shrunken center, my eyes widened. I knew this man. He was different now, but I knew him all the same. Sun-scarred and bent, filthy and ragged, but I knew him. This was Sadie's husband. Which meant the boy was...

My hands quivered. I had to consciously hold them back. My body demanded to lunge at the kid, to wrap him up in my arms, to press him to me in a hug. To feel what I hadn't felt since that part of me died. But I wasn't human. I was a meat golem. Doing that would literally crush the boy like a bundle of sticks. So I was left there to shiver in the hot sun.

Sadie's husband limped forward. I'd seen him limp in my memories, but here it was more pronounced; he was nearly dragging his left leg behind him. Whatever injury had grown heavier as his body had been eroded away. "Jerome, I need you to step back now. She's dangerous and she was just leaving."

I wanted to scream at him that I wasn't leaving, that I couldn't leave. Nothing could have made me leave him or Jerome. The urge to hold him was strong, too, to feel an embrace that I knew had the power to banish at least some of the hatred of the world. He'd never hold me like that, and he had never held me like that. He'd held Sadie, and me knowing was just a betrayal. My hands shook, and my vision started to wobble. The green battered at me.

"Daddy, no. She says she made that scarf."

"Maybe she did make it. I expect someone like her's good with stitching."

"Daddy, you ain't lookin'."

"Son, you gotta listen to me. Get behind me and let the lady get on her way."

"Daddy, you know that scarf!"

Sadie's husband blinked at the sudden force in his son's voice. He looked at the scarf, really looked for the first time, and recognition bloomed in him too. "Where'd you get that?" he asked me, more wondering than suspicious.

"She said she made it."

"She's lying, son. You know that."

Jerome shook his head. "I don't know that. Who's comin' to Daybreak, wearin' that, and lyin'?"

"She's a snatcher, boy! You know snatchers ain't to be trusted!"

I shook my head. *Sadie made this.*

The father's eyes turned to water, then to ice. "How do you know that name?"

"I want to talk to her," Jerome said.

"Yeah," said Sadie's husband. "Think I want to talk to her, too."

The old man shuffled over to Sadie's husband. "What do you want to do, Les?"

"I want to talk to this woman. If that's all right."

The old man nodded. "We bring her in, she's your'n, understand?"

Les nodded. "I got it. She ain't gonna do anything. Are you?" he asked me. I shook my head. Then, without knowing why, I mimed a cross over my heart. I watched Les's adam's apple bob as he swallowed, and he looked away.

"All right," said the old man, loud enough for his town to hear. "She's here with Les. Everybody go back to what you were doing."

The mob began to reluctantly break up. Some of the men moved back to the walls, where they lingered in the geometric shadows. Others went back inside. I saw now that the central building was up against a small hill and the town went around that, the adobe wall bolstered with the scavenged barricade. A single well stood in the wide-open space. A few old cars were parked around the corners of buildings.

The old man approached me. "You move your truck yonder," he said, pointing to a clean space by a wall. A few slender chickens wandered over the earth. "And that nose stays clean." I nodded to both, and moved the truck out of the way. Then I joined Les and Jerome where they waited for me.

"It's this way," Les said, nodding deeper into the town. Then he began to move, the limp slowing him down. I fell into step next to him, walking slowly enough that he wouldn't feel like I was trying to outpace him. Jerome was next to me, head craned up, squinting into the sun as he watched me.

"What's your name, ma'am?" he asked.

Jane.

"Hi, Jane. I'm Jerome."

It's nice to meet you. My hands knew him. No, not my hands. Tendons and muscles in my arms. The strings to my puppet. The green's violence could come from this confused love, too.

"Where are you from?"

Los Angeles.

"Hollywood! You seen any movie stars?" I nodded. I'd seen lots of them at the Nocturnist.

"Wow. I seen a movie, once," Jerome confided. "Over in Phoenix."

"You don't need to be tellin' her our business," Les said.

"Daddy, she knows movie stars."

I don't know them. Just seen them.

"Still, though," Jerome said.

The central structure was a two-story adobe building with many open windows, out of which I saw the occasional sullen stare. Other buildings were little more than adobe boxes or even simpler shanty huts. The edifices of Daybreak were just as exhausted as her inhabitants. Les nodded at the far end of the main structure, where an outdoor staircase led to the second floor. The stairs were steep and the steps were narrow, bowed in the centers from the tread of many feet. He climbed these with difficulty, stepping up with his good leg, then bringing the bad one up behind. I walked behind him, ready to catch him if he fell, but he didn't.

On the second floor, we found a hallway with a narrow doorway. Nothing was perfectly straight or square. The building gave the impression of being cobbled together, of slumping. Beaten by the desert, but somehow still standing. There were no doors in the hall, merely doorways. We went into the first and found a single small room. Two bedrolls, one for Les, the other for Jerome, sat against either wall. A small dresser, one I recognized from the back of the truck, loaded from Texas, stood against the far wall, under the window. The dresser was covered in new scars, but it was still there. The only thing that had survived, other than the two of them.

Two pictures, both in cracked frames, were arranged on the dresser. One was a shot of Les and Sadie. It had to have been taken only ten or fifteen years ago, but Les had aged multiple decades in that time. He wore an army uniform, standing straight, proud, and handsome. Sadie was on his arm. I picked the picture up off the dresser and gazed at it. I liked the looks of the two of them. There was love there. In my mind, I pictured me and Nick, him in his uniform, me towering over him. We would always be mismatched, but it tugged at a smile. I put the photo down and looked at the other.

This one was a bit later. Les and Sadie again, this time with a little boy next to Les and a chubby baby in Sadie's arms. "That's me," Jerome said, his grubby finger indicating the baby. I smiled at him and nodded.

"Don't really got anyplace to sit," Les said, "and nothin' to offer." I nodded. His shoulders slumped in shame as he sat down heavily on his bedroll. He hadn't wanted to take me here, but there was nowhere else we'd be out of sight of the town.

Les sighed, then rolled up his ragged pantleg. He undid a few straps and then, with a groan, pulled the bottom part of his leg off. It was old, made of wood. His stump, ending just below the knee, was bruised and callused. "At least I can get this thing off."

My eyes went to the lump of scarred tissue. My left hand went to the stitches of my right arm, so recently reattached. "Don't be shy," he said, shaking his head.

Sorry.

"No, I expect this ain't somethin' you're used to. Lost it in France." I nodded. "Quick ticket home, at least. I thought then that my fighting days were done. Don't think I ever been more wrong about anything."

I pointed at the picture of the whole family. "Late '45 or '46, I guess," he said.

"Before Leroy was taken," Jerome said, without the sadness of real memory.

Les, though, flinched like he'd been stung by a wasp. "Yeah, before that."

I pointed at Sadie. "That's Mama," Jerome said.

"But I expect you knew that," Les said. He stared at me. Though he was sitting on his grimy bedroll, his artificial leg off, he seemed to loom over me in judgment. I nodded. "You say you made that scarf," Les said, "but my wife made that thing. I know it, and the boy knows it. We buried her in it." Jerome nodded now. He reached for the tail of the blue fabric, catching it and gently caressing it between his fingers.

Some of me was Sadie Schroeder.

Les swallowed, and now his eyes were swimming. He was so small, dried out, the poised tears looked like the entirety of the water he could spare in his body. "Expect I knew that too," he said, his voice breaking.

I looked down at Jerome. The boy, at his age, was caught between childhood and manhood. The world wanted to grind him into something like his father. More than a little of him wanted to be cradled in the scarf, like he had the last time he'd felt truly safe. My hands shook now.

"What exactly do you want?"

I don't know. Sadie Schroeder is a name, but she's also a piece of me. I can feel her in my arms. I can feel her now, with you two. I know you, but you're strangers. You feel like dreams, but you're here.

Les shuddered, a small cry ripped out of him. His shoulders shook silently. "Get out." I scribbled a response on my slate, but he didn't look up. "Get out!" he shouted, and his voice broke again, crumbling wetly into a river.

I moved from the room. The scarf fell from my shoulders, held by Jerome. I came out in the sun, on the narrow staircase leading to the second floor. I stared out over the baking desert. So much of me wanted to run back into the room, to hold Les against me until he stopped crying. To touch him in the ways my body cried out for. Then, he became Fern in my mind. Then Nick, all jumbling together in confusion. But I wasn't his wife. Wasn't Fern's love. I was some of their corpses.

"Jane?" Jerome stood in the doorway, clutching the scarf. He held it against his body like a security blanket. I looked at him, unsure of what to say. "Is it true? You're my mama?" I didn't know whether to nod or shake my head. This was the kind of conversation that no one prepared for. No one knew it would have been possible more than a few years ago. It was too big, too subtle. "Jane?"

A piece of your mama was used to make me.

"What piece?" The question was so natural, so innocent. I couldn't tell if it was the natural resilience of a child, or the curse of what this new world had made normal.

I'm not sure.

The little boy watched me, the toughness bleeding away from him in seconds. The parts that quivered to hold him shook even harder. To comfort these old, raw places rapidly being exposed. "I can't tell if you look like her or not." I frowned, cocking my head. "We got them pictures. Those are the only ones we got. I look at 'em every day, but every day they look less and less like someone I know."

I'm sorry.

He shook his head. "I guess I can't tell what part of you was Mama. It's why I asked. I was hopin' you'd say your nose or your chin."

I think my eye. This eye.

Jerome nodded, light coming over his face. "I think so. It looks like the ones in the picture. I used to think there was no one with eyes like that. No one else in the world. Too light to even see. How do you see out of it?"

Pretty well. Hard when the sun's in it.

Jerome nodded solemnly. "I remember Mama used to squint. But at night, her eyes opened up so big they looked like two moons."

It's a good eye.

"You think with you seein' through it, my mama is still seein' a little bit? Seein' me?"

I wish it was that way. Your mama is just a name to me. I feel some things, but I don't really know them.

"Feel? Like what?"

My hand wants to touch your cheek. I showed him. My left hand shivered like an autumn leaf. I erased the message and wrote another. *Some part of me knows you, but it's not in my head.*

Jerome took another step. He reached for my hand. The green crashed around me, threatening to swallow me in a memory. But the child was here. It wasn't the same one, wasn't the little girl reaching for the orange or sobbing at the destruction of the idea of ever being safe. Jerome had a connection to some of me. A part of him came from a piece of me. And it knew.

Jerome reached up and took my hand lightly. He felt like a butterfly's wings. I let him move my hand down. I kept myself here, with him. Kept from losing what I had. I was still, terrified before this child. A twitch could kill him. He guided my hand to a place inches from his face. Tremors shook the limb. He brought his cheek up to the fingers and brushed it over them.

The skin was rough. My hands weren't quite right. But there was something bone deep in the gesture, something I knew the same way I knew how to breathe, understood English, knew who the president was. Those pieces of me that went through death but had shed context along the way. The brush of my fingers over Jerome's cheek was blessed context. In that touch, I knew more about Sadie Schroeder than I ever had. Than I ever would.

Jerome released the hand. "Jane? Are you all right?"

I touched my face and my hand came away wet. I hadn't even noticed when I'd started to cry. I nodded at him. I was fine. I was more fine than I knew how to be.

TWENTY-EIGHT

Les never came out of the room. I spent the afternoon with Jerome, and I could have spent much more. I knew I wasn't returning to Quartzsite or to the Frog Mothers that night. I was going to take every second with the boy until the inevitable mob threw me out. For now, though I was getting a few angry looks throughout the day, most of the people of Daybreak seemed content to ignore me.

Jerome and I discussed where they'd been. His first memories were of the refugee camps during the Night War. He had a kid's view of them, talking about the friends he'd made, what they liked to do, and whether he ever saw them again. He talked about camps that had food and ones where he'd gone hungry. There were more and more of the latter the longer the Night War went on.

I learned that Jerome was twelve. At times he looked anywhere from nine to fifty. His brother Leroy had vanished when Jerome was six, and he didn't remember him very well. His father still couldn't say Leroy's name, and when the boy went missing, both Les and Sadie had gotten smaller. That was how Jerome put it. His parents had gotten smaller in their grief and guilt.

Jerome asked me about Hollywood. He only had the vaguest idea of what a movie star was, but knew they were people to be looked up to in some way. So I told him stories about seeing different ones. The time I saw Imogen Verity, or that Turner Coates was a regular where I worked, or the time Leon Chamomile stopped in. He asked me who they were, and then wanted to know about their pictures. I ended up telling him the plot of three of the Vampiro pictures; he couldn't get enough of those.

Eventually, Daybreak went to sleep. Jerome said good night to me, and the town vanished inside. I was too electric to sleep. My time with the Frog Mothers had been restful, so I was ready for these and more mysteries to be revealed. For a time, I stayed on the landing, but soon, I wandered through a sleeping Daybreak.

It wasn't completely asleep, I soon learned. I saw it in the glint of moonlight off rifles lurking in the eaves along the walls. I couldn't tell if they were watching me or waiting for something to come out of the desert. As the night wore on, I found a place to spend it. I climbed up on the landing, up onto the railing, and from there to the roof of the central structure. The clay had been bowed by the passage of feet; I wasn't the first to take this route. I wondered if Jerome climbed up to the rooftops and thought about scolding him for it. I couldn't; I had no authority. I wasn't his mother, no matter how much parts of me wanted to believe it.

The roof was a series of thick beams forming a shallow arch, with more beams underneath to provide some support. Thatching was hay, glued with dried mud. I sat on one of the bigger beams. The sky opened up above me, bigger than I thought possible, and I thought about Jerome. And Harry Jenkins, and Pastor Dukes, and Fern Calloway, and Nick. The Frog Mothers too, and Sugar, and Frances. And even Burke, but I never wanted him to know about this place. Burke could live the rest of his days in Quartzsite without being aware of all the unrobbed graves out here.

I could keep my names. Those were the people I thought of the most. Sadie Schroeder and Haseya and Lorena Quintanilla and Rachel Prager. I called the stars by their names and wondered what the last two were going to be called.

It was going to be hard to leave in the morning, but I had to. Jerome Schroeder wasn't my son and Les Schroeder sure as hell wasn't my husband. As good as they both felt to a piece of me, they were alien to even more. Unlike Fern, Les had made it clear I wasn't welcome back. I wasn't doing them any favors by sticking around, either. Staying would be selfish. Knowing that wasn't going to make it easier. Family was something even monsters took for granted, but meat golems didn't. We lost the ones before, and the ones after, if they were anything like Burke, were hardly any kind of substitute. I couldn't think of a single one of the girls at work who had a warm relationship with the man who had stitched her together.

The cries of alarm, sparking along the walls like a half-broken wire, pulled me from my thoughts. A river of molten gold streaked out over the blue-black blanket of the night sands. A shooting star bound to the earth. I had seen it before, though not quite from this vantage. It had pursued me from the Dullahan rantch, hell-bent for revenge.

The suspicion was confirmed when the calls resolved into a single, shuddering word. "Dullahans!"

People emerged from their houses, wiping sleep from terrified eyes. Bells, tiny parodies of mission bells, began to tinkle desperately. The men who came out weren't armed. I wanted to scream at them, but I couldn't. And besides, what good were rifles against spectral horsemen? There wasn't enough water in this speck to give Tod Dullahan a hangnail. Women and children clutched at the men and at each other. I stayed where I was, lit only by moonlight.

The single smear of gold resolved into smaller streaks, each one betraying a rider. It was more than the four I was growing used to. This was nearly a herd of headless horsemen, all riding hard from the north, inexorably closing in on Daybreak. I began to recognize individuals, and my guts entwined. The stench of rotting fruit wafted over the town on an evil wind.

I didn't know the horseman at the head of the group, but I could guess. He was heavier than the others, barrel-chested and with thick arms.

He wore a double-breasted gray coat that looked almost military, and a cavalry saber rode on his hip. His horse was massive, a black charger with a single white star on his forehead. This had to be Ambrose Dullahan, the patriarch of the Dullahan Clan.

Tod Dullahan rode to the old man's right and just behind. The green roiled at the sight of him, wanting to swallow me up. The rest of Tod's gang thundered along with him. Morgan was the easiest to see, sitting behind the wheel of her pickup, but I spotted Shreve and Mal as well, riding close at hand. There were others, including one riding a spectral giant ant.

After the greeting I had got, it would have been easy to expect the town to come out fighting. But there were two things I hadn't seen since I got here: gold or running water. Granted, both would have been hard to come by for a community as poor as this one. Humans, though, had a way of getting their hands on whatever would fight their personal haunts. If these people truly had nothing against headless horsemen, it was by design.

And it was. The alarm cry of "Dullahans" hadn't been a call to arms. It had been a summons, and the people of Daybreak obeyed it. They filed out of their huts and the central pueblo, forming up in the center of town as they had done with my arrival, but there was no anger here. I saw only supplication.

Ambrose was the first through the archway, the other horsemen boiling in behind. The crowd recoiled as sure as a blob tasting alkali. The mob that had been a living thing the day before when it had greeted me was now a cowed, terrorized collection of people. Ambrose reined in his horse. The charger went up on its hind legs, blowing out twin gusts of brimstone.

"Citizens of Daybreak!" Ambrose boomed. His voice was deep, the vowels lazy, the consonants precise, a drawl from somewhere deep in the old south. "I regret to inform you of a recent tragedy. Three of my loyal men have been murdered."

From my perch atop the central building, the chemicals in my veins ran frigid. Three Dullahans had been killed. I ran through the inhabitants of Quartzsite, even momentarily considering one of the poor people in Fort

Meatstick before I remembered the mutants. Those three Dullahan dead could be placed squarely on the doorstep of Phobos and her ragtag group. No one else was crazy enough to try. No one but one bugsy skin-dolly, and Tod had already sliced that piece of me out.

Shame the mutants had missed Tod, but I knew real bastards always had the Devil looking out for them. When Tod died, I'd be there. It was the only way any of this made sense. One way or the other, I'd be there.

The crowd let out a horrified gasp. I took it as theater at first, that they were expressing the horror they knew Ambrose expected of them. But it wasn't that. It was genuine.

Tod reined in his sickly yellow horse. The beast whinnied, gnashing teeth that looked uncomfortably sharp. He threw himself from the saddle, standing to his full, unimpressive height. Morgan, Shreve, and Mal all pulled up as well, dismounting. The others stayed in their saddles, their invisible attention felt everywhere.

"I know, I know," Ambrose said, placating the mob with one short-fingered hand. "A cowardly attack that shall be avenged, I assure you. Avenged with the assistance of the men and women of this fine community."

As the horsemen watched the crowd, whatever aggression beat inside their chests was expressed through their steeds. The beasts pawed the ground, their hooves striking greasy sparks. The ant uttered an unnatural chitter, its mandibles bisecting the air. Every horseman's hand rested on their weapon, whether it was a sword, a knife, an axe, or a gun. None of them drew. I wondered if it was because they were that fast, or merely because they never had to draw. The only water was at the bottom of the well, and no one went for the bucket. The faces of the crowd, shiny with panic, watched the horsemen.

Something in the crowd started to move. A few murmurs rippled through the bodies as the shape advanced slowly. I couldn't quite see what it was. I went down on my belly, flat against the beam, slinking to the edge of the roof, where the wood poked out over the central square. Below were people, all wanting to see, but none wanting to be seen. The entrance of the town, not far, belonged to the Dullahans.

"Alvino? Is that Alvino?" Ambrose peered at the movement through the crowd, hand theatrically up, blocking nonexistent sunshine from nonexistent eyes. "There you are. Always a pleasure to see the fine mayor of this fine community taking responsibility for these fine people."

It was the old man who had greeted me. Then, his age had made him seem implacable. A part of the desert as constant as the wash where Quartzsite sat. Now, the age made him brittle, ready to collapse against what he faced now.

"Please, Alvino, come join me." Ambrose never dismounted, rendering the folksy invitation hollow.

Mal and Shreve approached the side of the crowd where Alvino walked through. The crowd parted as the horsemen approached. I had been wondering about Shreve. I knew headless horsemen were tough, but I'd dropped the better part of a barn on him. I had been hoping he had at least been laid up in bed. No luck; he looked as hale as ever.

Alvino, the old man, limped from the edge of the crowd. As he passed, the eyes of the people went from Ambrose to him, a momentary pleading, but then back to the horsemen in defeat. I knew then Alvino didn't have anything special planned, and that this had happened before. That this was a ceremony the people here hated in their bones.

"Now, Alvino, I trust you're going to tell me the good people of Daybreak are ready to pick the bones?"

"Mr. Dullahan," Alvino started, and even his voice had been broken since the previous day. "We gave only a month ago. You took Carlos Velez and Mary Carver from us."

"You gave Carlos and Mary to me, and I was grateful. And in return, I continued to give Daybreak the protection I promised."

"Yes, Mr. Dullahan, but we're a small community."

"You're small?" Ambrose said in disbelief. "Why, it looks like you outnumber my outfit at least five to one. More if I were a cruel man and started counting children."

Alvino swallowed. "Thank you for that."

"You see? I was getting concerned there for a moment. Thought you'd forgotten gratitude. Forgotten all the things I've done for you."

"We would never forget that, Mr. Dullahan."

"Good, good. Now it is a tragedy that brings me here, and it's a tragedy for both of us. Where I lose three brave companions, you lose three of those who selflessly guard your borders against a world of monsters."

"We understand."

"Good, good."

"But sir—"

Ambrose sighed. "I don't like to hear that word, Alvino. 'But.' I've heard tell that you can ignore every word until that one. That what comes after is the true intent of the speaker."

"It's nothing like that, Mr. Dullahan."

"I'm doing everything I can for you good people, and all I'm hearing is that you can't give me what we both need. What you promised to me when I allowed Daybreak to stay on my land. Do I charge you people rent you can't afford? No. I only ask from you what is in your ability to give."

"We can't give this."

"Can't, Alvino, or won't? Because it seems to me you have the numbers. Three of my people, savagely murdered. Now, I will have them replaced in the method we all believe is fair. But...if you're refusing to honor our agreement, perhaps it's time I bring you more closely into my outfit and let Daybreak select a leader more amenable to living up to his agreements."

Alvino's skin glistened like that of a dead man. I looked to the rest of the town. They watched their leader, and in some eyes I saw the guttering flame of hope. They wanted him to say no. They wanted him to fight. Pull the trigger on this war. Give them an excuse. But at the same time, they were terrified of it. They knew they'd be butchered and anyone who wasn't would be turned.

And then, underneath, was the saddest hope. I knew Alvino could sense it. He had to have sensed it from the very beginning. They wanted him to volunteer, because then at least that was one person who couldn't possibly be one of them. Instead, Alvino hung his head. "We'll do what you ask, Mr. Dullahan."

"Good!" Ambrose boomed. "I knew you'd listen to reason, Alvino. You always do."

"You heard the man," Tod crowed. "Time to draw the bones!"

Two horsemen, a man and a woman, dismounted and came up alongside their patriarch. Ambrose untied a gunnysack from his saddle and handed it to the woman. It rattled like porcelain. "As a special treat, I thought I'd let your most recent inhabitants help out. You all remember Carlos and Mary. Though they got different handles now, don't you?"

The two horsemen muttered assent, apparently far from eager about what they were doing, but going along with it nonetheless. I remembered what I'd been told about where their skulls likely were. They joined Tod at the mouth of the crowd.

"You all know the rules," Tod called. After Ambrose's sonorous tones, Tod's sneering voice sounded almost bratty. "You strike gold, you join us."

A frown rippled over my brow. Headless horsemen were terrified of gold coins. As far as I knew, they had to be minted, but I wasn't exactly familiar with the ins and outs. It was considered good manners to ignore monster fears and weaknesses as much as one could, but at the same time, keep one's home tidily free of them. Seeing as I didn't entertain company very much and I didn't make enough to be collecting coins, it hadn't come up.

Tod gestured to the gunnysack, reaching under it to give it a rattle. Something in it was heavy, but it was also diffuse, like a collection of pebbles. I scanned the crowd again, and finally, I found Les and Jerome, lingering near the back. Les's eyes were filled with fear, but I saw hatred there as well. Something I recognized, the green in him too. Ambrose had said children were off limits, but I had no idea what "children" meant to someone like him. Jerome was a boy, but he'd already experienced more suffering than a man should.

Carefully, I turned around on my belly, crawling up the beam on hands and feet. Below, the crowd had started to murmur.

"Where to start?" Tod asked. "How about over here. Miss? What do you think? You want to join the Dullahans?" The rattle of porcelain filtered up to me. Then a defeated sigh from the crowd. Disappointment. "No, it won't be you."

I reached the apex, where the biggest beam traced back to the landing. Below, I heard more variations on the same vignette: Tod, approaching someone, mocking them with the implication of his words, the rattle, then the verdict that no, this person wouldn't be joining the Dullahans. At the edge of the roof, I lowered myself off the side, my feet finding the low clay wall. There was no one on this side of Daybreak. They were all terrified, but they were also in full view of the Dullahans. No one was hiding.

I dropped onto the landing and picked my way down the steep stairs. The light was hellish, coming from Morgan's truck's headlights and the persistent sparks of the horses as they pawed the earth. Gave everything the stuttering quality of a silent movie, freezing the horror in moments. Overhead, the moon and stars were bright.

I stayed on the corner, peering around it. Les and Jerome weren't far. I could carry them both easily, one over each shoulder. If they stayed quiet, there was the ghost of a chance of escape.

I turned the corner, keeping to where the shadows loomed. Now I cursed my height. I could easily see over the vast majority of the crowd, all the way to where the Dullahans held court. At least Tod had picked the other side of the gathering for his bizarre game. Mary, that had to be Mary, held the gunnysack while Carlos flanked her. Tod was right up in the faces of the crowd, ordering them to pick their fate from the bag. A terrified man put his hand into the bag like it was full of rattlesnakes.

"Go on," Tod said. "Pick one and hope you strike gold."

The man winced, then pulled it out. I couldn't see what he held; it was only about the size of a fingertip. But it gleamed, and when one of the horses kicked up a fountain of sparks, the thing in the man's hand glittered like pure gold.

"We have a winner!" Tod crowed. The crowd groaned. I heard relief, but also loathing. They were happy it wasn't them, and hated what that had turned them into.

"No, please!" the man cried. He turned to run, but the crowd was implacable behind him.

Carlos grabbed his former neighbor by the shoulder, hauling him out. Tod slapped a hand on the other shoulder, kneading it with false friendship. "It's so nice to meet a member of the family."

Mal threw the noose around the unlucky man's neck and dragged him away, unhooking him only when he was surrounded by Shreve and Morgan. The man quaked in terror, too frightened to do anything else, a mouse among cats. Tod continued his path around the town, having everyone pick from the bag. As they drew closer to where I was, I moved faster, coming up next to Jerome and Les.

The crowed sighed as another man was picked. He bore it more stoically than the last. I ignored the horror unfolding, grabbing Les by the arm.

"What the hell are you still doing here?" he hissed at me. I twitched my head in the direction of the back of the town. *Let's go*, the gesture said. "What are you talking about?" I twitched my head hard enough to make me worry about the integrity of my stitches. At the same time, I widened my eyes. "You outta your snatcher head," he said.

"Daddy, Mama's in there. She wants to help us!"

"That ain't your mama, boy!"

"Listen to her!"

"She don't know what this is. She don't know who the Dullahans—"

"And what have we here?" Tod was right in front of us, the crowd having silently parted. The commotion was blood in the water, and the crowd had been more than happy to put his attention anywhere else. Now Tod stood in front of the three of us, and I could feel his mirthless grin. The stitches along my right hand burned with the memory of his bowie, now riding his belt. The fire turned to ice in my heart.

"Plain Jane, fancy meeting you here. Now, a lesser man would be cross, but I remember our deal. You were to stay out of Quartzsite, weren't you? This, plainly, ain't Quartzsite, so I can't even be mad."

"Tod?" Ambrose called. "Something wrong over there?"

"Nothing's wrong, sir. Just got a good feeling about this one is all."

The green crashed against me. Three horsemen, close by. Tod, and these other two. Carlos had moved against his former friends, but how fast would he be if I grabbed Tod? And if a falling barn wouldn't break one of them, could I? Maybe Les read my mind, because I felt his hand on my arm. Those places that were Sadie came alive. "Don't do it," Les mumbled.

I stayed frozen. I couldn't trust even a single movement. It might turn into a second, then a third. Become an avalanche. And then what? The Dullahans weren't going to take that well.

"What about you? You ready to hold up your end of the deal?" Tod asked Les.

"I'll do it, sir. Just like we all promised."

Tod chuckled. "Oh, I like this one. Got a good feeling about him, I do. Now reach into the bag. See if you strike gold."

"Daddy," Jerome said, voice wavering, small hand wrapping around his father's.

"It's all right, son." Les reached into the bag. The rattle was louder now, like a thousand porcelain beads all running against one another. He withdrew his hand a moment later, and I saw what he was holding. It was a tooth. A molar, from a human head. He handed it over to Tod, standing a bit straighter in this small triumph. The tooth was gray in the moonlight, shining wetly as Tod turned it.

My heart slowed its hammering. Les was safe. Then, deliberately, Tod dropped the tooth in his breast pocket and removed another one. One with a prominent gold filling.

"Looks like we have a winner," Tod said, holding up the grisly trophy.

"Daddy!" Jerome blurted. I hissed like an alley cat. The green crashed inward. Tod wasn't far. Three horsemen, all armed.

"Don't," Les said, putting a hand on my shoulder. His palm was electric on my skin. I knew the touch, as deep inside as my bones.

"You should listen to the man, Plain Jane," Tod said. The green thundered again at the sound of his voice. The horseman was still, the tooth in his right hand, the fingers of his left drumming on the hilt of his bowie knife. The searing agony of the wound leapt back to me, and I reflexively cradled my right hand, recoiling from the phantom pain.

"That's a good girl," Tod said. "Gotta gentle 'em. What am I telling you for? Looks like you got to know our Plain Jane pretty well."

"It's all right, I'm going. I'm going," Les said. He pulled away from Jerome and me. I wanted to reach for him, but it felt like reaching into a fire.

Jerome didn't let go. "Daddy, no! He cheated!" Somehow, that was the crime. Jerome could understand the rampant cruelty of the world, but in the wounded shriek of that one word, it only worked if somehow it was fair. Tod had robbed him of even that.

"It's all right, son. Just don't look. Promise me you won't look."

"Come on now," Tod said, grabbing Les by the shoulder and hauling him forward. He stumbled, Jerome still attached to his leg.

I wanted to attack Tod, but I couldn't. And it wasn't just worry over everyone else. It was fear. Pure fear of what he'd done to me. Now there were even more of him, in this place of power. So instead of grabbing Tod and breaking him, I knelt and took Jerome into my arms. He felt so right there, even struggling. He fit, the contours of each of us joining up like a puzzle.

"Jane! He cheated!" I nodded. The tears were running now. Tracks cut through the dirt on Jerome's face. He was screaming, reaching for his father. He couldn't get away from me. Not away from my strength. Les joined the other two men, and Shreve and Mal marched all three up onto the scaffold.

"Look at these three brave men," Ambrose said happily. "Ready to join the family. I couldn't be more proud. The bones always pick the right ones."

Finally, the big horseman slung himself off the saddle and landed on the earth. His footfalls were heavy as he climbed the scaffold. His left hand rested on the pommel of his cavalry saber. Jerome was sobbing now, the cries surrendering to despair. He'd stopped fighting me. I'd made him learn the most awful lesson of all: that he couldn't fight. That whatever a monster wanted of him was ours to take. I turned the fragile boy around in my arms. Les hadn't wanted him to look. That was the least I could do.

Ambrose reached the top of the scaffold. The selected men were all on their knees, their shoulders slumped and their heads down. All except Les, whose eyes passed between me and Jerome, ensuring I had the boy. That he wouldn't have to see what was about to happen. I nodded to Les, blinking more tears down my cheeks. He looked away, anguish where I had stamped it.

"Daybreak is a lovely place, and I'm glad to host it on my land," Ambrose said. "Humans need a place to go, the same as anyone else. This moment, this sacrifice of three of your sons, shows me that you are doing right by our agreement. It means that I'll continue to be happy to have Daybreak as a neighbor. I'll continue to keep the other monsters away from it. I'll continue to treat you with the care and compassion I would treat my own children."

Ambrose drew the saber. Fire ignited on the blade, wrapping around it like a lambent serpent. I recoiled. Even at this distance, I wanted to run. Something about that fire was worse than a torch. I felt it on my arm, playing in every one of the wounds Tod had carved into me.

"Gentlemen, tonight you leave your lives as men. Tonight you become headless horsemen. You take the first step on an endless road where you will know true freedom. True power. You aren't making a sacrifice; you're gaining a gift. A gift freely offered. You're joining my family."

Ambrose brought the sword back and with a single swipe, the first man's head tumbled from his shoulders. The thump it made as it hit the planks and then rolled over them was one I'd think of late at night when the good was far away. Shreve picked the head up by the hair, and I could see now that both edges of the neck had been cauterized by the blade.

"I welcome you as Dullahans," Ambrose said.

The sword fell again, and the second man's head rolled. Mal picked it up. The bodies of both men remained kneeling, looking almost like they were praying. Nothing would answer their prayers that night.

"I welcome you as sons."

Les didn't blink as the flaming sword came down. His head dropped and rolled over the planks. Ambrose picked it up, holding it aloft for the crowd. All three of the horsemen took hold of the wound at the neck, where the seared flesh had collected. The sheath swallowed the saber's flames.

Fire bloomed on the heads, emanating from the severed neck, beneath the palms of all three horsemen. I blinked away my tears, forced myself to watch even as the fear of the fire roiled in me, fighting the sorrow and shame. The flames rose, licking the cheeks. The flesh began to turn black. Not burned, it was too fast for that. It curdled to coal, then began to drift away in gusts, the ashes going skyward. Clumps blew away at a time, soon revealing ivory bone beneath. The last of the flesh was gone on wispy threads of air. Then the skulls stood exposed, gleaming.

Lines blazed into the bone itself, tracing new patterns into the skulls. Marking them as no longer human. Each one was unique, and as I watched, I memorized the swirls over Les's cheeks and cap. Ambrose gestured to Shreve and Mal, and both horsemen handed over the skulls in their hands. Ambrose worked a leather thong through them and soon all three trophies hung from his belt.

The three bodies continued to kneel, motionless. The horsemen were silent, waiting. If they had heads, it might have betrayed where they were watching, because there was the sense that they were waiting for something.

"Jane?" Jerome whispered. His voice was deafening now. Everything was silent. Even the horses were still. The crowd was still as a robbed grave. I held the boy against me, not letting him go.

In the distance, a sound began to reach us. The thunder of hooves over the desert. Joined with something else, a throaty buzz growing louder. The horsemen made room at the archway into Daybreak. Two horses and a motorcycle blazed into the town. One horse was pure black, the other a paint. Both sported red eyes and blew out gusts of brimstone. The motorcycle revved its engine, its single headlight peering into the night. Each new steed carried a weapon secured to the saddle. I saw a tomahawk and an axe on the horses, and a military rifle on the motorcycle.

The three corpses stood up. Only they weren't corpses anymore. They were headless horsemen. Their movements were smooth, sure.

"Welcome to the family, boys," Ambrose Dullahan said. "Now you three mount up. We're going home." The three horsemen walked off the scaffolding and went to their steeds. I watched as Les threw his leg over the motorcycle, the limp gone. The vehicle purred with the presence of its rider. "People of Daybreak, thank you all for your presence, and once again, I reaffirm my commitment to your safety. Have yourselves a lovely night."

Ambrose stalked off the scaffolding while the other horsemen mounted up, turned their steeds around, and blazed into the desert. Ambrose was among the last, pulling himself up into the saddle, the skulls rattling on his belt. His charger reared, and then he too bolted from Daybreak, north to his rantch. Tod was the final one to go, making a show of slowly tying the gunnysack to his saddle. He paused, and I knew the bastard was drinking in the lingering fear and resentment of this place. I felt his attention grasping at me, and the green churned around me. Hate, for him, but also for myself and my paralysis. Then Tod was gone, following the rest of the Dullahans out onto the desert.

I held Jerome as I watched them. I don't know how long he'd been hitting me, but by the time I noticed, he was already tired, his little hands beating against my chest in a frustrated tattoo. His sobs were dying in his throat. I pulled away, looking at Jerome with uncomprehending eyes.

"You could've stopped him! You could've killed 'em!"

I had no words for him. His fists slammed against my chest and the slate. I shook my head, wanting to explain that I couldn't. Even if I had succumbed to the green, I couldn't have stopped what had happened. I would have merely been cut to pieces, and Jerome would have watched as Ambrose Dullahan cut Les's head off. The slate shuddered helplessly against me.

I let go of Jerome, and he continued the useless attack. I looked around at the people gathered. Maybe I was looking for some kind of support. I found only hatred. The anger they hadn't mustered for the Dullahans was pointed directly at me, infernos behind every pair of eyes. A few murmured to one another. Then the shouting began. It started well away from me, shielded by a press of crowd between me and it. A shout of anger, followed by another, and soon the mob was feeding itself. The anger they'd kept on chains for the Dullahans was released now, and building strength. I stood up, not quite comprehending what I was seeing.

"You could've stopped him!" Jerome kept screaming at me, now on his knees in the dirt. "You could've killed 'em!"

A stone whistled overhead, landing with a puff into the dust. Others followed it quickly, and either aim or courage was getting better. I ran for the truck, and now the rocks were rattling off its dented hide. I started the engine, grateful when it caught on the first turn, and I hit the gas. I wasn't following the Dullahans, but I might as well be.

Monsters returning to the night, leaving the people behind.

Twenty-Nine

I drove north, trying to leave what I'd seen in Daybreak behind. I knew I wouldn't. Even as it was happening, I already saw it in my dreams. Already knew it would be an open wound, aching in the back of my mind until the end. Les Schroeder's face, while behind him the cavalry saber went through his neck. There wasn't even fear in his eyes when it was happening. Merely simple resignation, cut with grief, as though this was a foregone conclusion.

Jerome Schroeder was alone now. Brother, mother, and now finally father, all taken away from him. I didn't know what would be done with him in Daybreak. I hoped they'd take care of him, but with what? That town was desperately poor, the miserly earth already giving out as much as it ever would.

I had thought the humans in Los Angeles lived precarious lives. Well, after Nick showed me the truth of it. There was an entirely other level out here in the places time stopped caring about. As bad as Daybreak looked, as much as those people were trying to squeeze blood from the stone of the desert, it was a better existence than Fort Meatstick. Daybreak had community, and even safety against anything that wasn't a headless horseman. The Dullahans came, but it didn't look to be every night. The hopeless in Fort Meatstick were marking time until the inevitable night they simply ran out of the ward they needed.

My stomach turned over. I wasn't going to justify the horror out here. Wasn't going to praise the Dullahans for the vassal state they'd created. Better didn't mean good, and the people were still being used, treated like livestock. Even if Les had been the only one ever taken, I still owed Tod for him. I was heading for Tod and neither one of us could turn. He might not end it, but it wouldn't—couldn't—end until I had gone through him and seen what was on the other side. My hand burned with the memory of his slices. The hand that now felt as borrowed as it had always been.

I found the turnoff where the Frog Mothers had been keeping the truck and backed into it. It was around dawn when I walked into their camp and found them already up and around. Ooljee had the fire going, a steel kettle suspended over it and an old skillet sizzling on the embers. I kept my distance, and did my best to pretend it wasn't there. Gouyen sat at the opening of her tent, scowling as I walked into the clearing.

"Jane," Ooljee said with a smile. "Did you find what you were looking for?" I had no idea, and what I'd seen I couldn't explain. Words felt wrong. So I shrugged. "Are you hungry?"

I nodded, my mouth already filling with saliva at what she was cooking. The eggs hissing in her iron skillet were small, but they looked good. Ooljee poured me some coffee and I waited for the eggs. I sat on the other end of the clearing, on my old rock. I ate sparingly, but enough to put some strength back in my limbs.

"Expect you need a ride," Ooljee said. I nodded, gesturing up the road where I'd left the truck. "No need," she said. "Where are you going, Quartzsite?" I nodded. "That's easy enough." She stood up and called out, "I'm taking Jane home."

Sonseearray poked a sleepy head out of her trailer. "Good. Now keep quiet." The door slammed.

Gouyen merely grunted at the both of us. Ooljee picked up a broom leaning against the Model T. "You ever ridden one of these?" I shook my head. "Well, hold on. Not too tight, though. I don't want to break anything." Ooljee walked out to the open ledge overlooking the desert to the west. She put her legs on either side of the broom and waited. I picked up my bag, slung it over my shoulder, and stood behind her, wrapping one arm around her waist.

"Ready?" she asked. I nodded. The broom came up between our legs, and it carried us both a few feet into the air. My heart hammered against my chest as I looked out over the cliff. Far below, the wasted land stretched to infinity. "This is when it gets fun," Ooljee told me.

I had no response. The broom started moving forward, picking up speed. Soon, the sandy ground, dusted with pine needles, vanished behind us, and we were over a sheer drop to the floor of the desert. The sun was a sudden blast on our heads and shoulders. My arm curled tighter around Ooljee as the broom darted into the sky. I turned, and the alcove where the Frog Mothers made their home was just a few shadows against the side of the mountain. Above, the Springfield Shape glittered in pink crystal against the brutal sun.

The broom swept to the left, heading north around the mountain. Below, the ground ducked and weaved. It was merely colors from this height, all parched yellows, greens, and browns. In the distance, I thought I caught a glimpse of the river glittering next to the horizon, but it was gone just as quickly as we zoomed over the wash. Quartzsite approached rapidly below, the streets like ant trails, the clusters of buildings looking as beaten as Daybreak ever had. As I thought the name of the town, I looked south, trying to get a glimpse of it, and saw nothing. Now, in the daytime, it might as well have been a dream.

Off to the north, the swarms went about their daily wanderings, the anthills sprouting around them like alien plants. The Dullahans would be there, working at their ostensible jobs, riding between the columns of insects. And with them would be a few new headless horsemen. Les, trying to adjust to his new life. His thoughts would be with Jerome, and Jerome's with him. Separated now by existence.

The broom steadily lost altitude. I began to make out more details in the desert. Individual cactus plants rushing past, streets that now disappeared into the distance, buildings whose panels of aluminum and scrap wood could be easily catalogued. Then the broom simply stopped, only a couple feet off the ground. We were at the edge of Quartzsite, not far from Fort Meatstick.

"Here we are," Ooljee said.

I hopped off, stumbling as my nerveless legs remembered how to walk. *Thank you.*

"Oh, think nothing of it. Just a short ride."

For everything.

"You paid for it, Jane. Don't have to thank a body for what you paid for." I shrugged. "I hope you find some peace. And if you want to know more about Haseya, you know where you can find me."

I'll see you again.

"Wouldn't doubt it."

Ooljee picked up speed and the broom bolted into the sky. Soon, she was nothing but a speck against the blue, an insect zipping back to the Dome Rock Mountains. I was alone on the street. There were only a few places I could go here, only a few people who would be willing to talk. I'd start with the most friendly of the options.

As I walked on the dusty streets, I thought about Tod. I wasn't worried I'd find him. Some of that was that he only seemed to come out at night. But some was that it was inevitable now. I saw the tracks last night, and I was still on them. No way to get off. I couldn't leave this place, and he never would. I hoped to be prepared when the reckoning came, but it was happening regardless of what I wanted.

I walked up to the biggest cluster of buildings, looking for my friend's establishment. I didn't know what I would tell Sugar, but I felt like I should tell her something. Tell her I had a list of names and it was officially more than half of what I needed. That I was probably going to kill Tod Dullahan or die. That I'd doomed a family without meaning to.

My thoughts fell away like ash from a burn as I saw my destination. Or what should have been my destination. Where the Sugar Shack had once stood, now only a few beams, scorched black, reached up from the earth like rotted teeth. I picked up speed, walking and then jogging, as though getting there more quickly would change the reality of what I was seeing. The Sugar Shack had been burned to the ground. The sand beneath was soot, a few of the nearby plants also consumed. The structure had stood far enough apart that it was the only one damaged. A precise strike in the middle of town.

I came to a stop next to the wreckage. There was nothing identifiable left. The bar itself, as well as Sugar's apartment, were just completely gone, with a few charred beams left over to say there had once been something.

"Burned down the other night." Peter Wolff stepped out from the shadow of an abandoned shop. I stared at the star tattooed under his chest, nearly invisible under the layer of fluffy gray hair.

Who?

"You, I thought at first."

Me?

"Drifter comes to town, starts loitering at a spot, then that spot burns? Yep, sounded a lot like you."

I'm not a drifter.

"Everybody's a drifter, depending on perspective." Wolff hawked a wad of phlegm into his mouth and then spat it into the burned-out bar. The street was empty save for the two of us, as though the fire had driven off the inhabitants back when it ate the place up.

Meat golems don't like fire. Even writing the word was hard, bringing up its leaping orange evil in my mind. It wasn't Wichita I thought of then, it was my own legs, when my stockings caught fire. Right before Nick put me out.

"Plenty of ways to burn a place without being up close and personal."

It wasn't me.

"You got cuffs on? No, you do not. I know it warn't you. What I don't know is what you're doin' standin' there."

Sugar is a friend.

Peter shrugged, squinting up at the sky. "Don't see what that matters one way or t'other. I told you to leave town, and yet here you are."

I didn't have an easy response to that, so I just waited. After seeing the Dullahans at Daybreak, there really wasn't much this broken-down old wolf could do to make me nervous. If he wanted to try something, he might find more pain than he expected.

"What I don't think you're hearing is that this is all for your own good."

They always thought it was for my own good, and I learned pretty damn quick that when someone said that, what they really meant was it was for their own good. Wolff didn't seem the overly introspective sort, though. Maybe keeping him talking would tell me more. *What do you mean?*

"The Dullahans are done with the mutants 'round here. They're lookin' for 'em, and I don't know how picky they're gonna be when they find 'em. My guess would be not very."

I'm not a mutant.

"I know, but you also don't belong here."

I was reborn here.

"Maybe you don't belong anywhere," he said. "Not my business. I only know that you don't belong *here*, and I'm tryin' to get you to understand that. This war between Phobos and Dullahan is over, only nobody told Phobos that. She's gonna keep fightin' until Mr. Dullahan pulls her out of her hidin' spot and makes her realize what the rest of us already know."

Which is?

"This is Dullahan land. From those mountains there to those mountains there. This wash an' everything in it belongs to them."

Do you mean the town or the people?

Wolff snorted. "There a difference?"

There is.

"Not where I'm standin' there ain't. Maybe other places you got folks that care. Folks that can do somethin'. Out here? No one left."

You're the law.

"Ambrose Dullahan's the law. Me, I'm just a wolf without a pack."

Frustrated, I changed the subject. *What happened to Sugar?*

"Place got burned down. It happens. Now are you gonna listen to me and get back on that train?" I looked at the remains of the bar, and slowly shook my head. I was already on a train, and it was heading for Tod Dullahan. "What is your problem?"

I have a right to be here.

"I ain't talkin' about your rights. I'm talkin' about what you should and shouldn't be doing. This town ain't safe for you."

Safe isn't what I'm worried about.

"It should be."

Spoken like a coward.

The word was off the chalk and I was already showing him the slate before my mind caught up with me. Wolff stared at the markings, and I watched the beast surfacing. Gray and white fur sprouted from his skin. His lips peeled back over sharpening teeth. I merely stared at him, not even wondering if he would complete the change and lunge. There was only the mild interest that he might. I think he saw the green poised in my eyes. I think he knew what I would do to him. True to form, he swallowed the wolf and stood in front of me, a naked old man slowly desiccating in the sun.

"Your funeral," Wolff said, and with that, he left me, returning to the shadow across the street. My funeral was right. I'd been born out of six funerals, so I might as well have one more. "Go home, Jane. Wherever that is. Just go home," he called from across the street, but the deep shadow had eaten him up. He was gone, the voice a manifestation of conscience or something else.

THIRTY

I set off for Burke's, the only other place I could think to go. It was a relatively short walk from Sugar's, or else the town was growing smaller and smaller the longer I remained. Burke's place had changed only slightly. The ice cream truck was parked where it was whenever I hadn't stolen it, and the door to the office had been replaced with some old planks nailed haphazardly together. I opened it carefully and found that it wasn't on hinges. It had just been propped up in the doorway as a halfhearted attempt to keep the desert out.

The chains on the ant rattled as I came in. Burke was on the other side of the room, puttering around his weather machine. Frances sat on the stairs to the apartment. One of the hospital beds was occupied; Sugar lay in it, her eyes faded like worn velvet.

"Jane?" Burke rumbled.

I ignored him, going directly to Sugar. The human fly stirred, buzzing in recognition. She was in bad shape. Bandages wound over her chest and back. She was propped up, her weight off her upper back, where her wings would be. I didn't see them; either they were under her, or under the bandages. Sugar's human arm sported more than one ugly bruise and a few burns. Her fly arm was cracked in a few places, oozing a whitish yellow paste.

What happened?

"Jane here?" Burke rumbled again, shambling closer. I held up a hand, and heard him stop moving.

Sugar glanced around, then gestured to show me she had nothing to write on. I grabbed a legal pad off one of Burke's carts and found a pen nearby. Burke let out an angry growl, but I kept ignoring him. He could stay where he was.

I handed it to Sugar. She took the pad gingerly in the claw of her left hand, and carefully wrote with the other. *{Dullahans.}*

I tapped the message on my slate again, then erased it. *The Sugar Shack was burned down.*

She tapped the message on her pad. I don't know how she managed it, but it really seemed sarcastic. Then, she wrote underneath: *{When did you leave town?}*

I thought about it and did the math in my head. When I had been with the Frog Mothers, it had felt like forever. As soon as I had left, it felt like only a few moments. *5 days.*

Sugar nodded, buzzing thoughtfully. *{Couple nights after you left, some of the Dullahans were at the Shack.}*

Who?

{Tod and his gang, but a few others too. Drank most of the night. Drove off most of my customers too. Nothing unusual about that. Once the Dullahans get going, there's not much to stop them. Late in the night, they were leaving. I didn't see much. Door was open, and then splashing. A stream of water. Watched 3 Dullahans go up in smoke. Dissolve right away. Mutants got the Dullahans and didn't even get Tod, the dumb bastards. So something happens to the water cannon the mutants had, and the Dullahans go out chasing them.}

I shook my head in disgust.

She flipped the page and kept writing. *{Back when the war was really going, it wasn't weird. Fighting all over the wash. In town, outside of town. Mutants going after* *horsemen, horsemen after mutants. Rest of us just kept our heads down, waiting it out. Only it's supposed to be finished. Supposed to be won.}*

Wolff said the same thing.

Sugar buzzed in amusement, then stopped, cradling her many hurts. *{Hell, got me agreeing with Wolff? I should give up now.}*

Sorry, I wrote, smiling in spite of myself.

Sugar waved it off. *{Thought the fight at the Shack was it, but 2 nights ago Tod and his gang come in, telling me I must've helped the mutants. I never talked to a single one of them, but Tod didn't believe me. Or maybe he did and just didn't care. He told me that because I helped set up the Dullahans, some of the pain was on me too.}*

Sugar shuddered, the pen going still. Then she flicked the front page over for a fresh one. Her writing turned into a scrawl, memories making it harder to corral the pen.

{2 of the others held me down. Put me on my stomach. Tod pulled off my wings. Sounded like someone eating a lobster. Pop. Pop. Laughed too when they did it. Then they dragged me out onto the street. Got to watch them burn my place down.}

The pen went still. Sugar was shuddering, but trying hard to fight it.

Now the green was a storm, threatening to drown not just the promontory but everything else. Tod had gone too far. He'd lived too far, really, and was going to keep up his atrocities until someone did something. Every night, move the line just a little further. Until someone put him in the ground. It was going to end in blood between us. Now was as good a time as any.

The baby's arm reached for the orange. Wichita burned.

I was across the room, blinking the memories away. I had to stay in the moment. Had to be ready. Going against Tod when I was addled was a way to find myself tied up in another barn. One I wasn't going to escape. My hand went to where my stitches came free. My skin was baggy, sloughing off to reveal the workings underneath.

"Jane no." Burke stepped in front of me, one stitched-together hand out. Behind him, the doorway beckoned.

I hissed, gesturing at Burke to get out of my way. In my peripheral vision, I watched Frances get up, but she didn't move any closer. She knew what was going to happen, even if Burke didn't.

"Jane no," Burke said again. He shambled to his chalkboard, then checked to see if I had kept moving. I stayed still, but some of that was that I didn't trust myself. The green was seething around me now. If I gave into it, I would be completely gone, and only the tiniest chance of waking up with Tod broken underneath me.

«*Don't go*», Burke wrote. His eyes were actually soft when he turned to me. Pleading. He shook his head once, to emphasize what he'd said.

Why? I demanded, tapping the slate.

"Tod bad." «*If you go, they'll kill you.*»

Why do you care?

«*How can you ask that? I made you.*»

You made me as a toy. Can't even remember where I came from. Who I came from.

"Jane good!" «*It doesn't matter. You're Jane now. Someone new.*» I hissed, heading for the door.

"Jane please!" Burke called, and it was impossible not to hear the desperation in his voice. The weakness. I didn't bother to listen to it. Didn't bother to react. Burke's hold over me, whatever there had ever been, was entirely gone now. I'd found names, real ones, and they were who I owed, not the man who stitched me together. I strode purposefully for the door.

"Jane no!" The roar was close, and I had only turned partway around when Burke's hand closed over my arm. I whirled, finding him wordlessly begging me as he held on.

I stared at him for only a moment. Then I hit him. I pulled my wounded hand back, the same one I had put through my own wall, and hammered it into Burke's face. Where it should have been all along. He had to have seen it coming. I was no boxer. I didn't feint, didn't hide the direction of my violence. My skinned knuckles slammed into his face, between his nose and upper lip. His grip came free from my arm and he staggered backward a few steps. His hands came up to his face and he stared at me, uncomprehending at what I'd done.

"Jane," he rumbled, though the second word he could have spoken was gone. I suspect even he didn't know what to say. I nodded to him, wordlessly informing him that it was over now. That he couldn't touch me without expecting more of the same. His hands moved away, and I saw that I'd ripped a line of the stitches that pulled his lip into a sneer. His flesh was as bloodless as mine, looking like an old, torn piece of sailcloth.

I turned back to the door. I got two more steps, and then I felt a lurch. I hit the wall, and my vision went white for a moment. Then I was on the floor, half-sitting. The stitched-together ant wasn't far, straining on its chain for some reason. Maybe like a dog trying to help its master. Just above me was a brand-new dent in the roll-up door that functioned as the wall for half the lab. Burke was standing where I had been, and I put it together. He had hurled me bodily.

"Jane no," he said, his voice taking the maddeningly placating tone of a father to a daughter. I hissed, telling him exactly what I thought of that. "Jane no." Now he was pleading again, asking me not to. He didn't have to write it. I saw the words in his eyes. *No, don't make me do this. Don't make this happen. Stop what you're doing.*

I got to my feet and found my legs wobbling underneath me. It was a bad hit to be sure, but it was one I could take. I turned back to the door. I had a choice. I would either have to pass within arm's reach of Burke or the ant if I was going to leave this place. I picked Burke.

"Jane no," he rumbled again.

This time I grabbed him as he grabbed me. He went to my shoulders. I went to his neck. My left hand closed over his throat as he gripped me. Frances yelped in horror. Sugar was buzzing from her place on the bed. I hoped she was smart enough to stay out of a fight between two meat golems. I didn't think we were going to do this when I had come home, but Burke had chosen it. He'd been choosing it since I got here; I only just started listening now.

Burke roared again, and I was hissing. My right hand came back and slammed into his face. I felt something in his cheek snap, and as I pulled my fist back, I watched some of his stitches pop. One. Two. Three. His face coming as unzipped as the hand that hit him. With my left hand, I pulled, and something in his neck gave.

Burke snarled, and one of his hands reached downward, gripping between my legs. I would have cried out in pain, but I couldn't do that anymore. The other closed over my throat. And then I was up in the air, struggling futilely in his grip as he lifted me like King Kong. With a roar, he hurled me into the wall of his apartment. I bounced off the cinderblock, tumbling off the wall, hitting the rail by Frances and collapsing onto the floor. Agony bloomed all over me at distinct points, radiating outward to join one another in one encompassing hurt.

The green was roiling, but it wasn't going to swallow me. Something about this was horribly rational. It had to happen. I hauled myself to my feet by the railing of his stairs. My balance was even wobblier now. I didn't care. I'd hurt him too. I could see it in the way his face looked alternately swollen and deflated, the way his neck was hanging at just the slightest bit of an angle. There was more punishment coming his way.

"Jane no," he whispered, bracing himself for my charge.

My hand closed over the leg of his chalkboard, and I flung it. It slammed into his side, and I heard a crunch coming from him even as the board shattered. I followed it, flinging myself at Burke. He stumbled, then fell with me on top of him. My fists were pistons, rising and falling into his body. Something in his chest gave with a crack, then something in his face. I was going to hit him until he stopped moving. No matter how much it took.

Behind me, Frances sobbed. It was a broken sound. I'd heard it last night, but it came out of Jerome Schroeder. The loathing I felt was a living thing. That a boy losing the last person in his world could be the same as me beating this vermin was the worst insult.

Burke's hand closed over my arm, and I was in the air. He flung me into the far wall, where his shelves crumbled at the impact. They broke, fell over, covering me in stinging impacts. I fought to my feet only with difficulty, shedding the heavy objects in a rain. As soon as I did, Burke was on me.

The blow connected with my midsection, and now it was my turn to feel something give. So many connections inside, all the stitching and sutures. Making six corpses into a single living being. I didn't know what he'd popped. Which organ of mine wasn't going to be linked to the others. If he'd managed to do something lasting, or if it was merely an unpleasant sensation, a reminder that I wasn't human anymore.

The agony doubled me over. The second hit came down on the back of my head, and I was on the ground, vision spinning.

"Jane no," he said with more conviction.

I tried to get up, but he hit me again. This one was in the middle of my back, hurling me to the floor. The world blinked out for a moment. The green crashed, but it never took me. There would be no merciful darkness. No cleansing rage.

"Jane stop," Burke said.

I put my palms flat on the floor and pushed myself up. He hit me again, even harder. Something popped in my back. My head bounced off the concrete floor. The agony was all over me now, seething with the green. My arms felt so far away from me, it was taking forever to get them to respond. But I planted them on the floor and pushed.

And Burke hit me again. "Jane stop!" he roared. I couldn't have gotten up if I tried. The hole in the wall had me, pulling me down into its hungry mouth. I had nothing left in my arms. Nothing in my legs. All I had was my hatred. I put my palms flat on the ground and tried to get up anyway.

"Jane stop," Burke said softly. Another blow didn't come. "Jane stop," he nearly whispered.

I heard a scrape, and turned myself over only with difficulty. Now I was on my back, like a turtle doomed to a sun death. Burke limped back to me, holding a shard of his blackboard, a piece of chalk clutched in his hand. He squatted down next to me. I stared at the ruin I'd made of his face. The line of stitches was entirely split, showing off gum and broken tooth.

«*I made you. I don't want to break you.*»

I reached for my slate to respond, and only noticed then that it was gone. I spotted it by the stairs to the apartment. It must have come off when he threw me. I could only shake my head.

He smudged the message out and wrote another over the cloudy remains. «*If you go, the Dullahans will kill you.*» I shut my eyes and nodded. The scratching on the chalkboard opened them. «*Stay here.*» Barely legible over the cloudy white of his former words. I fought to stand, getting my wobbly legs under me. Burke tensed, his free hand clenching into a ball.

"Jane no."

I shook my head, staggering not for the front door but for where my slate had fallen. Only then did I remember Frances and Sugar were in the room. Both watched Burke and me silently, taut as guitar strings. As though either one of them could have done anything about the two raging meat golems. I bent over with difficulty, picking the slate off the ground. A corner had snapped off, and the chalk had been broken down to a nub.

"Jane what?" Burke rumbled.

Tod needs to pay.

Burke let out a frustrated growl. He stared at me, the wheels moving behind his eyes. Finally, he lurched out the door. A moment later he returned, clutching one of the rusted shovels in hand. I braced myself, resolving to be ready if this was the end of things. Instead, he tossed it to me. Then he picked up another piece of his broken blackboard and scrawled on it. He threw that to me as well. It was a map, and X marked the spot.

"Jane go."

I traced the path of the map with my finger. It led out to the endless fields east of town. I limped from the office, clutching the shovel. I threw it in the back of the ice cream truck and once again stole the vehicle. It felt, as I turned the keys, that this would be the last time. I left Quartzsite behind and found the place the map indicated: a piece of the desert that looked exactly like the rest of it. There wasn't a saguaro cactus that looked like a devil's fork, but there should have been. I stopped the truck and started to dig. Out on the horizon, the swarms of ants went about their business as I found the last little piece of myself.

Jane & Burke

Thirty-One

The trench was twenty feet long. Its sides were ragged, like the edges of my broken skin. I had been digging all through the day and deep into the night.

I found the first bone at the beginning of my labor. A fingerbone, small and yellowed. I knelt, picking it off the ground with reverence, and turning it over in my hand. As though I could see something within it. I thought of taking it to the Frog Mothers, to connect it to me. Then I thought I should get the rest of the bones, whatever hadn't made its way into my body. The pieces of the woman that Burke had judged unworthy to be part of his child. He hadn't bothered to drive her back to wherever he had dug her up. He'd just taken her here, a short way out of town, and put the leftovers in a shallow grave.

So I kept digging, and when I found another bone, I carefully placed it at the edge of this grave. Initially, I kept them separate, laying one bone next to another, but there were too many. Soon, it became a stack. I'm no good at anatomy, despite what people think when they see my stitches. I couldn't be certain what I was looking at, but the pile seemed a little big.

When I dug up the second skull, I knew I was looking at more than one woman.

I kept digging, and I kept finding bones. I placed them on the edge of the growing trench and went back to work. I was chest-deep in the hole before it stopped giving up bones, but I found more in the walls. So I hollowed it out, my meat golem muscles chewing through the soil easily. My body was little more than a collection of pain, but pain couldn't stop me. Not even the shard that twisted in my heart every time another desert-battered bone came up on the end of my spade.

Twenty feet long and five feet wide. The night sky gave me enough light to work by, the way it never would have back home. All of Harry's stars overhead, blind but bright. Enough to see the swatches of sad white. Enough to know this wasn't merely a grave. It was a mass grave, giving up body after body as I dug. Some of it was me. Or almost me. Or could be me. I didn't have a word for any of it. Even after everything, I didn't know what to call this. I didn't want a word, either. Whatever this was, it was too awful to name.

Rachel Prager. Lorena Quintanilla. Haseya. Sadie Schroeder. I thought I had over half of them, but there were so many more here. More than ten. Maybe more than a hundred. My heart tangled up in my chest. These remains deserved better than some pit in the middle of nowhere. They deserved to be back where they came from. Somewhere at least a little sacred. Somewhere they could rest.

I heard the truck coughing from far out. I ignored it until the headlights splashed over my struggling form in the trench, becoming obvious it was here for me. It wasn't Morgan Dullahan's truck; I knew that as soon as I didn't see the line of gold beneath the tires. The brakes squeaked and the door groaned as it opened.

"Jane?" The voice belonged to Barrow White. The ghoul's feet crunched over the sand, and his skinny legs made the headlights of his truck momentarily blink. Barrow stood over me, little more than a shadow in the gloom. I was slow. I was beaten. I was exhausted, in both body and heart. But I felt no danger from him. Nothing that raised my hackles. He was the one who looked defeated, his narrow shadow slumped in its place.

"I'm sorry you had to see this," he said finally, sounding almost sad. He gestured to the side of the trench where the bones were piled. "I didn't realize it was so many. You lose track when it's happening. You don't mean to, but you lose track of them."

I kept digging while he talked. If he was going to say anything, it would be to absolve himself. That was fine by me, but he wasn't going to find forgiveness here. I think I might have been the one person who could offer it, but I was out of mercy. The hole I'd punched in my wall had started the meal, and Quartzsite had eaten whatever was left.

Barrow's next words, though, surprised me. "I never wanted to be a ghoul," he said. "Y'know, once we knew that such things were possible. I wanted to be a vampire. I saw that Bela Lugosi picture when I was a bit younger. Not really a kid, but younger. Most magical thing I'd ever seen. I know he's supposed to be the bad guy, but I cheered for him. I didn't want the hunters to get him. So when the monsters came, I wanted to be the mesmerizing nobleman with the power. Everyone wants to be Bela Lugosi. No one wants to be Dwight Frye."

Barrow began to pace, out of the headlights, then back into them. I didn't know how much of what he was saying was really for me, or if it was only because he had no one else who would listen. His former verbose manner, so ostentatiously articulate, was gone, the mask dropped. Now he spoke like the man he had been rather than the monster he had sculpted himself to be.

"This was in '46. I don't know if you remember what it was like then. People knew something was afoot, but not everybody wanted to believe. *I* believed. Thought there was finally a pot of gold at the end of that rainbow. So I waited and waited for a vampire to find me. To make me rich and handsome and all the things I never was. Left my window open. Cut myself so he could smell the blood. Didn't work, but I never lost faith. Albus White got me instead. The White family was already pretty well established then. Not as big as it is now, you understand, but we were already in two states. Of course, I didn't know that then. Just that I got taken out of my house one night."

He chuckled. "Do you know how ghouls are made? I found out. I had myself a little shack back then at the edge of Quartzsite, where I kept my beetle zoo. Still have it, if you're interested. Well, I wake up, and my bedroom's full of the smell of grave dirt. Tall, skinny shadows are all around my bed. Then they grab me, tie me up, blindfold me, drag me off. When they remove the blindfold, I'm in this big house in the middle of the desert. White Manor, they call it, but it's a manor the same way my truck is a limousine. We do have such grand words for things, but really, it's just a crumbling bit of life the desert forgot to eat up. Anyway, we have a traditional ghoul meal. I'm fighting it, but they hold me down, and they force every last bit of that person down my throat until I'm going to burst. Then they bury me."

Barrow chewed over the memory. "Like every other ghoul, I dug my way out. Maybe that makes you go a little crazy. Maybe it's just that being a ghoul changes your mind inside. I don't know. Don't know what it means to be any other kind of monster, either. We're all alone. It's like being out in the desert, when the headlights are the only light anywhere. And you stand in them, and can see others, out there in the night, standing in their circles of light. You can call to each other, but you can't really hear what anyone else has to say."

Barrow cleared his throat. "I didn't want to be a ghoul, but that was what happened. I thought I should just play the hand I was dealt. Anyway, it wasn't the first time I felt that way. I didn't want to be me, either. If I could have picked, I would have been Rock Hudson, but I couldn't. I was me. It's all we can ever be, I guess. And you, you would have been nothing unless Burke dug the pieces of you up and brought them to life."

Barrow coughed, suddenly self-conscious, like he had only just remembered there was someone else present. "Burke said he sent you out here. Said it was either that or he'd have to kill you. He doesn't want to kill you, Jane."

I found another bone, picking it out of the dirt and holding it up. It was slender, maybe from an arm or the lower part of the leg. It was scarred. A lot of them were, from the brutal desert conditions. I ran a thumb along the scarring; it was rough with irregularly-spaced notches, but the same length of cut.

"Burke isn't a sentimental man. I've had to accept that the longer I've known him. We've been partners for longer than you've been alive." That last had barbs on it. I kept digging, knowing I would find another little piece soon enough, to be added to the collection.

"I mean, it wasn't just you. It was never just you. There were so many, I lost count. I never paid that much attention. Wasn't for me, anyway. He kept making you over and over again, hoping that the next one would stick around. And you know what? She never did. Some of them stayed for a week. One of them stayed nearly a month. I don't know how long you stayed. I don't remember."

A petty part of me wanted to reach for my broken slate and tell him, *I didn't.* It continued to bounce against my chest as I dug.

"I don't know why he kept making you. He never saw what was staring him in the face: that none of you would ever stay. The next one would abandon him, and the next one. Kept breaking his heart, and then he'd glue it back together, and the next one of you would break it all over again. I don't think the damn thing is in any kind of shape anymore. It's been broken and reset so many times, it's just glue."

Barrow sighed. "Then he finds Frances. I suppose she's the next best thing. But what kind of monster moons over a human? Humans are food, potential ones of us, but they're not us. Burke looks like a fool parading around with her. The whole town laughs at him behind his back, you know."

I paused. Burke knew, because I knew. When I started bringing Nick around the Nocturnist. Oh, some of the girls liked him because they thought he was a gangster. Some of the other girls liked him because they wanted to cut him up and add some part of him to a new meat golem. But there was always a blade on it. That I was easy because my boyfriend was a human. We all had regulars with crushes, but I picked a breathing pink-skin whose only power was not being scared of wards. When I walked into rooms and everyone was suddenly silent, I knew. When eyes followed us on the streets, I knew. Burke knew too, and he took it. For whatever reason, he took it.

"He's stopped trying, but it's like I told you before. I don't think he's stopped hoping. It's because he's running out of raw materials. Not enough pretty girls dying anymore, I guess. He hasn't said so, but I think that's why he wants that money. From Phobos and the Dullahans, and for his resurrection process. So he can move somewhere with enough pretty dead girls to start a family." Barrow barked out a bitter laugh. "It's not going to end up any different. Why would it?"

The last was so quiet, I almost missed it. I paused, looking up at Barrow's silhouette and cocking my head in question.

"Why do you reject him?" Barrow sounded honestly curious but there was a broken edge to his voice, like a teacup with a chipped lip. I pointed to my chest and cocked my head again. "Yes, Jane. I'm asking you a question. I don't have the others here, do I? Of all the ones who left, you're the only one who ever came back."

I didn't know how to tell Barrow that I didn't come back for Burke. I didn't know if I wanted to tell him. If he didn't already know, that truth felt too personal to share. Too much of me for someone who hadn't earned the right to know. So I went back to digging.

"Well, you've found the big secret. All of them are buried here. The parts we didn't use. This place is almost like coming home for you. As close to one as you'll ever have."

The needle was there, in the comment, but then it was gone, because the blade of the shovel bit into the earth and I felt something on the end. I lifted it out of the sand, and there, the desert rolling off it, was a skull. It wasn't the first skull I had found in this mass grave. They studded the lip of the trench, staring off into the dark.

This one was broken. The face was intact, but the rest of it had been cracked open from the top. There had been a couple others I'd found in similar shape through the course of the day and night. I reached down to pick it up, and as I did, my fingers recoiled. A physical force, like two magnets turned the wrong end inward, pushed my hand away. Above me, Barrow was still talking, but I didn't hear him. I knelt by the skull, taking in the contours of it, barely lit by the moon and stars. As though I could see a face in it. Divine how the flesh had attached, see the eyes, if they were blue or green or brown, whether the hair was long or short, free or styled. But it was a skull, lying in the thirsty dirt of the desert. It couldn't tell me anything. It. She. Every bone in this trench had belonged to a woman, discarded because it hadn't fit Burke's needs.

I reached down to the skull. A faint electric ache traced my fingertips. I touched bone, taking the skull into my hands like an injured bird. The break was ragged, eating up the entire back end. He'd needed the brain intact. The brain. My brain.

I stared into the eye sockets. And they expanded, the darkness in them the dark of a movie theater. I felt the curtains parting, and it was showing me what this was. Maybe it was an ecstatic connection to the remains, or maybe it was the lingering power of the Frog Mothers' spell. It didn't matter, because I was gone.

Thirty-Two

The weight in my arms was so familiar. I felt it every time the green crashed in on me. It was the little girl, and I waited for this memory, one that I knew so well, to leave me as it always did. To strand me in the present without any care. Sunlight rippled through the leaves of the orange tree, and the little girl reached and reached, like she was trying to touch the moon.

"Nora?" I turned. Nora. Nora was me. The joy of being known to another exploded in my chest. A man stood in the doorway of a house. A cozy house, with a tiny back porch. He looked like the kind of handsome all-American man who should be holding a football. He was wearing slacks, a checked shirt tucked into it. His hair was short, receding a little bit, but I thought in an attractive way. Could have been the square jaw.

"What are you doing?"

I felt myself smile. I wanted to touch my face, to know that this was truly my smile. Me. "Viv likes the oranges. She was bawling, and I thought this would calm her down."

"You were right," he said, coming down the two wooden steps onto the lawn. We had a lawn. We. A ring sparkled on his finger, and I could feel a matching band on mine.

Then it hit me. Viv. Vivian. The baby's name was Vivian. Having a name to match with the memory that had haunted me for five years was like sunlight through those leaves. I turned to look at the little girl. Really look. She was grinning at the man. Her father. I saw parts of him in her face, and then there were parts I couldn't identify, but were familiar. Me. I was there. Nora.

Vivian's hair was pale blonde, sparse over her scalp, and she wore a floral print dress over her diaper. Her hands opened and closed to her father as she grinned with two teeth. Beyond the border of our street was an endless orange grove, the trees eclipsing the horizon, filling the air with tangy citrus.

I turned to my husband and his face was somewhere else. We were in the living room of our house. I knew it, though I'd never seen it before. It was small, but it was all we needed. The three of us were on the floor, between the couches. It was night, only a single candle lighting the three of us. Vivian sat nearby, her chubby finger tracing patterns on the wood of the floor.

"We have to go," my husband whispered.

"Where are we going, Cal?" I asked him.

Cal. Calvin Lis. I knew his name all at once, and forgetting it felt unnatural. Though he had been married to Nora, not to Jane. I was a different person. But I knew this man. I could rattle off everything about him. He was from Kansas, and he came out west to build movie sets. He was good at it, too. He liked the dry weather because he had a baseball injury in his right elbow, and it would swell up whenever it rained. I met him at a studio party that I'd gone to with my friends, trying to meet stars, but instead I met Cal and fell in love.

"These monsters, they're from the pictures."

"You think the pictures made them?"

Cal shrugged. "Maybe. I don't know. But we need to get out of here. Go back east."

"Who do we know back east?"

"I mean Kansas. I got family there."

"What are you gonna do there?"

"I'm a carpenter. I'll make real houses instead of fake ones. I think I remember how it goes. You add four walls instead of three."

The flame was somewhere else, and then it was huge, covering the horizon. I knew where I was now. The Glassing of Wichita. We'd made it to Kansas, just like Cal had wanted, came the bitter thought as I watched the tripods stalk through the flames. They disappeared in the pillars of smoke only to reappear, the pale rays from their weapons lighting fires and melting metal wherever they swept.

Vivian was heavy in my arms because she was several years older. She was a baby no longer, now a little girl, her hair thick but still pale blonde. I saw her father in her face, but there were still the maddening parts that had to be me. Tears streaked through the grime on her face as she watched. All around us, the tall prairie grass whipped in the hot winds as Wichita was consumed.

"Nora. Nora, we need to go," Cal was trying to pull me along. A line of survivors, battered and terrified, fled out into the prairie. We were all armed, but what good were weapons? How could we possibly survive in the face of that? When they had their tripods, what could we possibly do?

We could run. In a hideous irony, we ran west. Right back where we'd come from. I saw this now, in much the same way I'd seen the trail of the Schroeders. This, though, was from behind my eyes. Nora's brain had been harvested from her body and put into me, and it had brought with it these memories. So I could live them. Watching helplessly as tornadoes writhed over the prairie, the deep comfort of Vivian's too-thin arms wrapping around my neck. Her weight that I'd carry no matter what. We stayed in refugee camps, always mobile, and always shrinking.

Then we made it to the desert. Our group was small by then. Only a handful of people who had somehow survived the nightmares. We were camped out in the hills, what little we had for wards strung up around us.

I realized that I knew those hills. I'd driven into them on an errand for Burke. This wasn't the same place exactly, but the mutant clan had been close by. Lightning crawled across the sky, but there was no rain. That, at least, was mercy.

As I made the realization, I saw them in the flashes of lightning, insect faces emerging from the dark. Not just mutants, but the giant ants as well. They made a high-pitched warbling sound, as maddening as a banshee's wail. That fake rotten smell I'd never forget hung in the air.

The stench of ammonia hit me, and one of our screams found a shrill pitch. In horror, I watched a man whose face I knew dissolve, an advancing ant spraying him with acid from its jaws.

"Nora! Get Viv and run!" Cal screamed.

And I did it. Vivian was sobbing. I clutched her to my chest and I forced my exhausted legs to run. Cal was shouting, ordering the others to flee. But it was too late. I knew it and I think Cal knew it too. The mutants and their creatures descended into the camp. I don't know how much of their purpose was to turn us, or if this was just some compulsion to mayhem. I suppose it didn't matter. We were running, Calvin, Vivian, and me, not really running for anyplace. There was nowhere to run. Nowhere we could escape to.

Cal was just behind me, exhorting me to go faster. And then he was gone. I turned to see a giant ant lifting him from the ground, mandibles around his abdomen. He was still screaming to me to run, even when his voice went wet and red. The ants were all around him in a hellish wave, their exoskeletons clattering against each other, the vinegar stench as loud as my blood in my ears. Vivian was sobbing now as I clutched her. I ran until I thought my lungs would burst. Then a hiss hit my ears along with the smell of burning flesh.

Mine. I howled, staggering and nearly dropping Vivian. My arm smoked, threading white into the air. My skin curdled and split. The ant that had sprayed me had stopped, and now others were pulling up as well, their acid streaking over the desert. I cradled my daughter close to my chest and forced myself to go, even as I felt more caustic streams splashing against my legs and arms.

It couldn't stop me, not when I had Vivian in my arms. I ran until my legs felt like little more than bloody stumps. The sounds of the ants, and the screaming of my companions, receded behind me, and the streets of Quartzsite were ahead. I made for them, not knowing where it was. Just knowing there might be a place to hide out the night. A place that the mutants and their creatures wouldn't follow.

The streets were deserted. Behind me was an impenetrable cloak, silent now, the insects content with what prey they had managed to take. I moved as quickly as I could, holding Vivian to me. My limbs were on fire, and becoming lighter with every moment. Bits of me turned to air. I staggered into the streets, looking from building to building, the slumping shacks of this outpost in the desert. It looked even lonelier then than it did now. By that late in the war, the monsters had taken the houses. Now they were on the other sides of doors and it was humans living in the shadows. But out here, I thought maybe. Maybe I could find someone to help.

And then I saw a light. I knew the place. It was Burke's office, but Nora had never seen it before. To her, it was just a chance at salvation. She crept toward it, going as silently as she could. After the long night, the horror of what she had seen, the light was an atavistic comfort. A signal that everything could be all right again. That she'd see the sun. That Vivian would.

Nora—I—the question of identity blurred. I wasn't Nora, but I was. We shared the same brain, though it had been pushed through the veil of death on a bolt of lightning. I carried Vivian to the edges of the property, then I remembered pausing, setting Vivian down. The little girl's eyes were wide, and they looked silver in the moonlight. I thought of Sadie's eyes then, a connection Nora couldn't have ever made. I touched Viv's cheek.

"Stay here. Hide. I'm going to check that place, and I'll be back."

"Mama," she protested, but I touched her cheek. My arm was ruined by the acid, hideous burns stretching from wrist to bicep.

"Viv, don't worry. We got this far, and we ain't gonna stop. I promise you. I'll be right back. Hide here until then." I indicated the piles of garbage that hemmed in Burke's place.

Vivian nodded. She'd become good at hiding. It was the first game we ever played, and I suppose, in many ways, the last too. She slunk into a cave formed by old car parts and a rusted bicycle. I left her behind, limping for the door, cradling my burned body. I was in bad shape. Death probably wasn't far off from me if I couldn't find a doctor. I didn't know what to do with Vivian. Something. She had to live. I—Nora—thought of her chubby hand reaching for the orange. The last true moment of peace. Then the Glassing of Wichita, the moment hope died. Those memories burned themselves into Nora's brain, writ large for the next user.

The roll-up doorway from the garage was open, and I reached it, leaning heavily on the jamb. I couldn't believe my eyes. It was a doctor's office. There were hospital beds and everything. Not terribly clean, but by the standards of someone who had been sleeping in a ditch, it was immaculate. It was a place I could go, be healed. Be saved.

Then a monster shambled into view from behind a curtain. Hunchbacked and misshapen, Burke O'Hare gave me a smile, his lip pulling back from a line of stitches. I stepped back in horror. Burke—I knew him even if Nora didn't—held his hands up.

"Lady safe," he said.

"I am?" I felt myself saying.

He nodded. "Lady hurt."

"There were giant ants. They got me with acid."

Burke nodded again, turning to his equipment. He went to a tank and filled a jelly jar with a strong-smelling clear liquid. "This help."

I took an unsteady step forward. "You'll help me." He nodded, then gestured to one of the beds. "Thank you, sir. Bless you. Bless you." I was already thinking about Vivian, about getting her inside, to this apparently safe place. Burke was moving around, but I didn't think of him. Vivian was far too important. I heard a creak of metal, and then I turned.

Burke was moving quickly, holding a steel bar over his head. A steel bar he'd shown me—Jane—once before. The skullcracker he said was for the mutants. It came down, and my vision went white. I was on the floor then. My head was numb, crimson streaks over my eyes in stinging waves. A pool spreading by my head. I peered out into the dark and I saw Vivian watching me. Tears fell down her cheeks. I tried to tell her not to look, to close her eyes, just to run, but my mouth worked without sound. Just open and close, open and close. The skullcracker came down again and it was the last thing Nora Lis ever heard.

THIRTY-THREE

I held my own skull in my hands like a talisman. I stood in the trench as above me, Barrow rambled on. I set Nora's skull on the lip of the trench with reverence. Then I surged up onto the ground next to Barrow. His confused muttering turned into a scream as my hand wrapped around his throat.

I think he thought I had lost control, but I hadn't. I felt Nora with me, Vivian in my arms, but I wasn't out of control. I knew precisely what I was doing. My hand found a home right under Barrow's chin, and his words were choked off. I lifted him like he was a paper doll, then hurled him into the front of the truck. He hit the fender with a thump and fell to the sand, writhing in agony. It would have been so easy to finish him then. But he knew. He knew what had set me off.

"I never killed them!" he wheezed.

I took a step forward. *No, you only buried them out here. Treated them like trash.* Maybe he heard my thoughts. Out here, in the desert night, anything was possible under an infinite sky.

"I was only helping a friend, Jane! And if it meant a little extra food, that's all it was. I didn't do anything! Nothing that makes me deserve this."

I moved forward, dropping to one knee. Then I held the slate in front of the headlights. He blinked through the beams swirling with dust and tiny insects. *Remember?* It was the only word I could manage. I wasn't a creature of communication then. I was a spirit of vengeance. I was a Fury. For Nora Lis and all the others. All of those Burke didn't wait for. All of those he'd killed and defiled.

"I remember them. Kind of." My brow furrowed and he quailed from me, hands up in terror. "Bits and pieces from all of you, I remember. Your legs...I remember exhuming them up from that boneyard in Ehrenberg, but they weren't quite right. Burke added some muscle on your calf from another girl. There was a rotten spot. I remember because Burke was so mad. She had the perfect legs, except for that spot. Like a bruise on a banana. So we dug up another girl from the same place, and lucky us, she had a workable liver and spleen too. I remember that part."

I tapped the word.

"I'm sorry. You see how many there were. Another girl was missing some teeth, and so Burke found a girl whose teeth were intact. She was fresh, but I didn't think to ask."

You knew.

"I never knew!"

I tapped the words. Then added *You lied.*

"No, I never knew. I could guess, but I never asked! What was I supposed to do? He's my friend. He's the only friend I have."

I stared into Barrow's watery eyes, and I saw something in them. Saw something that I'd seen in Nick's eyes, and in Cal's eyes. Saw just what Barrow meant when he said the word "friend." I already knew, if I was going to be honest, but now it couldn't be denied. Barrow was broken before I'd gotten there, and breaking more every single day. Burke would keep at it until there was nothing left of the ghoul. And Barrow'd be happy for it.

"Don't kill me," Barrow whispered. I stood up. Now I knew he was seeing those legs he had remembered. The ones with the bruise like a banana. "I didn't want to be a ghoul," Barrow whispered. "But now I can't be anything else. So I want another night of it. As many as I can get."

I picked up the remains of Nora's skull. I couldn't leave it out there. I'd have to do something about these bones, but not right then. They had kept for years. They'd keep for one more night. But Nora's skull couldn't stay. It was a talisman of sorts, connected to me in a way none of the others were. I put it in the freezer of the ice cream truck and drove back to Quartzsite. Burke and I needed to have one last conversation, and I could end what I hadn't before.

Thirty-Four

I pulled up in front of Burke's office, seeing everything with a new old mind. Adding context to this place made it sinister. It was deep in the night, the same it had been when Nora Lis found it. I was in pain, too, my body coming unraveled. Burke had been broken to make me, and in the process broke me as well.

The green crashed around me, but it never once threatened to submerge me. I operated with chilling clarity. I was here to kill my creator. Wouldn't take them long to find me either, if I thought for one second Peter Wolff would care who tore Burke apart. The only one who did was that little ghoul, left crying in the desert. That would be the end of him, too.

Something was wrong, though. I couldn't point a finger at precisely what. Merely that the office looked off. The plank that had served as the door was simply gone. As I pulled up, I saw that it lay not far from the doorway, on top of the sand, not yet eaten by the desert.

I stalked over it, my rage giving way to a bit of caution. The light was on inside, just like the night Nora had come here. Death lived in this place, and maybe that's what slowed my steps as I came to the portal. Or maybe I knew. That it had only been a matter of time, and that time had run out.

The ant was on the other side of the doorway. It had been cut to pieces, each joint expertly sliced. It lay on the ground, looking like a wooden toy some child had gotten tired of and then ruthlessly taken apart.

The lab was in chaos as well. Most of the beds had been turned over. Some sported cuts through both mattresses and metal. Frances lay among the wreckage, her head cleanly removed from her shoulders. The woman as much a discarded toy as the ant. An act of shocking callousness, but in many ways expected. Every monster who knew her, from Burke to her murderer, had seen her as little more than an object to be used and discarded.

A rattle drew my attention. The closet door opened and trash came spilling out, along with Sugar. I ran to her, helping my friend to her unsteady feet. She swayed drunkenly, her human hand holding my shoulder for support. The bandages wrapping her body were stained, but not wet.

I gestured to the room and raised my eyebrows. Sugar nodded to me, and then to the blackboard that I had shattered. The pieces still lay willy-nilly about the room. I set her down against a wall and she leaned forward, to keep the places where her wings had been torn from touching the cinderblock. I retrieved a bit of the blackboard and a nubbin of chalk and handed it to her.

{The Dullahans,} she wrote. As though it could be anyone else. I raised my eyebrows and gestured more emphatically. Sugar's fly face was unreadable. Her mouthparts worked compulsively as she rubbed the words away and wrote a new message. *{They thought Burke knew where Phobos and the mutants were hiding. They came to ask.}*

Where is Burke?

{He wouldn't answer, so they took him.}

I rocked back on my heels. The Dullahans would be torturing him already. My creator deserved everything they gave and more, but it rankled.

Tod didn't have the right to do that to Burke. He was mine. Whatever pain he was going to suffer was mine to cause. For Nora Lis and whoever else he hadn't waited for. I stood up, and turned only when I heard the whisper of chalk.

{*Where are you going?*} Sugar demanded.

To get him back.

Sugar got up with difficulty, hauling herself to her feet with the railing of the stairs. She shook her massive fly head, then took another step, reaching for my arm. Her grip, her human grip, was soft. There was no presumption in it, the way others had tried. A pleading to the touch, one that would go away in a stiff breeze. She shook her head again, slower this time.

I took my arm back gently, and I touched her hand once. I gave her a nod I hoped was reassuring. I had no intention of dying, but if I did, it would be what I had to do. I didn't learn that from Nick, but I'd seen him do it. Knowing there was no one left to finish a vile task, but if you let it go undone, then someone would get away with it. I'd read the books, but I'd never really known what that little phrase meant. That shard of fire in my soul that would never stop hurting if I let it burn.

At least they were all in one place now. I went to the cabinet. The last time I had seen this, Burke was taking out the weapon he would use to kill Nora. I hesitated, feeling like I was walking over my own grave. I forced myself to open it.

The skullcracker hung there on its rack. "For mutants," Burke had told me. Had lied to me. I don't know if he realized he'd killed the woman who gave me my brain. Or if he had killed all of them, and it was some kind of joke when he showed me the weapon. I don't know if that even mattered. Even if Nora was the only one he had murdered, she was one too many. I couldn't touch the weapon, though. It was too close to the violence I'd seen. To the violence Vivian had seen.

Fortunately, that wasn't what I wanted. I took down the water cannon and its backpack. The metal canister sloshed nearly full. I pulled a single strap over my shoulder and held the gun itself. Headless horsemen hated running water. Dunk them in a river, and they died. Supposedly. I'd never seen it, but I'd be testing it that night. Tod wasn't going to let me come onto the ranch again and live. He knew, same as I did, that we were going to collide. He just didn't know it was tonight.

Sugar leaned heavily against the railing. Her face was unreadable.

Thanks Sugar.

{For what?}

Not stopping me.

{Honey, I can barely stand. Do whatever you got to.}

I got into the ice cream truck, shrugging off the backpack and setting it in the cab next to me. The engine rumbled, coughing and sick like the rest of this place.

Thirty-Five

It felt like I should be driving on a field of fire, but it was just an ice cream truck on the dirt roads north of town. The night was endless now; the sun would never rise on me again. I'd seen too much. The sad part was I didn't even know everything. There was still one name in the wind, still a part of me that I couldn't know. I'd held her bones, I was sure, but there were too many to sift through, too many to ever know for certain. It was Nora I held close now, her final moments cycling through my mind like a movie theater that only played a single feature. At the end of each repetition, it froze on the broken expression on Vivian's face. Though it filled me with a rage stormier than I'd ever felt, the green never threatened to swallow me.

No one stopped me as I crossed the nebulous border onto the Dullahan Rantch. The road wound through electrical fences into the fields of artificial anthills. Passing the anthills, like voids in the night, was an admission, an admission that I was there to kill or die. From their fences to their antprods, the Dullahans had the power to kill me with a touch. It didn't really matter. Nora Lis had died for me. Only fair if I died for her, I guess.

As the road snaked over uneven ground, I peered into the dark, ready for the sparking hoofbeats of the Dullahans. I saw nothing in the preternatural gloom. They were out there, somewhere. Waiting, perhaps. An hourglass in the backs of their thoughts, the sand nearly all collected at the bottom. Sand that was alive with ants.

I crested a rise, and the Dullahan compound spread out before me. Closest was the barn, the site of my torture. It had been partly fixed, the wreckage of the collapsed half in relatively orderly piles, the walls beginning to be repaired. If this was where they took their prisoners, the place the Dullahans designated for such work, Burke would be in there. The stitches along my formerly severed hand burned with the memory. The hand was still far away, twitching with the life of the other women, playing at the echoes of a dead will.

I pulled off the dirt road and shut the car down. Now all I could hear was the wash of wind in the desert, and the faint clatter of the ants off in their anthills. Their rotten-fruit scent permeated the dry air. I pulled on the backpack, buckling the belts over my chest and abdomen and tightening the ones at my shoulders. My hurts bloomed anew as the straps cut across the bruises covering me. I hefted the cannon, feeling its negligible weight. My borrowed finger found the trigger and I convinced it to squeeze.

Nothing happened. My heart stuttered as, for a moment, I wondered if the thing was broken, mentally cursing Burke for letting his weapon against the hollows go to pot. Out here, in the middle of Dullahan territory...now the green crashed inward, ready to consume the thoughts of Nora. The thoughts that kept me there.

I forced myself to breathe. I thought of Nora, of the feel of Vivian in her arms, the smell of her hair. I thought of Les and of Fern, who loved pieces of me. And I thought of Nick, asleep on my couch. How he was too far away to touch.

Burke was too arrogant to keep a broken weapon. He had been expecting the horsemen. Too slow when they arrived, sure, but he believed himself to be ready. The cannon wasn't broken. I just wasn't using it right.

By the light of the stars and moon, I found a catch along the silvery surface. I flipped it, then pulled the trigger again. This time, a stream of sour water sprayed over the sand. It stank of mildew, but it was running water.

Armed, I approached the barn cautiously. The horsemen were cautious, so there would be at least one guard, no matter what. Wouldn't break my heart if I had to hose down any of Tod's little gang. I was only bringing what they had coming. That's what I told myself, but the truth was I'd never killed anyone, and although the rage whispered it would be easy, I knew it wasn't. The look Nick got on those rare occasions when he talked about the war, Night or Day War, told me it didn't go away. I'd carry whoever I killed tonight with me forever, tucked away in a black place in my heart, next to the names. No matter what, though, I couldn't hesitate, because none of them would.

The front of the barn had been freshly restored, the new door hanging open in an invitation, a bit of lamplight spilling out. I shook off the heebies climbing up my spine; I was being paranoid. They weren't expecting me. They couldn't be.

I crept to the door and peered inside. Lanterns lit the room. I was grateful the flames were small and behind glass. The barn was looking better than I was. The skin on my hand had unraveled to my wrist, forming a lacy cuff of dead flesh. I ached from the beating Burke had given me, and my limbs were heavy from the day and night of hard labor. Phantom pain still ran up and down the forearm Tod had cut from my body. The Dullahans had fixed the barn up in a way I hadn't managed with myself. Maybe couldn't.

Burke was there, shackled a post on the other side of the barn, a mirror of where I had been held. His head slumped down, his shoulders limp. I saw no guard.

I slunk in, gaze fixed on my creator. He was as utterly still as the night itself. His shirt had been partly torn off his body, revealing his misshapen torso. Whoever his creator was had been indifferent at best to what they had made. Muscle and skin had been stitched together with no real desire to make it look beautiful, or even functional. It protruded in unnatural places, the bones themselves at awkward angles. His flesh wasn't like my patchwork skin, either; his was a uniform jaundiced yellow, as though he had been left in the sun to rot before he had been assembled and brought to life.

That wasn't what held my attention, though. It was the scorch mark over his heart. A black smudge on his chest, that at first looked like nothing more than a smear of soot. I came closer, helpless to do anything else. The flesh around the hurt was cooked, bubbled, grayish fading to red, haloing it. An electrical burn.

I made the only sound I could as my trembling hand gently lifted his head by the chin. Burke's eyes were sightless, his face slack. The place where I had burst his stitches flapped limply. He was dead.

"I gotta admit, Plain Jane, I'm pleased as a fly in shit you're so goddamn predictable."

I whirled. Tod Dullahan stepped out from behind the shelves by the door. He'd been lurking there the whole time, watching me. Probably enjoying my mounting horror as I realized that Burke was gone. That every bit of revenge, of truly understanding who I was, why I was, had been stolen.

The horseman toyed with the antprod in his hand, the end arcing blue lightning back and forth. "All them others thought I was plumb loco to miss out on the raid." Like I said, something about a woman who couldn't speak always brought out the raconteur in men. I was frozen in terror, suddenly back to the moment when he had tortured me in this barn. "Your old friend Burke told us where to find Phobos and all her little friends. The boss wanted all of us to go along with him, wipe out those bugbrains all at once. But I started thinkin' about my girl Plain Jane. I started thinkin' she was just crazy enough to come and rescue her old boss."

It was almost funny. He thought I was here for a rescue. I suppose I was, but only so I could kill Burke myself. But I couldn't laugh. I couldn't make that sound. Tod advanced on me, lazily twirling the antprod, but it was his bowie that I watched, sheathed on his narrow hip. The instrument of my agony.

"Something off, Plain Jane? Because here you are. Only there's nothin' to rescue. The doc here's been playin' both sides all the way back to when the war was a lot hotter than it is now. You know how many Dullahans he's had a hand in killing? Too damn many, I'll tell you that. So I did the only thing left to do with him. You understand, right?"

Tod didn't care whether I understood or not; he just liked hearing himself talk. He had been getting closer and closer as he continued his monologue, the sparking point of the antprod now down by his feet, as though I would forget about it if it wasn't right in front of my eyes. Inside, I was screaming to myself, *shoot him shoot him shoot him*. But I couldn't. I might as well have been shackled to a post. Tod had me bound just with his presence and the sizzle of the antprod cutting through the air and the promise of the blade on his belt.

"You know what the funniest part of this is? The doc gave Phobos up without a fight. We didn't lay a blade on him. Didn't have to. He was cryin' over what I did to his whore. Can you imagine? Some meatstick. We got a whole town of 'em, and he's blubberin' about that one. He didn't take it like a man. He didn't want to rip me up, and god knows he had the strength to do it. No, he whined like a woman and begged me not to hurt him. So I didn't. I just killed him."

Tod stopped a yard away from me. I knew he could bring the antprod up and lunge at me as quick as a striking rattlesnake. He hadn't yet only because he was enjoying this. My fear was what he drank.

The green roiled around me, but I held tightly onto Nora to push it back. She had given me the context of her memories. I knew the name Vivian. Knew why I held her to the oranges, knew why we stood outside Wichita. Knew why we came here. Knew how I died. As much as I wanted to remind myself Nora wasn't me, not really, she was, and she held the green back. Kept me from losing control and lunging at him with bare hands, right into the sparking tip of the antprod. Right into what my fear and anger wanted. So instead I was frozen, unable to do anything at all.

"So what's it gonna be, Plain Jane? We been makin' a lot of promises to each other, and I figure it's time to keep one of 'em, don't you?"

I was perfectly still, and so was he. I couldn't move, and he was waiting, tensed like a note a phantom let hang in the air. The cannon was still clutched in my distant hand, but I didn't know if I could move it. He was so fast anyway; at the first twitch, he would be on me. I cursed myself for letting him get as close as he did, but the fear, the torture, had put me there. Burke was dead, the whole purpose of coming here lost. And not for anything. Because Tod was as ruthless and petty as he always had been.

Tod's fingers drummed against the handle of the antprod. He was waiting. Watching. Daring me to do something and knowing I couldn't.

He had no face to see. No eyes to watch. Merely the maddening void where they should be. Still and silent, he betrayed no intention or emotion. He was probably content to wait there all night, until that instant when my eyes hardened and I brought the cannon to bear. I wasn't a gunfighter. I was a waitress and a seamstress. He was a killer.

Tod had been nothing but cruel since I arrived. I saw him, in my mind, pocket the tooth Les Schroeder had drawn, replacing it with the gold one. The token that had decided Les would join the Dullahans. That wasn't frightening; it was contemptible in how small it was. That was a Tod I could fight, not the one who had burned my arm off my body and laughed while he did it. The one who needed to hurt so bad because there was a hole in some wall somewhere that he was too damn scared to try and fill properly. So instead he threw pain—other people's pain—into it, and he never knew that only made the hole hungrier.

My eyes didn't narrow. It was my hand, the hand he had cut from my body, that moved, all of its own accord. The hand, puppeted by tendons and muscles that had mostly belonged to Sadie Schroeder. That tensed around the cannon's handle, bringing the barrel to bear. Tod moved a second later, the antprod coming up, tip sparking with murder. The barrel was leveled, and I squeezed. My skin recoiled from the lightning as it swept closer. The stream of water spat out. The antprod was nearly on me.

The stream scythed through his arm before coming to rest on his chest. Tod howled as his arm fell off at the elbow, thumping onto the ground. An arm for an arm. His flesh sizzled, vanishing in the water, quicker than Nora's skin had dissolved in the stream of formic acid. Of course, that's why I used to be so frightened of humans; they were so much tougher than monsters.

The stream erased Tod in a mist when it settled over his heart. The water churned, leaving Tod's betrayed scream to hang in the air. The antprod clattered to the floor, the arc clicking off. Now it was nothing. He was nothing.

Burke's broken body sagged against the post. My decision was made. This was going to end. All of it. I left the barn and started toward the manor house.

Thirty-Six

The manor was a large two-story Spanish ranch house, the kind that feudal landowners had been building in this place for hundreds of years. The porch was wide, dotted with chairs. On a pleasant day, it would have been an inviting place to sit in the shade and enjoy something cool to drink. Now, the emptiness was eerie. The invitation felt like one for the dead alone. I was dead. I was six dead women in one living one. The house called to me, welcoming the one who would empty it.

The house was silent as I walked up the front porch. The door was unlocked. And why not? Who was crazy enough to break into the Dullahan manor? Apparently only me. Only one goofy skin-dolly who didn't know when to quit.

I stepped inside and turned on the lights. The walls were whitewashed, nearly blinding. The floors were tiled, with Navajo—Diné, I reminded myself—rugs punctuating it. The walls were decorated with Mexican ceramics and the occasional stuffed animal head, ranging from antelope to giant ants. I hadn't seen a place this rich since I had come to Quartzsite. I hadn't thought there was a place like this out here, as though the desert bled away wealth as surely as it did water. But this was a place for money, the hoarding of it. Whoever owned the rantching land here had more than they would ever know what to do with.

No sound greeted me. This place was deserted, just as Tod had said. I imagined them off hunting Phobos and her clan. After seeing what happened to Nora, I had no sympathy for the mutants. Let the horsemen ride them down.

I knew what I was looking for, but not quite where it would be. One thing would end it all, and Ambrose Dullahan, in his arrogance, had left it unguarded. He had spent the last several years terrorizing the whole wash, and no one other than the mutants had responded. He assumed it would be safe, the towns too cowed to take advantage. Tonight, the mutants would be gone, leaving only the Dullahans. And me.

As I walked through the house I found more glittering opulence. In my life in Los Angeles, I didn't see places like this outside of magazines, but it was even more jarring looking at it after the rest of Quartzsite. This place shouldn't exist alongside Fort Meatstick. Shouldn't even exist next to Barrow's desert shack. It looked to be entirely for a single person: Ambrose Dullahan. I imagined the rest of the Dullahans would be in the outbuildings, probably some kind of dorm or barracks. A private military for a rich man.

I found his bedroom on the second floor. A wide canopy bed dominated the room, and the southwestern decor continued here as well. Something about it all looked put on, as though Ambrose was desperate to cultivate an image, and elaborated on it to the point that it rang hollow, no pun intended. Nothing drove that home like the pillows on the bed. What did a headless horseman need with a pillow? To prove he could afford them.

The jail cell on the other side of the room was what I was truly after. Half of the room was cordoned off from the other with iron bars stretching from floor to ceiling, a cell door set into it on the other end and bolted into the walls themselves. On the other side of the door was a massive floor safe, and all around it were shelves, covered in skulls. Each one decorated with whorls and other markings, the skulls were the missing heads of the headless horsemen. The whole Dullahan clan. The collection numbered about twenty, and most were clustered at the other end of the room, right by the safe, squatting blackly in the center.

An open space on the shelf was directly to the right of the safe, as obvious an absence as a missing tooth. Where there should have been a skull was a small pile of dust. As I was watching, one of the skulls on the wings fell apart into dust, with one more on its heels. Another pair of Dullahans had just been killed.

I unhooked the backpack, set the water cannon down, and walked to the cell door. My hands curled around the cool bars. I tensed, and pulled. The bruises were electric over my battered body. The iron groaned, but didn't give. I relaxed for a moment, catching my breath. Then I tried again. This time I put the image of Vivian in my head. I let her stoke the green. Let her call the inexorable tides to come and take me. I felt her in my limbs, coming on the permeation of the waves, calling to the power inside me. The power that the other monsters feared when they saw me. When they thought I was little more than a dizzy skin-dolly, ready to break a person with no provocation.

My hands tightened over the iron, my muscles turning to steel. With a heave, the iron door shrieked from its hinges. I dropped it, where it cracked the hardwood floors. I was little more than aches then, aches held up by anger and some misguided sense of justice, but I was standing and the door was gone. The safe was too strong for me. Picking it up would be impossible, and there was no way to batter it open. I turned my attention to the skulls.

I picked one off the shelves, one next to the safe. Red swirls over the brows and spirals over the back of it rendered it almost pretty. It was art, albeit of a grisly variety. I crushed it between my hands. It fell apart like it was make of chalk. Something howled through my fingertips, but I couldn't be certain if it made a sound or if I merely felt it. It was a cry of rage and frustration, a helpless shriek into an uncaring void. The pieces of the skull swiftly crumbled, turning into desert dust in my hands. I brushed my hands off and crushed two more skulls, the ones closest.

That should do it, I thought to myself. I fetched a couple pillowcases from the bedroom and filled them with the rest of the skulls. I left the water cannon behind. I no longer needed it. I'd wait for Ambrose Dullahan on the porch. He'd have heard my call.

THIRTY-SEVEN

I watched his arrival in streaks of gold coming out of the mountains to the east. That was the same way Nora Lis had gone, fleeing in her mortal terror, looking for a bit of mercy the world would never give. It was beautiful, that molten gold against the blue-black of the desert night. And overhead, all the stars I could ever imagine twinkled in their velvet cloak. As last sights went, they were good ones.

Nick's picture was with me, tucked into the breast pocket of my shirt, right over my heart. I didn't need to look at it. I could imagine it, the peace on his face as he slept. It wasn't strength I took from it, but rather calm. If Nick could sleep with monstrous me in the house, he could steady the hammering in my heart.

I was ready to die, but I didn't want to. Some of me still wanted to tell Nick what I'd found. That I'd managed the impossible. I'd found five names of women who had been dead and forgotten. Found them when the world had thrown them away. Learned the name of the storm inside me. That meant something. Whatever else I did with my life, before or since, that meant something.

This was how it had to end. The Dullahans were a poison on this place. Quartzsite wasn't my home. Wouldn't ever be my home, either. But I'd never feel peace if they were still out there. Yes, Tod Dullahan was dead, but another Tod wouldn't be too far away, ready to follow Ambrose's orders with a terrifying eagerness. Cruelty was like that: permission watered it like a flower. It's why all the worst in the world were the ones who'd been given leave, by money or by status or by god. Or by some tinpot bastard in the desert.

I watched them get closer, the improvised sacks of skulls hanging by my side, preternaturally light even to my aching muscles. I fidgeted, the skulls clattering together, shifting and moving like the strata of earth.

Soon, at the head of the golden streaks, I could make out the individual horsemen. At the lead was Ambrose Dullahan, up in his saddle and riding hard. I saw others I recognized from Daybreak, including the two that had obviously been with him under duress. Les was there as well, his spectral motorcycle roaring through the night. It was with grim pleasure that I didn't see Mal, Shreve, or Morgan. Seemed I'd picked the right skulls.

Inside, I was little more than seething green, my secondhand organs twisting into burning shapes. I didn't show that to the horsemen; I showed them a patchwork statue. I showed them an immovable woman. Showed them someone who had been taken apart and put together again.

Ambrose reined his stallion in at the bottom of the porch, and the beast went up on hind legs, whinnying and blowing brimstone smoke from its nostrils. The other horsemen reined up behind him, fixing me with their eyeless attention.

"You!" Ambrose bellowed. "You're the one Tod told me about, ain't you?" I nodded at him. "He said you was trouble, but he didn't say anything like this." Ambrose paused. "Tod is dead, ain't he?" I nodded again. "So tell me, skin-dolly, how do you want to die? I can make it slow or I can make it quick. Lady's choice." The saber snarled from its sheath, fire igniting around the blade.

I felt myself flinch. I put Vivian in my mind, holding up the shield of memory. None of the other horsemen moved. Frozen by the showdown between their boss and an angry waitress.

Ambrose faltered, the blade of his saber wavering just slightly. He was probably wondering what I had in the pillowcases. Wondering what kind of weapon the crazy skin-dolly had brought. Wondering how I was so goddamn calm. I thought I'd show him. I upended first one pillowcase over the porch, then the others, a cascade of skulls clattering out over the wooden planks. Some of them tumbled down the stairs to land in the dust in front of the Dullahans. I tossed the pillowcases aside.

Ambrose Dullahan froze. The night held its breath. Even the ants in their distant anthills stilled. All of us silently waited as the source of all of Dullahan's powers spilled all over his front porch.

"Now hold on," Ambrose said, his once powerful voice brittle. "This don't change a single thing. We're still kin now, all of us. All she's done is put your lives in danger with some damn fool stunt." I waited, once again a statue. The horsemen were as still as I was. A rotten wind swept through the night.

"You son of a bitch!" That was Les, still astride his motorcycle. He brought the rifle up to his shoulder, and the crack echoed all through the wash. Ambrose stumbled forward, a hole in his chest. He put a hand to it, finding black, venomous blood leaking out. The patriarch turned, raising his blade, ready to kill the traitor. But the gunshot had given them permission. It pulled the vital brick from the dam holding their rage, their helplessness, their will in check. The flood was on Ambrose Dullahan, and he couldn't stop it now.

Two horsemen charged him with axes, weapons ringing as they clashed. Despite his bulk and the wound, Ambrose was an incredible swordsman, turning aside far more attacks than landed. But there were too many. More attacked Ambrose, but there were a few others fighting one another, perhaps settling old scores that they never could before. Some ran for the skulls on the porch.

I took a step back, watching them sort their own problems out. Some of the horsemen grabbed their skulls, leapt onto their chargers, and surged out into the night. One broke two skulls apart with a sledgehammer, causing two horsemen attacking Ambrose to turn to dust, but she was quickly torn to shreds by a larger group of her former family.

Finally, Ambrose dropped to his knees, covered in wounds, his left arm hanging limply by his side. His mount had similarly been battered into the earth, its unearthly screams finally cut off when Les put a bullet through its head. I recognized the horsemen surrounding Ambrose, finishing the grim work of killing him. It was the five I knew from Daybreak, taking their vengeance on their tormentor. Ambrose cursed them as traitors but that didn't stop them, and after more punishment than any human could take, he fell into the dust and soon joined it, his body dissolving away.

The horsemen watched him die, some of them reaching out to one another, seeking a little bit of contact their new changed state hadn't taken. The remaining horsemen picked their skulls out of the dirt, brushing them off. I left them to it. I had a few things I had to do.

"Jane?" I turned. It was Les, or whatever his name was now. A different man than Sadie had married, and I had certainly no claim on him. "Thanks," he said.

I wanted to tell him it was the last thing the Sadie part of me could do for him, but I think he knew. I hope he knew. I never had a chance to ask him, because I never saw him again. I like to think he returned to Daybreak. Jerome needed someone, and so did Les. Maybe with a gang of headless horsemen looking after them, they'd never be victims again. But that wasn't how people thought. If the horsemen did return, at some point they'd see how much more powerful they were than the humans, especially with no gold or running water around. They might decide they should be in charge. They might think they needed more of them to fend off the mutants that were suddenly stronger, or some vampires coming from the south, or who knows what. I had to hope Les was better than that. That he could hold off the need for power that poisoned us.

Instead, I just nodded at him, because all I had was hope.

Thirty-Eight

I set Burke's body down on the slab that had once given me birth. This was a mad idea, but Burke had been insane by any rational metric. Maybe the apple didn't fall far from the patchwork tree. I'd retrieved his body from the barn and driven back to his office in his truck. I supposed it was my truck now. I didn't know if Burke had a will, or if anyone really cared one way or the other. Or if I did.

I cared about Burke. Or at least the answers that rattled around in his brain. I still wanted those, and I thought, if there was a time for them, it would be when there was no time left. No reason left to lie to me. Nothing between us but the truth.

It was a moral anathema, but I could comfort myself that Burke had done it to others. This whole night seemed to be about people getting what was coming to them. Really, though, this wasn't about him at all. This was about the five names I knew and the one I didn't. It was about the mass grave he'd sent me to, knowing what I'd find. That I was one of many and his callousness really was as complete as I had always assumed.

I hadn't cleaned the office, other than placing a sheet over Frances and another for the ant. I would bury them later. No other monster would care enough to bury a human properly, and to the humans, Frances had been like Nick, a real Christine Daaé. The respect she was due fell to me.

I closed the restraints over Burke's wrists and ankles, gave him the injection, then pulled the chains, raising the slab to the ceiling, the skylight opening it back up. I turned on the machine, the bass hum shivering through my entire body. Electricity crackled in the air, a promise of death, and at least temporarily, life. Soon, thunder boomed over Burke's office, followed by the sizzle of electricity. A bolt hit the body at the top with a crack like a cannon, and the whole platform wobbled. I turned the machine off, and the storm began to dissipate almost immediately. I felt no wonder in the act; that had been bled away by the exhausting night. This was merely a task, the last little barrier between me and the final answers. Then I brought Burke down into the office.

The skylight stayed open, showing the dawn sky, the stars beginning to be swallowed up by the first tendrils of the waking sun. With the machine shut down, this was the light in the room, a fitful dawning. I watched the corpse of my creator. The electrical burn on his chest should have marked his death. The end of him. But Burke was already stirring on the slab. He was alive, just like his process had promised, struggling back to wakefulness through the big sleep of death.

I picked up a shard of the blackboard and fetched a piece of chalk. This was going to be more complex than his simple two-word grunts could handle. I unlocked the manacles over his hands and stood by the side of the slab, waiting for him to rise. Questions rattled through my mind, and I couldn't decide which would go first. I feared they'd just spill out of me, but better questions than violence. I'd had more than enough of that.

Burke's eyes opened. They were milky with death, and they didn't move, staring resolutely straight up.

"Hello?" Burke asked. "Is anyone there?" I stared at him in mute incomprehension. "Why can't I see? Hello? It's dark in here. Can anyone hear me?" My hand crept into his. His hand squeezed mine reflexively, then released, a short, automatic gesture. "Hello? I can feel you. My hand feels strange. Can you help me?"

I couldn't. But I couldn't tell him either. I couldn't do a single thing that I hadn't done already. "My name is Arthur McCall. Can you hear me?" I squeezed his hand. "Oh, good," he said, the hint of a smile in his voice. "I sound strange." He paused. "Can you talk?" I squeezed his hand twice this time, hoping he'd get the code. "Oh. I'm sorry. This isn't my voice. I wish you could tell me what's going on."

I wished the same thing. I should have known. The Frog Mothers had told me, and before them, Wyeth. Meat golems weren't one person. We were six. No reason Burke's process should work on us the way I intended.

"Miss? I don't want to sound crazy, but…is there a Frankenstein around?" I patted his hand. He seemed to get the hint. "It's the last thing I remember," he said. "A Frankenstein, like from the pictures. Thought I was going crazy when I saw him. Could be I was." He paused. "I wish you could talk." I blinked away a tear. I squeezed his hand.

"I'm a little scared, miss. I can't see, and you feel far away, even though you're holding my hand. I can't really explain it. I wish you could tell me what happened. Is there someone else around?" I patted his hand. "Oh. Just us." He stopped speaking and when he started again, his voice was jagged. "Am I dead?"

I squeezed the hand. He wasn't dead at that moment, but it was true enough. Burke O'Hare had lied to me constantly, but Arthur McCall had been as honest as Nora Lis had been. He was worth telling the truth to.

"This ain't heaven. Guess that says everything I need to know. I suppose I never done enough in my life to warrant it. Is it just like this? I can't move, I can't see, forever?" Not forever, I thought at him, but merely stroked his hand.

"At least you're here. Don't know what I'd do if you weren't there. Don't know what you look like, so I'm just going to imagine. Is that all right with you? Good. You don't mind looking like Gene Tierney, do you?" I patted his hand. That sounded all right to me. "Thank you, miss. I really do think I'd be going mad without you. Is that what you see before you die?

Frankenstein?" I merely held his hand. I didn't know how to answer that. Fortunately, he didn't need an answer.

"Funny thing is, I had a neighbor. Simmons. He said he saw a Frankenstein, and I thought he'd gone bugsy. Now here I am telling Gene Tierney that I saw the same thing." He paused. "I'm scared, Gene. I'm real scared. It's dark here, and it's cold, and I know I'm never leaving this place."

I put his hand between mine.

"Come to think of it, you're cold too. I guess an angel's hands would be. That's what you are, right? You're an angel? Have to be. What else waits for a man after death, hears his confession? So I suppose that's what this is going to be then? All right. I'll tell you everything."

Arthur McCall confessed his sins to me, and none of them were terrible. I won't ever repeat what he said, because that's between Arthur and the angel he thought looked like Gene Tierney. I gave him what absolution I could, patting his hand whenever he fell silent. Once, the silence went on too long, and Arthur was gone. Back beyond the veil.

I cried for him. Maybe a little for Burke too. And I cried for Nora and all the others whose names I would never know.

Thirty-Nine

The sun was hot on my shoulders, but the beer was ice on my lips, and that was the important thing. Sugar and I sat in two old chairs out in front of the burned-out wreckage of the Sugar Shack. The beer was from a shipment Sugar hadn't cancelled, and she figured we might as well drink it. She wasn't wrong. A beer in the sun with my friend was only right after all the awfulness going before. Every part of me hurt and I was more exhausted than I'd ever been, but this would do. It would do for now.

A white wolf loped from across the street, changing as he arrived. Soon he was Peter Wolff, squinting in the sun.

"Still in town, Miss Stitch?" he asked me. I looked around, then gestured to it. He sighed. "I expect I'm telling you something you already know, but the Dullahans are missing. The whole damn clan. Went out there this morning, and you know what I found? Piles of ashes. Ashes that smell a whole lot like the Dullahans used to." I smirked, not bothering to ask how often Wolff had been smelling them, or precisely where, to know their scent so well.

"Seems like several of them have been murdered, if you ask me. And there's a pretty obvious suspect with a pretty obvious motive. So I'm bringing you in. Get up, Miss Stitch." I raised my eyebrows at him. I didn't even bother to push my sunglasses down my nose. I watched the faded star tattooed to his chest. "You heard me. Get up."

What Wolff had apparently forgotten was that I knew him. I knew what he had been to this town for years. He wasn't fooling me, especially if he truly believed I'd done what I'd done. But I needed to show him. So I stood.

"Good. Now are you coming quietly, or do you need to be cuffed?"

I let him get the sentence out before my hand closed around his throat and I lifted him off the ground, as light as air. I barely squeezed, letting the pressure from holding him do the work for me. Then, with a flick of the wrist, I cast him away. He hit the dust with a plume and went rolling. When he came back up, he was a white wolf, lips skinning over his sharp teeth. I waited calmly for him to lunge, taking off my sunglasses and sliding them into my breast pocket, wondering just how much of him I was going to break before he cried uncle. I hurt and I was tired, but I was done taking his shit. I was done taking anyone's.

He must have seen it in my eyes. Or he knew that if I had wiped out the Dullahans, I wouldn't mind doing the same to the town wolf. Wolff took his human form, panting in the sun, watching me with barely concealed fear. "What the hell do you think you're doing?" I sat back down and picked up my beer, taking an icy sip.

"If you think this is over," he sputtered. "I'll come back." And he was a wolf again, loping over the desert sands, away from the crazy skin-dolly. I put my sunglasses back on, my fingertips brushing the edge of Nick's picture.

Sugar buzzed. I turned, and she held up a note. *{Not smart, pissing off the law.}*

He isn't the law, and you know it.

Sugar's buzz took a staccato tempo: laughter. *{What are you going to do?}*

Go west, like they say. What about you?

{Rebuild this place. Shouldn't be too hard. Everybody needs to drink.}

Now I laughed. A shadow touched my feet. I turned, thinking that maybe Wolff hadn't gotten the message and I might have to do a little hissing, but it wasn't Wolff. A mutant stood before me. I caught a flash of Nora's nightmare of a memory, but I held it down. This wasn't Nora, and I wasn't in any danger. It was so much easier dealing with my memories now. Now that the hole wasn't trying to gobble me up anymore.

"Jane?" the mutant asked. "I'm Ophelios. We met earlier?" I vaguely remembered the name, but I didn't have the energy to put up with much.

The mutant looked around, his goggle-eyes showing nothing close to a readable emotion. Then, in more conspiratorial tones, he said, "We know what you did to the Dullahans. We're grateful. Phobos is dead, but there are enough of us to rebuild here. These lands are going to belong to the mutants again. The swarms are gonna be ours." I shrugged. None of this mattered to me.

"Well, like I said, we know what you did, and we want to offer you a place here. Quartzsite needs a deputy, and Wolff is too old. We want to make you the law. What do you say?"

I shook my head, then waved at him, *Go away*, the wave said.

"Jane, wait. This town needs you. We need you."

I'm not a cop, I wrote, showing him the slate.

"That don't matter," he said. "We know you're on the right side and we want to reward you. We're gonna have money again, once we take the next swarm to slaughter. Name your price."

More corruption. Corruption for me, but corruption all the same. Ophelios didn't want the law, he wanted someone who would do whatever the mutants wanted, the same way Wolff had served the Dullahans. I shook my head again. *Find someone else.*

Ophelios's shoulders slumped. "All right, Jane. If you change your mind, you can find us out on the old Dullahan property. Guess you know where that is." He said the last with a knowing smirk in his voice, then turned and shambled away.

{Turning down cushy gigs?} Sugar wrote.

I don't want it. Nobody should.

{Doesn't mean nobody will.}

The more things change, I wrote.

Sugar laughed, and we drank more beer. That, at least—time with my friend—was right.

FORTY

pulled the ice cream truck, now my ice cream truck, in front of the church in Ehrenberg. It wasn't the first time it had been loaded up with bodies. I had buried Burke and Frances earlier in the day, at the cemetery they had originally taken Harry Jenkins from. I don't know if that's poetic justice or not. All I know is that it was hallowed ground they had a connection to. I planted them side-by-side, and whatever connection they'd had in life they could have in death as well. A few humans watched me do it, probably thinking to themselves it was the first time they'd ever watched a meat golem put someone *in* the ground. Then I'd smashed Burke's machines and dissolved his notes in formic acid. No one needed to know what he knew.

The truck was full of the remains from the trench. I pulled out every bone I could find. Some had no doubt been lost to the desert, but there wasn't much I could do about that. I hoped the women would understand. I'd tried. I'd tried as hard as I could.

I entered the cool darkness of the human church, and it wasn't long before Pastor Sherman Dukes emerged from the back. He started when he saw me, then caught hold of himself. "Jane, right?" he asked. I nodded. "I didn't think I would see you again. I thought you got what you needed."

I did, but I need to ask you a favor.

He turned to stone, folding his arms over his chest. "I don't know how many more favors I can do for you."

I beckoned to him, and reluctantly, he followed me out into the sunlight. I led him to the truck and opened up the back, pointing to the freezer. He looked at me with a challenge in his eyes until I stepped away from the truck and put my hands up. Only then did he climb into the back and peer inside the icebox. He was looking at bones. Piles of bones chewed at first by Barrow White and then the desert.

"What is this?" he asked breathlessly.

I wrote out the message, periodically rubbing it away to write more. *My creator made a lot of women like me. He killed. He robbed graves. Then he buried them in the desert. This is them. I wanted to bury them here. Some of them came from this place originally. Others came from other places, but I don't know who is who.*

"You're worried about their souls," he said softly.

I wasn't. I wasn't worried about mine either. I wasn't sure I had one, but then, I wasn't sure anyone had one. After talking to Arthur and Harry, I didn't know if there could be anything behind the veil. I wasn't going to tell that to Pastor Dukes. He didn't need that burden, not if his faith was all that was keeping him sane. All I wanted to do was something right for the women they had been. So I nodded.

"Yes, Jane. You can bury them here."

Thank you.

And I did, taking the plot he had marked and giving them six feet of peace. I laid the bones in the bottom of the hole as gently as I could, trying to show them the respect they'd been denied in their first death. From the shadow of his church, Dukes watched me as I worked.

The last bone was Nora's broken skull. I lay it reverently with the other skulls, some broken, others whole. Pastor Dukes asked, "Do you want to say anything?" I pointed to my mouth. He chuckled, shaking his head. "I'm sorry. It's something I ask without thinking. I didn't mean anything by it."

I shook it off. He was right; I needed to say something in the only voice I had. My chalk scratched against the slate as I wrote what was in the heart I'd gotten from one of them. When I was finished, I held it up for Dukes to read. *These women were used. Some of them were killed. None of them deserved it. I hope they'll find peace here, whatever peace there is to find.*

Dukes read the words and nodded appreciatively. "Thank you, Jane. Now we'll pray." He hung his head and so did I, and I waited patiently for it to be done. Dukes didn't understand that this wasn't about God. It was just about them. About treating them as more than garbage.

"Amen," Dukes mumbled, and then nodded to me.

I filled in the hole. Dukes never left me as I worked, looking faintly bemused the whole time. Later, I would add a wooden marker and I'd list the names I knew, adding a message that there were others who would always be mysteries. When I was done, I was filthy, hot, and dry as a meat golem. I looked at my stitches. The hand had stopped unraveling. It still felt somewhat far away from me, but it was working well enough. I thought that I could finally fix it for good.

"Are you hungry, Jane?" Dukes asked. I was. I nodded. "I can make us some sandwiches."

I followed Dukes around the front of the church. The little blonde girl who had escorted me to the church on the second day here, when I met Richard Quintanilla, was waiting out front. Her hair was long and wavy, filled with desert dust. Her dress was more patch than dress now. The sun had given her freckles, her green eyes a squint.

"Pastor?" she asked when she saw me, fear quavering in her voice.

I knew that voice. I'd never heard it precisely like that, but I knew the voice deep in my stolen synapses. The sounds echoed through me. A chubby hand reached for the orange. Arms gripped me tightly in the winds of hell.

"It's all right, Vivian," Pastor Dukes said to the girl. "This is a friend."

That name was even more sublime. I knew it without knowing it. The way I knew how to speak English or who the president was. That name was next to my heart always.

Green roiled around me, but it wasn't anger. It was tears. I felt them in a great ball in my throat, threatening to push its way out and send me crumbling to my knees. I should have known she couldn't have gone far. She was so little then. She wasn't much bigger now.

"She's a friend?" Vivian Lis asked.

I nodded as emphatically as I could and I wrote her a message. *My name is Jane Stitch.* And then I paused. *I knew your mother.*

FORTY-ONE

The picture of Nick sat on the end table of my workshop, right on top of a letter addressed to him. The letter said all the things I wanted to, but were impossible to tell him. That I loved him. That I wanted him to come find me in my dress shop in a tiny town just across the border called Ehrenberg, Arizona. That what I'd done was truly behind me, because I knew the names.

But I hadn't sent the letter, because I didn't quite believe it. I had to be certain that the rage was truly behind me. The apartment in Los Angeles was no longer mine, and the hole had been filled with five names, five women who had died and now had a headstone in an Arizona desert. There was still one that I'd never know, a part of me that would remain an enigma. I had to be at peace with that. There was nothing left to find. Nowhere else to look.

I had moved into that storefront I'd seen, and five names were scratched on top of the doorway. There wasn't much call for dresses, but I could mend things, and I'd do it for cheap. Word had gotten around the humans that I was safe. I think both Dukes and Fern Calloway had helped with that.

Vivian Lis wasn't my daughter, no matter what I remembered. She was Nora's daughter, and Nora was gone. I was something to her, and I would be there if she ever needed me. She didn't. Not yet. I couldn't blame her for being scared of meat golems. Not after what she'd seen. I'd just stay in town, and when she wanted me, I would be there. And if anyone ever bothered her, I'd rip them in half.

If the violence came, it would be because I summoned it. That meant something. So every day, I looked at the letter and wondered if that would be the day I sent it. It hadn't been so far. But it would be.

One day.

THE END

Jane Stitch will return in...

Dolly Come Lately

ACKNOWLEDGMENTS

This book is a bit of a departure for me both in terms of the series and in terms of the kind of book it is. I am incredibly grateful to everyone who has had a hand in allowing me to do this. Candlemark & Gleam of course, who continues to be a source of support and a model of what a small press should be. My family, who puts up with my moods and understands that we can't go see dinosaurs every day. Kate Sullivan, who originally took the chance on the City of Devils and remains a trusted editor and friend. And of course, the readers, without whom I'd just be some guy yelling at passing cars. All of you have my deepest thanks.

About the Author

Much like film noir, Justin Robinson was born and raised in Los Angeles. He splits his time between writing and taking care of a small human. Degrees in Anthropology and History prepared him for unemployment, but an obsession with horror fiction and a laundry list of phobias provided a more attractive option. He is the author of more than 15 novels in a variety of genres including noir, humor, fantasy, science fiction, and horror. Most of them are pretty good.

Follow the Author Online

Website: http://www.weirdnoirmaster.com
Twitter, Instagram, Patreon: weirdnoirmaster
Facebook: facebook.com/weirdnoirmaster

The ADVENTURE CONTINUES ONLINE!

Visit the Candlemark & Gleam website to

Find out about new releases

Read free sample chapters

Catch up on the latest news
and author events

Buy books! All purchases on the
Candlemark & Gleam site are DRM-free
and paperbacks come with a free digital version!

Meet flying monkey-creatures
from beyond the stars!*

www.candlemarkandgleam.com

*Space monkeys may not be available in your area. Some restrictions may apply.
This offer is only available for a limited time and is in fact a complete lie.